Dolores Stewart Riccio

The Divine Circle of
LADIES
PAINTING
THE TOWN

The 8th Cass Shipton Adventure
by Dolores Stewart Riccio

ISBN: 1463510659
ISBN-13: 9781463510657

Printed by CreateSpace, An Amazon.com Company,
Charleston, SC.

Also by *Dolores Stewart Riccio*

Dedication

For the one and only Rick, extraordinary husband and partner,
and the companion of my own Italian adventure

Acknowledgements

I'm especially grateful to the knowledgeable, careful first readers and fabulous editors who have done their best to smooth out the rough edges of my story: Joan Bingham, Anna Morin, Lucy-Marie Sanel, and Ottone Riccio.

Special thanks to Maureen Massetti Rothwell for suggesting a visit to the *strega* of Benevento, to Diane Robinson for the use of her name, and to Linda Lauren for the slightly altered lyrics of *Que Sera.*

Bright blessings to all friends of the Circle who inspire me to keep writing with their kind comments and encouragement.

A Note to the Reader

This is a work of fiction. The characters, dialogue, events, businesses, love affairs, criminal activities, herbal remedies, love potions, and magic spells have all been created from my imagination. Recipes for dishes enjoyed by the Circle, however, may have been taken from actual kitchens, probably my own. Plymouth, Massachusetts, is a real place, but some of the streets and locales in the *Circle* books are my inventions, which is also true of the cities and towns in Italy featured in this adventure. Greenpeace, too, is a true crusading organization, but any misadventures here described are fictional.

In a series, families keep growing, changing, and becoming more complex with time, so that even the author has to keep copious notes. For my eighth *Circle* book, therefore, I'm including a cast of primary characters and their families—to be consulted when confusion reigns. It will be found at the back of this book, along with a few recipes from the Circle.

The experience of the sacred is profoundly connected to love. Magick is ultimately the art of living consciously, connected to all life. In this enraptured state... moonrise, sunrise, or star rise, every blade of grass... echoes within our cells.

Akkadia Ford

If we thought a bit
Of the end of it
When we started painting the town...

Cole Porter

CHAPTER ONE

Magic is believing in yourself. If you can do that, you can make anything happen.

Goethe

"*When shall we five meet again, in thunder, lightning, or in rain?*" Phillipa cackled over the hefty Le Creuset bouillabaisse pot she was stirring on her Viking range. The witch's laugh she'd perfected—reminiscent of Disney, the wicked stepmother, and the poisoned apple—was quite infectious. We all chuckled with her.

"It's Esbat of the Harvest Moon at my place," I reminded her, "so never mind whistling up a storm, Phil. Full moon rising over the Atlantic in September is a glorious event."

Our circle of five had gathered at the long marble table in Phillipa Stern's kitchen around a heap of crackling French breads and an extremely pungent rouille waiting to accompany the glorious fishy stew. Phillipa tossed in the last additions— scrubbed clams, mussels, and shrimp—turned off the heat, and covered the pot.

"Five minutes," she decreed, glancing at the old copper wall clock.

"Ah, lunch with the ladies and a little dignified spell-work—it's high time I opened the wine," Heather said, helping herself to bottles of Graves chilling in the Sub-Zero side-by-side. She opened two of them with her usual expertise, tasted the wine with a nod of approval, and began filling glasses all around. "So...what's on the docket for today?"

"A little problem I'm having with a neighbor," Phillipa confessed. "Liam O'Reilly, next door, has three teenagers whom I suspect of being rather clever thieves. Well, maybe not the girl, but what a foul mouth, and loud, too, just like her father. You should have heard what she called me when I asked if her dad had 'borrowed' my wheelbarrow. Apparently she'd got wind of our Sabbats and such, so there was the usual Satanist invective."

"The usual Satanist ignorance, you mean," Deidre said. "Is there quite a lot of garlic in this rouille?"

"Yes. Enough to ward off vampires and lovers, my dear. At any rate, you'd think her brothers would be wary, what with my husband being a Plymouth County detective," Phillipa continued her tale of neighborly woe. "Maybe they like the challenge, I don't know. During the last month, my GPS and the laptop I left in my car one night have disappeared. Stone reported the theft, of course, but no fingerprints were found in my car, which implies a certain amount of expertise. Then a chain saw, a power drill, and a cat carrier we kept in the garage all disappeared. My best leather jacket and two unusual geraniums, actually cerise in color, from the back hall. And last week, the smaller of my two gas grills, which was covered and stored in the shed, vanished into thin air. Stone questioned the young men informally, but with no evidence of their involvement, any further interviews might raise a cry of harassment. The thing is, *I know* they're a pack of thieves."

"Psychic knowledge doesn't count as evidence," I said.

"Not since Salem," Fiona said. "Spectral evidence hung a lot of good women. But now the law has swung too far in the other direction. Folks won't even believe their own sixth senses." She shook her head sadly and broke off an end of baguette to nibble.

"At least you've still got your big grill," Deidre said. "I'd have liked to see them try to cart that monster away. Must weigh a ton. You could rotisserie a whole pig on that baby."

Zelda, Phillipa's sleek black cat, once a dumpster rescue, sidled into the room following her nose to the delectable aroma of fish. She mewed plaintively and snake-walked her way through our ankles. Phillipa already had a china bowl of cooled white fish from the stew to place on her mat.

"Tch tch, people food. She'd be much healthier on a diet of nutritionally balanced cat kibble," Heather declared.

Zelda licked up every shred of fish and looked at Heather with an expression of feline disdain.

"But what you need in the present emergency is a good guard dog," Heather continued. "Remember Boadicea? I'll bring her over first thing tomorrow, and I guarantee no one will get away with any neighborly thievery while she's on patrol."

"That ferocious old boxer?" Deidre exclaimed. "Is she still boarding at your place? I don't know how you get away with having that noisy dog pack living with you in your exclusive neighborhood."

"Cousins and friends at town hall," Phillipa muttered. "Heather, I am not, repeat *not*, adopting one of your canine protégées when a little spell-work will probably do the trick." She began ladling the fragrant soup into bowls. "So put on your pointed thinking caps, ladies—how should I banish this larcenous crew?"

"Was there anything—you know—not for mundane eyes on that laptop," I asked.

"Well, not my book of shadows, if that's what you're worried about," Phillipa said. "Perhaps the odd cryptic note, but couched in the form of a recipe among ordinary recipes."

"Very sensible," I said. My own entire grimoire was stored in the PC in my home office. *Perhaps not such a great idea.*

"Good luck to the O'Reillys," Fiona said, tucking her napkin into the neck of her coat sweater of many colors and picking up her soup spoon.

"What do you mean, *good luck?* Aren't you going to come up with some potent incantation or something?" Phillipa demanded.

"Phil, dear, we will simply banish them with good luck, thereby saving ourselves from any troublesome karmic backlash. Yes, that will work best. You catch more flies with shoofly pie than vinegar pickles," Fiona observed sagely.

Phillipa raised a winged black eyebrow and winked at me. "Good luck, eh? And how exactly do we manage that, Fiona?"

Fiona gave a quick smile, put down the hunk of bread she was dipping into broth, and rummaged around in the old moss-green reticule from which she is never parted. At last she fished out a beautifully polished black stone. "It's an Apache Tear," she said. "You want to bury this somewhere on their property. Under the kitchen threshold would be best, but I suppose…"

"You suppose correctly," Phil said. "Imagine if I were caught! How would I explain *that* to Stone? And those hypocritical buggers would probably sue me."

"Well, get as close as you can," Fiona continued imperturbably, "and then we'll call on the angels."

"Sure, why not?" Deidre agreed. "And what about the Holy Mother as well?"

"There are many holy mothers, but I think we can put this particular prayer for good luck safely in the hands of the angels," Fiona replied while forking up a plump clam. "Mmmmm."

"That's all very well, Fiona, but shouldn't we also summon some kind of protective light to guard the Stern estate—before the O'Reilly boys start walking off with the doors?" I tasted the

Graves; it was cold, fruity, and dry—well able to stand up to the spicy bouillabaisse.

"And bring in Boadicea," Heather added.

"An altruistic prayer for someone else's good fortune is one of the most powerful spells in the Cosmos. Of course, a vigilant animal is a good protective measure, as well," Fiona mused. *"A dog's bite is worse that his bark*, I always say. Phil, dear, do I detect a hint of orange peel and saffron?"

Not one for revealing her secret ingredients, Phillipa smiled enigmatically.

"So then, would ten be a good time for you?" Heather asked.

"What part of *no way* don't you understand, Heather?"

"Or would eleven be better?"

∽

When I got home after our raucous lunch and a Fiona-inspired good luck prayer for the O'Reillys, Scruffy, my insouciant canine companion, and his offspring Raffles, were waiting for me at their usual sentry post on the window-seat in the living room.

Hey, Toots! About time! Where you been? I gotta pee real bad, and the furry-faced guy is still snoozing on your bed—I don't know if you should allow that. He's got sawdust on his paws. Scruffy jumped down and presented his big shaggy head for a pat.

"Joe is allowed on the big bed, and you two are not, ever. You have your own lovely L.L. Bean faux sheepskins in the kitchen. Get over it."

Scruffy sniffed the legs of my jeans with a disgusted expression. *Pah! My superior canine senses detect that you've been hanging around with that black hairball again. We don't need you bringing home her fleas and other crap!*

Other crap! Other crap! Raffles always repeated his sire's words. Twice.

Not that they spoke aloud—exactly. But one only has to *listen* in a certain way to hear what one's animal companions are saying.

"We need to learn to co-exist with the feline species," I said. "Cats are our friends."

Speak for yourself, Toots! Personally, I never met a hairball that I didn't want to chase up the nearest tree. There's not one of them you can trust, and they smell like three-day old fish.

Old fish! Old fish!

"Well, don't worry, Scruffy. Adopting a kitty-cat is not in my immediate plans. You two go outside now and take care of business, so I can have a little rest myself." I opened the back door so the dogs could avail themselves of the pet flap off the porch, thoughtfully installed by Joe in one of his home-improvement forays. After I settled the dogs, maybe I'd curl up with my furry-faced guy on that big bed for a nice afternoon nap. The Graves had given me a pleasant warm and woozy feeling in my second chakra.

It was not to be.

An old Buick Regal had pulled into my driveway. As the dogs rushed outdoors, Patty Peacedale was just coming up the porch stairs. I opened the door for the Presbyterian minister's wife and her inevitable knitting basket of copious proportions.

"Patty! How nice to see you. And just in time for coffee… or would you prefer tea?"

Patty's earnest, heart-shaped face shone with the zeal of good will. A lock of brown hair fell in an oil swirl on her forehead. She was dressed, as always, in an outfit guaranteed to blend into any wall, a beige cardigan and skirt that fell just below the knee, a silver circle pin at the neck, and sensible shoes that matched her scuffed brown leather pocketbook.

"Hell-o!" she said cheerily, although her hazel eyes were filled with the usual anxiety. "Coffee would be a blessing, dear. I think we all need a boost from time to time, don't you?

Thank the good Lord for caffeine, I say." She sat down wearily, immediately took out her current project, and began knitting. A large plain oblong covered her knees in an indeterminate shade of gray. "It's a prayer shawl," she explained. Her lips murmured silently, no doubt adding the requisite spiritual ingredients.

"How lovely! Who's it for?"

"Mrs. Pynchon," she said with the barest hint of a satisfied smile. Mrs. Chester Pynchon, Treasurer of the Garden of Gethsemane Presbyterian Church, where Patty's husband Selwyn was pastor, had been the most obstructive thorn in his crown ever since he began his ministry in Plymouth. "Poor thing has been laid up with gout this fall. She'll like this color, I think, don't you? Sort of soothing and pearly."

"How does that work, the prayer shawl thing?" I put on the coffee—a good strong brew was just what I needed to clear my head.

"It surrounds one with the inexpressible comfort of a mothering God."

Or Goddess, I was thinking.

"Selwyn is not entirely in favor," Patty said. "*Hope and help for hurting women* is the prayer ministry's motto. Smacks of the feminist, he fears. But never mind that—I've come on another mission today."

Uh oh. I recalled some of Patty's other "missions for Cass."

Rescuing the forest girl Sylvie and our subsequent dust-up with her psycho boyfriend had been Patty's doing. And it was she who had invited me to give a talk on the origins of Halloween, Samhain, to the Gethsemane Ladies League, which had been followed by poisoned brownies at the hospitality hour. Having one's stomach pumped out is a truly nasty experience.

But, in all fairness, not all of Patty's projects were that disastrous. The Garden of Gethsemane Presbyterian church being just around the corner from our old house, on several occasions Joe and I had been "volunteered" by Patty to help out with various uneventful events—such as Thanksgiving Dinner for the Lonely and Elderly. And somehow I'd become the kind of confidante every pastor's wife needs, a sympathetic listener who does not belong to her husband's congregation—someone to whom she could vent her feelings about Mrs. Pynchon et al.

Looking at Patty's ardent, kindly expression as she clicked away blessings for the old dragon, I knew I would probably be a sucker for whatever good works she wanted to foist onto me today.

"So, who's in trouble this time, Patty?" I poured our coffee and filled a plate with Joe Froggers, spicy molasses cookies from an old recipe of Grandma Shipton's.

"I always feel so at home in your cozy kitchen, Cass," Patty said, eyeing the bunches of herbs hung up for drying from the beamed ceiling. The herbal lore of generations of Shipton women had been another of Grandma's gifts to me. "I rather wish the parsonage weren't such a rattling big place, and cold, too, with those high ceilings. I think it was originally built with one of those cheaper-by-the-dozen Victorian families in mind. Mrs. Pynchon has often commented that she prefers a pastor who fills up the parsonage with children and not hobbies. She means my knitting and sewing room, of course. And my writing aerie, the dear little turret. Oh well, one mustn't complain. Others have it worse. Poor Ada Richter now. Ada Feuer, as she calls herself these days. She comes to us with the story that she's been possessed by the devil, and Wyn is not best pleased that she's asked him for an exorcism. So, I wondered, you know, Cass, if that's something that you and your friends might be better able to handle. Didn't I hear that you performed an exorcism for a young widow a while back?"

"Actually, Patty, Wiccans don't believe in the devil, or Satan. That's more of a Christian sort of thing."

"You don't say. Well, *a rose by any other name.* I always say. You'll like Ada. She's a woman of hidden depths, and that's always so admirable, don't you think? Pity about Jerry, what a cross to bear."

I felt myself getting more confused by the minute. This was almost like a conversation with Fiona—a toss-up, who could be the more pixilated. "Okay, Patty. Who's Jerry, and how does he figure in Ada's alleged possession?"

"Jerry Richter. Her husband, naturally. When a woman is feeling the urge to fire up the marital bed supernaturally, well...it surely suggests a troubled home life. Especially if she fantasizes that her husband is taking a nap at the time."

"Supernaturally?"

"The devil tells Ada she can ignite a fire simply by thinking about it. And while she knows she shouldn't listen to such an evil notion, she's tempted to give it a try."

"Pyrokinesis," I murmured.

"What's that, dear?"

"Igniting and extinguishing fires with one's mind. Does she have any talent for it at all?"

"Well, when Wyn turned down her request for an exorcism, his left shoe did get rather hot." Again Patty permitted herself a tiny smirk as her knitting needles flashed. "Quite a dance before he got the shoe off. Something between a tarantella and a highland fling. And such language! Mercifully, Ada had just left his study as I was bringing in a cup of tea, so no one else heard Wyn taking the Lord's name in vain."

"A hotfoot would be quite the provocation. Did Wyn suspect Ada of zapping his shoe?" I poured us both another cup of coffee, admitting to myself that this was getting mighty interesting.

"It *was* rather coincidental," Patty allowed. "We do say that coincidence is just the Lord's way of remaining anonymous. But in this case—Satan?"

"What sort of a guy is this Richter?" If push came to shove, there were easier ways of getting rid of one's husband than practicing pyrokinesis. Not to mention the danger of spontaneous combustion singeing one's own self. And lifetimes of bad karma. "And why doesn't Ada simply consult a very good divorce attorney?"

"Because Jerry Richter *is* a very good divorce attorney. I'm told he's clever and unscrupulous, and Ada would be turned out in her shift. And it's she who put him through law school, working all the hours God gives." Patty sighed and stuffed the prayer shawl into her knitting basket. "Perhaps I'd better take this up again when my thoughts are purer and more charitable. God doesn't judge people until they are dead, so neither should we."

"Does Ada *have* grounds for a divorce? She must be pretty burned up over something."

"I fear that Jerry is having an extra-marital affair and flaunting the other woman in public," Patty whispered as if my walls were taking notes to be read out in church. "Of course, men will be men. Many are ruled by their privates instead of their higher natures."

"How true," I murmured. I hoped Patty wouldn't swear me to secrecy—I could hardly wait to call Phillipa. "Who's Richter having an affair with?"

"His secretary, Nevaeh Nichols. Travels with him, entertains his clients, accompanies him during court proceedings, and generally leaves poor Ada in the cinders." Patty sighed and picked up cookie crumbs with her finger.

"Nevaeh?"

"That's *heaven* spelled backwards. One of the trendy new girls' names. What's wrong with something simple and serviceable like Mary, Wyn wants to know."

"It's a grand old name," I agreed. "So what is it you want me to do, exactly?"

"Just have a little talk with Ada. About this possession business, and the fire obsession. It's all far beyond me, but I just know you and your friends will come up with something helpful."

"A little talk, when?"

"I'll arrange something," Patty said. "And soon. I'm a teensy bit worried that Ada's situation is fast becoming too hot to handle."

I thought the myth of Medea sending her husband's new bride an enchanted robe and crown that burst into flame and burned the girl to a crisp. And the scorned wife killing their two children to cause Jason even more pain.

"Do Ada and Jerry have children?" I asked.

Patty shook her head sadly. "God has not blessed them in that way."

Sigh of relief.

Joe wandered into the kitchen just then, still tousled with sleep in an especially sexy way. He greeted Patty warmly, helped himself to a monster mug of coffee, and kissed the top of my head before he sat down at the table. "So, what are you two gals up to this afternoon?"

"Patty is showing me a prayer shawl she's knitting, and we've been talking about one of Wyn's parishioners who's turned to her for counseling." No need to alarm Joe about the fire-starter wannabee before absolutely necessary.

"That so?" Joe raised a suspicious eyebrow. Patty took out her knitting again and clacked away, her eyes downcast. "I thought Wyn took care of parish counseling."

"Some problems could be too personal and intimate, a woman might prefer to talk to another woman," I said. *Especially if it involves immolating one's husband.*

But Joe, although not exactly psychic, has that lover's ability to zoom into my thoughts in a most disconcerting way. "All fired up about her husband, is she?" he asked. "And Patty's consulting you? Now that suggests…"

"Never mind what that suggests," I interrupted. "It's a confidential matter, honey. So...what fabulous project have you been working on while I was out having lunch with the girls?"

Patty left soon after while Joe was still describing the wonders of the gazebo he wanted to build beyond my herb gardens, to take advantage of the ocean view. Or perhaps I would prefer a pergola, a structure of lattice suitable for training woody plants, possibly grape vines. *Thank the goddess for this brilliant idea that wouldn't involve tearing up anything inside the house, especially the kitchen.*

"Cheeri-o, Cass. I'll be in touch," Patty said with a surprisingly conspiratorial wink.

CHAPTER TWO

And hand in hand, on the edge of the sand,
They danced by the light of the moon...
Edward Lear

Lady Luck was with us on the Esbat of the Harvest Moon. The sky was clear and starry, the air was just cool enough to invigorate us without chilling our middle-aged bones.

Esbats are dedicated to the moon and the Goddess, whereas Sabbats celebrate the seasons of the sun. That makes an Esbat an ideal time for magical workings. For banishings, we might have met on the dark of the moon, but at the full moon, especially the Harvest Moon, a wish or desire or figment of imagination could be conjured to fruition in reality.

We built a lovely fire on my beach and chanted and danced until we'd raised a cone of power that soared upward to the thousand goddesses—who are, in essence, all one, the mothering force of the Cosmos. Among other spells, we'd renewed our good luck prayer for the O'Reillys, and I sent out an unspoken wish that the burning thoughts of Ada Richter...or Feuer... whom I hadn't even met yet, would be dampened and cooled.

We all had personal wishes, sometimes shared and sometimes kept hidden. Deidre's smile was shining and secret, and she herself seemed to have shed the last few years, a golden girl in the firelight. I think we all guessed that her wish had something to do with her new love, Conor.

Phillipa desired her newest poetry collection to follow a charmed path to publication. She tossed a handful of sage into the fire and muttered a rhyme of her own devising. Rhymes gave a more potent force to a spell, so we had learned, and Phillipa was mistress of improvising verse in the midst of action, like Cyrano.

Fiona burned rose and cinnamon incense for her grandniece Laura Belle, who still had a speech problem (elective mutism), although the little girl was speaking more normally now, if rarely.

Heather lit one of her handmade candles for a new housekeeper, having lost again another marvelous cook and dog person, Ashling, who was marrying Maury Irving and moving to Vermont. Maury had been Heather's husband Dick Devlin's assistant veterinarian at the Wee Angels Animal Hospital, so now Dick as well as Heather had been left high and dry. Dick's plight had not been overlooked, however, in Heather's candle magic. Tiny silver charms winking in the wax included a miniature stethoscope as well as a frying pan

"I implore Hestia, goddess of hearth and home, to send Dick and me some good people who won't get blown up or spirited away into witness protection or go into business elsewhere, or for goddess' sake, elope to another state." Heather's record of keeping household help had been ill-fated, to say the least.

I allowed that small vague desire to travel somewhere evocative and inspirational to surface from my subconscious. "An adventure in a foreign land, that's what I wish for most right now. Joe has traveled all over the globe, to every exotic place imaginable, and I'm still here, stuck in the same old rut."

Beware of what you wish for, as the saying goes.

Afterwards, we clambered up to my gray-shingled saltbox cottage overlooking the beach. The moon, gone high and bright, provided all the light we needed on the new stairs Joe had built to replace the former rickety ones. For "cakes and ale," we drank a delicate Soave with brie and pears and Phillipa's delectable Fall Fruits Bread.

৹ৡ

"*Travel,* my dear, comes in many forms." Fiona gazed thoughtfully at a beam of sunlight striking her thistle-painted teapot. "Could be as mundane as a trip to the Massasoit Mall. Or as exotic as a camel ride across the Egyptian desert to view the Sphinx at dawn. Or we could be talking about the transcendent travel that comes from deep meditation. Or that sublime soaring of the spirit that we feel when we release our goddess energy to the Cosmos. Then there's astral travel, of course—an out-of-the-body experience can be rather fun. I remember one time when I..."

"What I'm asking about specifically," I interrupted a bit impatiently, "is *why* you gave me this traveler's grimoire for my birthday last year, to keep magical notes and reflections— *during my trip,* you declared. You'd penned a few chants and rhymes for safe travel in the first few pages. In dragon's blood ink, no less. I'm still waiting for that trip to materialize, and I don't mean to the mall. But if all you had in mind was some flight of fancy, I have plenty of those. I could start writing now. The Goddess hates a blank book."

Fiona smiled that infuriatingly knowing smile. "I believe what I said, my dear, was *someday, somewhere, somehow.*" She poured me another steaming cup of lapsang souchon and opened the shortbread tin. Out of nowhere, her Persian cat Omar Khayyám, oozed into the room and jumped onto the much-scarred cherry coffee table. "Why don't you have a look at the future yourself, Cass?" She smiled impishly, breaking off a cookie corner for Omar.

"Because, as you know very well, Fiona, a clairvoyant rarely sees anything useful about her own future. No *heads up* on imminent danger or a winning lottery number. The Sight comes and goes in its own whimsical way." I savored my tea—fragrance of apple wood and pine—and settled in to enjoy the moment. The brilliant leaves of October dancing in the breeze outside the living room windows—which, for once, were sparkling clear, not cobwebbed.

Fiona's little fishnet-draped cottage in Plymouth Center was cozy, comfortable, and, at present, spotless. It hadn't always been thus. In fact, some members of our circle of five had privately dubbed her place Chaos Cottage, what with its heaps of books and pamphlets stacked in chairs and doorways, and the cluttered, buttered kitchen! But now that Fiona was again fostering her grandniece Laura Belle, all was transformed into a child-centered haven of order and cleanliness. One that I hoped would never be visited by a fanatical social worker. Laura's little rocking chair was painted with magical spiders and snakes. Winsome trolls, imps, and faeries peeped out of her toy box. And the girl's own special shelves brimmed with books like *The Little Wiccan's Book of Magic, Changeling Child, Mother Goose for Pagan Use,* and *Wanda and Glenda: A Tale of Two Witches,* and in the corner, a wooden rocking unicorn winked a blue glass eye.

"Well, I hope something exciting happens to me soon. There's been rather a long lull," I complained. My sea-going husband Joe Ulysses, who worked as a ship's engineer for Greenpeace, got all the fun gigs. At this very moment, he was packing up his old duffle for the good ship *Gaia* where he would sail to Indonesia to protest the destruction of peatland and forests to make way for plantations. *Indonesia!* Did that ever sound exotic! I sighed and nibbled a delectable shortbread.

"I fear you've become hooked on thrills, my dear. No damsels in distress have turned up on your doorstep recently.

No evil-doers have threatened our peace of mind and well-being. There's been no one to hex for truth, justice, and the American way."

"We don't do hexes," I protested. Well, almost never. I couldn't speak for Heather, though. Any hint of cruelty to animals brought out her dark side. "Actually, Patty Peacedale wants me to exorcise another of her possessed parishioners. She seems to think of me as a kind of psychic personal trainer for spiritually abused wives."

"And no one could do it better, my dear!" Fiona patted my hand, her silver bangles ringing chimes of approval. "Always remember that you are the center of the universe. As am I. And each human being is the heart of her world, circles within circles. This is what I learned from the Navajo."

"Sure. I am totally unique, just like everyone else. But I may need your help with this Ada Richter, Fiona. Ada imagines she's a fledgling firestarter. Well, actually, she's already given Wyn Peacedale a hotfoot. So one assumes she has some talent for pyrokinesis. But Ada believes that the devil made her do it."

Fiona looked thoughtfully into the middle distance. "Hmmm. A dangerous notion. I think I may have a pamphlet on pyrokinesis somewhere." At once, she rose from the couch and followed her own abstracted gaze to the bookcase across the room, laying her hand unerringly on a slim red booklet. "Yes, indeed. The very thing."

Life with Fiona was full of these Eureka moments.

"*Cool It! Learn to Quench Psychic Fires in 3 E-Z Lessons*," Fiona read off the title with approval. "But what's the devil got to do with it?"

"Ada says the devil's talking to her."

"Poor girl is obviously listening to the wrong voices, wouldn't you say? I mean, I have nothing against the occasional schizoid communication—can be quite inspiring, you know. St. Bernadette, St. Theresa, St. Joan of Ark..."

"St. Joan is not an ideal example," I protested.

"But we will have to steer Ada away from that blatant fantasy. *There is no devil, and Satan is his name*," Fiona continued with full authority. "Have no fear, Cass dear. I'll help you do the quenching and banishing thing."

There would be a dark of the moon right after Mabon. Perfect! "Oh, good. I knew I could count on you."

"Yes, dark of the moon right after Mabon." Fiona zeroed in on my train of thought. "Mabon will be at Heather's. A perfect setting, the Morgan mansion. That lovely hill, the dark woods, and her great stone circle. As Jane Austen so aptly said, 'A large income is the best recipe for happiness...' "

"Heather's certainly made a bunch of needy dogs happy with hers—Goddess bless her," I said. "But getting back to the subject of travel..."

"Who knows what the future may hold? A Wise Woman fixes her attention on the present moment. We must concentrate on Mabon—the feast, the harvest, communing with the Dark Mother. After that, we'll deal with Ada's devil and your gypsy notions."

"Not to worry. I'm communing, I'm communing. And Phil is whipping up enough gourmet whole grain and apple goodies to feed the multitudes, Heather is dipping orange and gold candles with Goddess-knows-what hidden spells, and I'm drying the last harvest of my herbs. Faeries will gather the rest—so I'm told."

"And Deidre?" Fiona smiled knowingly.

"Dee is making corn dollies and replicas of the Dark Mother, of course, but with only half her attention, what with Conor hanging about day and night."

"I do think we really tried *not* to meddle in Deidre's love life, or lack of it." Fiona polished her spoon with the hem of her coat sweater of many colors. "But some of us may have slipped from time to time and muttered the odd incantation. Anyhow, *all's well in a love spell*, that's what I always say."

I made a mental note of that one to add to our collection of *Fiona's Fractured Proverbs.* Watching the leaves sailing down to the moist earth in Fiona's little backyard, I suddenly felt the passing of the fertile seasons into the oblivion of winter with a pang of regret.

CHAPTER THREE

...walk among long dappled grass,
And pluck till time and times are done,
The silver apples of the moon,
The golden apples of the sun.
W. B. Yeats

Mabon ushers in the sign of Libra, equal day and night, balance in all things, my own sun sign. The evening was chilly but clear and brilliant with visible stars as we celebrated the autumn Sabbat in the circle of stones on Heather's hill. Our fire was small and carefully contained against a brisk breeze stirring the pines. The hooded robes we'd finally ordered kept us warm, especially with sweaters bundled underneath. Dancing kept our blood circulating nicely as well as building up some magical energy. We sought the blessing of Pumona, goddess of apples. We honored the Dark Mother, Persephone, and other dark goddesses, Hecate and Kali. Then, when wind shifted and grew bitingly cold, we hurried into Heather's house to warm up with mulled wine and apples in various delectable baked guises.

In keeping with Mabon, Fiona's round cheeks were as bright as apples and her gray eyes sparkled. The many silver bangles she wore tinkled merrily as she threw herself on her favorite red velvet fainting couch in Heather's Victorian living room. "That was quite uplifting, don't you think? I *felt* Pumona and the other wood nymphs dancing along with us in the shadows, and none of those negative forces, the strangelets."

Phillipa rolled her eyes upward as she sliced an apple cake flavored with Grand Marnier and candied orange peel on a Limoges platter, but an amused little smile played around her lips. "Golly, Fiona, I must have missed those wood nymphs, but I will say I feel infused with something—cosmic energy, I guess."

"Whatever did we do to celebrate the natural cycle of things before we got together and learned about, *you know*—the old ways?" Deidre asked.

"Jewish and Christian religious observances have been instituted at the same times as the old Pagan festivals, of course," Phillipa said, "but I admit I was never a regular at temple."

"Will and his mom jollied me along to attend mass with them when I wasn't too exhausted from caring for the children," Deidre said, "but it wasn't like this, really elemental. Still, I did…I do…find comfort in the Holy Mother."

"Feminine spirituality, feminine power. That's what was missing, what we encountered in Fiona's study group. The history of women's issues led us right into goddess myths and matriarchal religions," I remembered.

"And magic," Heather enthused. "Oh, I do love magic! If I'd discovered magic earlier, I wouldn't have had to suffer through those three ruinous marriages. I could have practiced Divorce Strega Style on those bastards. But never mind—now I have dear Dick, the best of partners—sometimes I think I summoned him into my life. Dreamed up the perfect teddy bear man and conjured him into reality. Now if I could just materialize a real cook and housekeeper! Well, thank the Goddess that Dick loves to fire up his grill and broil his heart out."

"We've all put in a good word for you with the Cosmos," Phillipa said. "Someone will come along very soon—with any luck, someone fated to hang around for a while."

"Let's see...after the old family retainer was regrettably murdered by the bomb meant for Heather, along came the sour-faced Italian in the black dress who made such marvelous pastries, then the old sea captain who could cook every fish known to Neptune, and finally the delicate Irish nymph with a talent for airy scones," I mused. "Whoever could be next?"

"A goulash king? A sushi master? A French chef?" Phillipa suggested. "I can hardly wait."

"Don't forget that the perfect housekeeper for me must be a dog person as well," Heather reminded us wistfully. "Not so easy to find in combination. So many good cooks get downright edgy about canines in their kitchen."

"Damn straight," Phillipa agreed.

"Keep the faith, girls," Fiona said. "Could be a Scot, you know. Haggis, oatcakes, lamb pasties. I like a good Scotch broth myself—shanks and barley."

Phillipa made a sour-lemon face. "Some hairy-legged Caliban piping in the haggis! What a perfectly dreadful notion. I'd rather have a golem in the kitchen."

"A Scot retainer would be very good with border collies," Fiona defended her phantom houseman. "And other doggies, too, of course."

At that moment, I had a glimmer. A fleeting vision flashed across my third eye. Someone different, indeed. *Would I say something? No, after all, I might be wrong this time. And why spoil the fun?*

"What are you smirking at?" Phillipa asked tartly.

"Oh, just imagining you facing a slice of haggis on your plate," I said.

"Talk about awful offal..." she murmured.

"Shhh, Phil. Don't let Fiona hear you. I seem to remember that she cherishes an old family recipe...from her Pictish Auntie Gracie."

∽

Ada Feuer Richter was not at all as I had imagined, which just goes to show the vast holes in clairvoyance. A glimpse here, a glimpse there, and an expanse of darkness between.

She was thin as a wraith but elegant and attractive, with wonderful bone structure—like one of those anorexic models in fashion magazines. Her dark eyes were emphasized by sooty eyelashes and straight black brows; her silver-gray hair was worn in a sleek A-line bob exposing a vulnerable white neck. She wore a striking blue mohair sweater, slim black pants, and ballerina flats. *In her middle or late fifties,* I thought. The lines around her eyes were minimal, but then Ada didn't look as if she laughed much.

Patty Peacedale had arranged for us to meet in the parsonage parlor, an ark of a room furnished with cumbersome ornate furniture that had probably been there since the reign of Queen Victoria. The pastor's wife served oolong tea and mincemeat cookies, confiding in me that she'd completely lost her taste for chocolate since that incident at the Halloween hospitality hour.

"I'm not much of a baker myself," Patty admitted, "but the girls of the Ladies League are always so prolific—heaps of goodies left over after the coffee hour every week."

Meanwhile, Ada's tea went untouched while she gazed into the cold, empty fireplace with quiet disturbing intensity. In my mind's eye, I was imagining the ashes springing into flames that jumped into the room and set the old worn Turkish rugs ablaze. I jumped up and shook my hands to rid myself of the disconcerting image. "Cramps in my hands," I explained, forcing myself to sit down and behave calmly.

Ada looked at me for a long moment, expressionless. "I want to start fires," she said finally. Her voice was low and dramatic. *Good Goddess...it's the Garbo effect,* I thought.

"*He* tempted me. He told me I could do it just by taking thought. Start fires. I'm afraid of what will happen next," Ada continued. "The Reverend Peacedale was unwilling to help me, so Patty suggested that I talk to you."

"How would I be able to help you, Ada. I mean, what is it you really want me to do. Rid you of this intrusive voice?" I was truly at a loss here. I should have brought Fiona.

"*He* is talking in my head all the time. Telling me to concentrate my anger. It will be like a laser, he said. It will purify my home, and Jerry." The darkly-fringed eyes looked at me helplessly. "What can I do? Perhaps I won't be able to stop myself."

"Does *he*—the spirit who talks to you—have a name?" I asked.

"*He* calls himself Abbadon." Ada looked down at her slim, expressive hands. She pushed back the plain gold ring that seemed to have become loose.

"How long have you been hearing this Abbadon's voice?" Meanwhile, I was thinking, *what do you imagine you are doing here, Cass? This is schizophrenia. This gal needs a psychiatrist, not a witch.*

"Oh, weeks and weeks. Ever since...Patty said you could say a spell or something. I don't really want to hurt anyone. I'm afraid to go to a psychiatrist, if that's what you're thinking. If Jerry finds out I'm seeking therapy, he'll have me committed for sure. He tells me my suspicions about him and that girl in his office are evidence that I'm crazy, that I ought to be in an asylum, but I ask you, what about finding lipstick on his underwear? He's just dying for a chance to be rid of me. *Dying.*" Ada laughed hoarsely, in a voice unused to levity.

Even facing the most damning evidence, some husbands will stonewall it and almost convince a gal that she's being unreasonable. As if there are so many innocent ways a guy could get a red smear on his underwear. I felt a pang of sympathy for Ada. After a few years with a man like Jerry, a woman might lose faith in her own perceptions.

"Now, now, dear," Patty said soothingly. "No one is going to make you do anything you don't want to do—are you, Cass?"

"Has Jerry asked you for a divorce?" I've always wondered, when a marriage turned vicious, why the warring couple didn't simply go their separate ways. Admittedly, it had taken the better part of a year and a few bruises for me to split from my ex, Gary Hauser. The weeks between raising the subject of divorce and someone actually vacating the marital home are always fraught with raw emotion and danger.

"He has not...*yet,*" Ada said, looking at me directly at last. "There's a difficulty with his real estate holdings. Papers he had me sign two years ago, something about taxes. I think he's worried that I might walk away with some property of value. Now he wants me to sign more papers, but I have refused. So I think he has in mind to question my competency, have himself named my conservator so that he can sign everything for me and put me away in some snake pit."

"Yes, I see. But the problem right now is for you to rid yourself of this Abbadon and his temptations. That would be called a *banishing,* which is best done at the dark of the moon. I have a very talented friend who is willing to help. But meanwhile, just out of curiosity, do you believe, as Abbadon says, that you do have the power to start fires?"

Ada smiled grimly and turned her attention back to the dark hearth. Patty clutched the Celtic cross she wore secretly under her blouse. The unsanctioned pendant had been a gift from the circle. We'd taught Patty how to use it as a dowsing tool when there had been a poisoner running loose in the parish, convincing her that it was a new way to bless the food, and, incidentally, to be sure it was wholesome.

"It's as if everything I touch is dry as tinder," Ada explained, "and I feel I've only to blow on it to start a small flame."

Rising from her chair, she walked over to the fireplace, knelt before the hearth, and began blowing softly, the way you might do to get a few sticks of kindling going. Was it my imagination, or was there a thin plume of smoke rising from the blackened remnants of logs? "Abbadon, Abbadon," she moaned.

Curious as I had been to see if Ada actually could start the thing burning, I was getting distinctly edgy. "Banish that thought!" I declared firmly, holding up my hands, little fingers pointing outward, to stop the fire spell. I'd already had enough of fire-starting in my life, and possibly in my past lives as well.

"Oh, goodness me, isn't it surprising how those embers will stay hot for days," Patty exclaimed nervously. "Yes, I think Wyn and I had a fire in here just a couple of nights ago. This parsonage can be a pretty chilly place in the fall before we're allowed to turn on the furnace. Well, *allowed* may not be quite the right word. But Mrs. Pynchon *suggests* that we refrain from turning on the heat until Thanksgiving. To save on the parish oil bill, you know. But never mind my little troubles. Perhaps it would be a good idea, Ada, if you'd lay all your problems— Abbadon and whatnot—in the hands of the Almighty just before you go to sleep. The Lord is up all night anyway."

"Good plan, Patty," I agreed. "Let's pull out all the stops on this one. Meanwhile, I'll set up something for the dark of the moon. You really don't want this kind of magic, Ada. It's far too risky."

The dark eyes turned to me with such a look of desperation and anguish, I felt for the first time that afternoon a bond of sympathy with this unhappy woman. "It's going to be all right, Ada," I assured her. "Just keep cool until the moon is in the right aspect. Which is only next Tuesday."

But a funny thing happened on the way to the banishing!

෬

"Conor has a new assignment, and, Cass, you'll never in a million years guess where!"

Actually, I could have guessed quite easily. Clairvoyants are good guessers of other people's secrets. But I didn't want to throw cold water on Deidre's moment of dramatic suspense.

"It's Rome! He's going to Rome!" Her grin revealed two charming dimples. At once, the years of motherhood fell away, and she looked like her yearbook photo again, the high school sweetheart who had once given Conor the heave-ho for the sake of the basketball team captain she'd married—Will Ryan, dead two years ago of sudden coronary arrest.

I didn't have to be a clairvoyant to see what was coming, but I let Deidre spill the rest in her own good time. I merely said, "He's finished the book then?" *Conor O'Donnell's Plymouth,* commissioned by W.W. Norton, had tied down the footloose photographer to our South Shore for almost a year as he photographed the mystique of our town in every season. An old flame from Sacred Heart High School in Kingston, Deidre had run into him last November. With her Mazda. Their friendship renewed by accident or karma, romance had bloomed like a winter rose. Their affair was observed with relief and misgiving by her closest friends in our circle of five. It was high time that her grief and guilt were assuaged, true—but who knew how the mercurial Conor would adapt to being weighed down by Deidre's young family of four?

"Yes. I'd expected Conor to close up his Plymouth pied-à-terre and take to the road again, all his possessions in a backpack, but he says no," Deidre said. "He's keeping the apartment after all. He says 'I've allowed myself to buy some books. I'm a man of property now.'"

"And that's not all?" I prompted.

I could still see the corner of her smile as she turned away to pour boiling water from the kettle into the double-walled French press that had been an early gift from Conor and had greatly improved Deidre's coffee-making skills.

"*And*...he's asked me to go with him. A change of scene will do me a world of good, Conor says. Not only that, but he went right over my head to ask Mother Ryan if she was up to taking charge of the kids while he squires me around on a little Roman holiday. Can you imagine? You'd think she would have expected me to throw myself into Will's grave, not encourage me to take up with a new guy. But you know how he's enchanted the woman. She calls him *the dear little leprechaun*. Always wants him to run his fingers through her bucket of quarters before she rumbles off on the free bus to *Mohegan Sun* with her blue-haired gambling cronies. And Conor even hinted that there might be a special blessing forthcoming from the Pope for her, the nerve of the man. All objections melted away like a child's sand castle at high tide."

"Conor has an exceptional talent for...for..."

"Slinging the bull?"

"For honeyed words. Blarney, perhaps," I said. No woman in love wants you to agree that her new Mr. Right has any nicks in his white armor. "Sounds like a delightful trip to me, but how tied up will he be with work? What's his assignment?"

"Secret passages of the Colosseum. It's for *National Geographic*. Some new tunnels decorated with mosaics have been discovered. Probably for the royals to escape if the mob turned ugly or the lions got loose. Sort of like Air Force One and the Presidential Bunker."

A small snake-like slither of apprehension slid down the back of my neck. *What's wrong with this picture?* The only thing I could bring up consciously was Deidre's newfound gift—or curse—of seeing dead people. "Eh...I'm not so sure you will feel comfortable hanging around the Colesseum. Not the best of vibes, all those sadistic games, gladiators with merciless tridents and war chains, Lions versus Christians."

"Mother Ryan wants me to bring back a little sand from the floor of the Colosseum, which is supposed to contain the blood of martyrs." Deidre winked in her old mischievous way. "Although it's hard to tell one packet of sand from another."

"But, Dee, aren't you afraid you'll be overwhelmed by the ghosts of the place?"

She passed me a plate of the children's animal crackers. "Concerned, maybe. Not afraid. I've never been visited by more than one specter at a time, and those gals had an agenda. They were after justice. Surely all the martyrs of the Colosseum have been spiritualized by now and gone on to greater glory. They're not still out for revenge."

"Well, if you feel the least bit uncomfortable in the bowels of the ruin, I hope you'll get out of there and let Conor deal with the spirits," I said.

"Of course. He'd be the equal of any phantom, I'm sure. Probably try to get the thing on film. Maybe *Nat Geo* would pay extra for that!"

"I suppose you have your amulets all ready to go," I said.

Deidre put down her cup and, from the work basket at her feet, removed a doll she was finishing for her shop *Deidre's Faeryland* at the Massosoit Mall. She sewed on gossamer wings of translucent dusty pink. "This is Rosamund who has the power to enchant and enslave. A favorite with little girls. Yes, Cass, I have created new amulets especially for our trip. The problem is getting Conor to wear his."

"What do they look like?" I nibbled on a giraffe; the mild vanilla flavor brought me straight back to the years when I was a young mother, running a garden shop with one hand and taking care of three youngsters with the other.

"Roman gargoyles. To keep Roman strangelets at bay."

"Tell him it's a charm to enhance his photography."

"Maybe. He can be quite a stubborn guy about some things."

"But you'll wear yours?"

"And Conor's, too, if I have to."

"Why don't you tuck it into one of those many pockets in his khaki vest," I suggested. "Under a roll of film or something."

"Not to worry. I'll find somewhere to stick it. Conor may be one of those guys who leads a charmed life, but it's a dangerous life, too, and anyone can use a bit of magical armor now and then."

"Yeah, I know what you mean. I buried a little medicine bag in Joe's duffle bag. Herbs of protection, and some Navajo gizmos I got from Fiona," I said. "I don't know if he's noticed, but he's never mentioned the matter. It's still there, too—I check every once in a while. Especially before a major trip, like this Indonesia thing."

Diedre clapped her hands together like a child in rapture. "But here's the really exciting part, Cass. Conor has already made our reservations, we have confirmed seats on Alitalia leaving a week from Monday."

"Well, then," I said, "We'd better have a little blessing for you before you leave. Not to mention, a party. Whose deep pockets are paying for all this, anyway, Dee–*Nat Geo?*"

Deidre took an elf out of her workbasket and began to sew on its little brown vest. It, too, had many pockets, rather like Conor's. She did not raise her eyes as she said, "I'm not sure about the money source. Not entirely *Nat Geo.* But Conor says I'm not to worry about it."

Whenever a man says, "don't worry about it," I'm inclined to worry more. But that's me, ex-wife of Gary Hauser, who left me pretty much in financial ruin.

∽

"She's gone!" Patty Peacedale's voice on my kitchen phone did not exude its usual cheery bonhomie. "Ada's gone. I've called and called, and I've been to the house but there's no answer all week. There's a housekeeper, but all she says is, *No casero, no casero. Señor Richter. El doctor. El doctor.*

"That doesn't sound good, does it? What about *Señor Richter*? Have you asked him about Ada?"

"No. I'm afraid Jerry Richter already thinks I'm a terrible busybody. He's a Lutheran, you know. Well, they both are, actually, but Ada and I got to know each other at the Plymouth soup kitchen, and she didn't want to go to her own pastor with the exorcism thing. To tell the truth, I rather hoped you'd give Attorney Richter a call, since he doesn't know you from Adam—or Eve."

Patty's voice was getting shriller and shriller. I certainly didn't want to see her driven to distraction by concern for her incendiary friend. So I found myself agreeing to ask Richter about his wife.

"Oh, God bless you, dear," Patty said. "I'm praying for poor Ada, you know. May the Lord protect her from that …that…"

"Hard-hearted bastard?" I suggested.

"Misguided. Misguided sinner." Patty said. "Good luck, dear. Call me right back afterwards."

I decided to approach the misguided sinner in his den of iniquity, so I struggled into my olive linen suit and drove downtown to the offices of Richter and Beiber, Attorneys-at-Law, in a converted mansion near the historic district of Plymouth. The receptionist looked aghast when I confessed to not having an appointment.

I gave my name and Patty's name to the svelte young woman sporting an amazing cleavage for a business person. "Some of her friends are very concerned about Mrs. Richter," I explained. "She seems to have gone missing. There's probably a very simple explanation, if I could just see Attorney Richter for a moment. No need to involve the police, I'm sure."

The receptionist teetered away on spike heels with little white plastic flowers on the toes and spoke to another woman in the inner sanctum. I wondered if that was the secretary Nevaeh Nichols and if I'd catch a glimpse of Ada's nemesis. The receptionist shut the door between us firmly, however, while I cooled my heels (sensible black pumps) in the lobby. I took the opportunity to page through a pamphlet on exorcism that Fiona had pressed into my hand at our last meeting. *Get the Devil Out of Here*, it was called. After twenty minutes or so, the great man himself came out to greet me, all smiles. *That one can smile, and smile, and be a villain,* occurred to me.

"Mrs. Shipton," he said.

"Ms.," I corrected.

"Ms. Shipton, then. I understand that you and the Reverend Peacedale's wife have some concerns about Ada. Very thoughtful of you both. But let me assure you that she's in very capable hands now."

"*Hands?*" I didn't much like the sound of that.

"Yes. As friends of Ada's, you must have noticed that she's been visibly disturbed these past weeks. A few days ago, her agitation reached an insupportable level, and we had to call for assistance. I promise you that Ada's getting all the help she needs now, and she's resting comfortably in a safe place."

"What place?"

"I'm sorry, Ms. Shipton. This is a private family matter, and I have no intention of sharing with you and Mrs. Peacedale any more details of this troubling incident. So, if you'll just relay my message to her, I think that should be the end of the matter. Unless, of course, you'd like me to call the Reverend Peacedale and inform him of his wife's continuing interest in someone who is not even a member of his church."

The vibes this control freak was giving off were giving me the psychic whim-whams. I had to be careful not to look him straight in the eyes which might have thrown me off balance. Clairvoyants seem to be missing some useful armor that protects other people from naked evil intent.

"No, that's okay, that's okay. I'm glad to hear that Ada's resting after all she's been through recently. I'll talk to Patty." I murmured my good-byes and got out of there as fast as my sturdy pumps would take me.

CHAPTER FOUR

Stone walls do not a prison make,
Nor iron bars a cage,
Minds innocent and quiet take
That for a hermitage...
Richard Lovelace

But I wasn't willing to let the matter rest there. Something had to be done about Ada. Clearly, her husband Jerry got her out of the way so that he could redeem his assets and be rid of her hysteria in one oily maneuver.

The first step would be to find out what incident had allowed Ada to be consigned to "capable hands." Perhaps there had been a police report filed by Richter to cover his ass. The second step would be finding where exactly Ada had been stashed. So then...Phillipa and Fiona, in that order.

When I got back from my visit to Richter, I found Joe at the kitchen table drawing plans for a garden pergola while the two dogs were watching him nervously from their respective faux sheepskins. He looked up for a hello kiss. "You're going to love this," he said. "It's really more in keeping with a Colonial saltbox than a gazebo would have been."

Hey, Toots, just a flea-hopping minute here. The furry-faced guy isn't going to mess up our good place, is he? A canine's kitchen is his castle.

His castle. His castle. Raffles jumped up between Joe and me. He was getting to be remarkably big and shaggy, just like his sire.

"You've got the dogs pretty worried," I said. "They're afraid you're going to tear up the kitchen again."

"Cass, do you really believe those two know what I'm drawing here?"

"Let's not get into that again. Just don't leave those plans around where they might get accidently chewed to pieces, honey. I'll be in my office." I beat a hasty retreat to the old borning room that housed my PC and the files for *Cassandra Shipton, Earthlore Herbal Preparations and Cruelty-Free Cosmetics,* the online business that supported me. I called Phillipa on my cell. Could she ask Stone to check if any police report had been filed recently that involved the Richters?

"Oh, goodie. Another crusade, I assume?"

"You remember, we said some words for poor Ada at the Esbat of the Harvest Moon? Her husband's had her put away in a padded cell facility because she caused some kind of 'incident.' I think it's highly probable that he lodged a specious complaint with the police for an excuse to commit her to a mental institution."

"Where?"

"Don't know yet. I'm going to consult Fiona on that one."

"Okay. I'll see what info I can shake out of my beloved but close-mouthed husband."

Next, I called Patty and pledged to continue our investigation into Ada's fate. "But you'd better keep a low profile, Patty. Richter as much as threatened that he'd complain to Wyn if you got any more involved."

Patty sighed. "Oh dear. I'd so much rather Wyn would not be bothered with my small concerns when he has many much weightier matters on his mind."

"Amen, Patty. Amen. But you'd better leave Ada to me for now. Plausible deniability, you know."

Later that day, when the sun was over the yardarm and glasses all over the South Shore were being filled with a relaxing adult beverage, Phillipa called me back. Stone did indeed recall that particular police report because the complaint had been unusual and the investigating officers were joking about it. A well-known and respected attorney claiming that his wife had set a fire in their home. *Little kids might do that, but wives?* There had been some corroborating evidence, however, and when questioned, the woman had seemed distraught. The matter was settled by the husband arranging for his wife to be committed for observation at a suitable facility. Which one? Stone didn't know. When the husband decided to drop the charges in favor of medical intervention, the case had been closed.

కింా

Ada's story had an upsetting effect on Fiona, as evidenced by an uncharacteristic scowl and an agitation of her silver bangles.

"A competent exorcism by a trained Wise Woman, that's what the poor woman needed. Far better than to have some psychiatrist meddling with the woman's psyche in matters about which he would know nothing, namely pyrokinesis." Polishing her crystal pendant with vicious energy, she set to work at once dowsing amid maps of Plymouth and surrounding areas.

Nothing!

"*Leaping Lords of the Wildwood!*" Fiona exclaimed, tossing the Plymouth maps off the coffee table in a rare fit of pique and sending Omar scurrying upstairs like a gray streak. "You're the

clairvoyant, Cass—give me a clue, some general idea of locale.
I have hundreds of maps—this will take forever if you don't
narrow the possibilities."

"Okay, okay. Give me that thing for a minute." I held
the faceted crystal to the sunlight and stared at it until, as I
knew it would, its brilliant rays sent me off into a semi-trance,
something I generally avoided doing like the plague. A vague
landscape passed before my eyes. *What in Hades was that? Ceres
save us—the gallows tree!*

"Try the North Shore—maybe even Salem," I said finally,
fighting off the usual nausea and disorientation.

Fiona flung open an old trunk that served as an end table
next to the sofa; maps spilled out in every direction. No
matter—a minute later, Fiona's hand had unerringly found the
very one she sought, Essex County. She spread it out carefully
on the coffee table and took back the crystal pendant. Soon
it was swinging purposefully over Salem, then swung over to
Danvers and came to a rest.

"What's in Danvers?" I asked.

"Let me Google that," Fiona said. She reached into her
reticule, pulled out a mini-notebook, and booted it up. Fingers
flying and bangles chiming, she soon found what she was
looking for. "Tranquility Lodge, a private psychiatric facility in
Danvers. Sounds like the perfect place to lock up an erring wife.
What did he say she did? A bit of firestarting?"

"Apparently Richter called the cops, and there was
some evidence. A couple of charred items in Richter's study,
nothing much really. A smoking chair, not exactly a smoking
gun, but it was enough. Should we...could we...spring
Ada?"\

"No problem, dearie. Do we have someplace to hide her
afterwards? Some kind of wife protection program?"

"Serena Dove owes us both for the Ashling Holmes affair,
the gal who was haunted by her dead husband. And Serena's in

the business of giving refuge to abused wives at St. Rita's," I said.

"Sounds like a plan," Fiona said.

∽

Before we could infiltrate Tranquility Lodge and rescue Ada, however, we had another urgent matter—the spiritual protection of one of our own. Deidre could not be allowed to take off on Alitalia with Conor O'Donnell until we had surrounded her with a suitable psychic defense.

We gathered at Phillipa's for Deidre's farewell ceremony. It had been a long time since we'd seen Deidre quite so beaming and excited as she had been recently, and we were delighted for her—although I couldn't help a pang of envy thinking of her flying away with a new love to the Eternal City; it did sound like a fantasy come true.

Phillipa cast the circle, called the quarters, and rang a small silver bell to focus our spiritual intention. Heather lit the four directional candles she'd made, white for protection and purification, blue for peace and serenity, and for the altar, a dark blue Goddess of the Crossroads Hecate candle that Heather felt would be especially appropriate for travelers. (Later Heather would wonder if she shouldn't have added a courageous red candle as well.) Miniature quartz stones and charms were embedded in the wax for additional power and protection.

The basic defensive ritual involves sage smudging, and while we were at it, we smudged ourselves as well. Deidre showed off the new Roman amulets she'd created—amazingly ugly little faces with red eyes. Phillipa remarked that those little gargoyles should put the fear of the goddess into any malevolent influences! Fiona sprinkled corn pollen over our petite traveler and insisted that she carry an Apache tear as well. It seemed as if we'd left no magic stone unturned.

Afterwards we lounged around on silk pillows in Phillipa's living room and sipped flutes of Prosecco that Heather had deemed to be quintessential *eleganza Romana*.

It was all perfectly traditional and reassuring, but I had an uneasy feeling in my third chakra. I was almost tempted to gaze at one of Phillipa's Moroccan brass tables long enough to bring on a light trance, but in the end I thought better of it—no need of being a psychic spoilsport.

"If you get a chance to take a side trip, you might visit Benevento—in the hills south of Rome," Fiona said. "I could contact an internet pen pal who lives there to show you around. Anna Amici is a healer and a finder like myself.

"Why Benevento?" asked Phillipa. "I'm sure Dee will be much too busy exploring Rome. So many art treasures, so little time…"

"In ancient times, Benevento was the site of a temple dedicated to the Egyptian goddess Isis whose worship was popular with Roman women," Fiona said. "It was also the location of a sacred walnut tree where Pagans gathered for ceremonial dances. Naturally when Christianity took hold, priests had the tree cut down, but other trees secretly took its place through the years. Obviously, the grove is now imbued with great spiritual power. A medium as sensitive as Deidre is bound to be inspired."

"A medium, I am now? Holy Mother, I've only seen a few ghosts, Fiona. And what kind of a busman's holiday would that be!" Deidre exclaimed tartly.

"Well, dearie," Fiona said mildly. "Just remember Anna Amici's name in case you find yourself in need of a bona fide Wise Woman."

Clairvoyance being the unreliable art it is, I was utterly clueless when I hugged Deidre good-bye. As were we all.

Well, maybe not Fiona, who hardly knew what she knew.

༚

"It's Cass, Serena. I have a favor to ask," I said as soon as I heard the ex-nun's crisp "Good morning! St. Rita's Refuge. How may I help you?"

"Do you, dear!" Serena's tone took on a cautious note.

"Would you consider taking in a fugitive friend of mine? I know you guard the identities of abused wives and children staying at St.Rita's with great care. And we would need the utmost discretion. The woman's husband is a prominent Plymouth attorney with excellent resources, and he'll be moving heaven and earth to find her."

"Heaven help us—you don't mean Jerry Richter's wife, do you?"

"Hey, Serena, I thought I was the psychic here, not you. Do you know the Richters?"

"Yes, Cass—you can't do much business in family court without encountering that great white shark, the bane of all poor women seeking custody and child support."

"Is that a 'no,' you won't give refuge to his wife?"

"No, that's a yes. A little frustration will do him a world of good. I don't know if we can pull it off, though. The man regularly employs some slimy detective out of Providence to get the dirt on his opponents and find hidden assets, of which his wife may be considered one. With Richter's divorce experience, I would think that he'd know better than to slap around his wife—or was it something else?"

"He signed her into a psychiatric facility so that he could take control of their mutual real estate holdings and enjoy his mistress, too."

"Figures. What's the wife's name? How're you going to get her out?"

"Ada. You don't want to know. I hope you won't mind that this may be considered a little illegal?"

"It's only illegal if there's a court order keeping her in custody. Chances are this is an involuntary commitment for the purpose of evaluation. If Ada is found to be a danger to herself and others, Richter can then request a court order to hold his wife indefinitely. If not, if she's simply been committed for examination by a psychiatrist, it's a different story. Once you get her here, Sister Mary Joseph, our psychiatrist, can declare her *compos mentis*, and Sister will have colleagues to back her up."

"Great, Serena! I knew I could count on you. There's just one other teeny problem"

"I can't wait to hear."

"Just keep in mind that I took on Ashling and her levitation last year on your request."

"I believe that you owed me for hiding Rose Abdul and her son from her crazy husband. Perhaps we should stop keeping a scorecard, and just do the Lord's work as we see it."

"Right. Speaking of which, Ada Richter, who belongs to the Lutheran church, believes that the devil has been whispering in her ear."

"Jesus help us! What's the devil want with Mrs. Richter?"

"Pyrokinesis. He tells her to start fires with the power of her mind alone.

"*As if!* Can't you and your circle handle the exorcism?"

"We would if we didn't have to spring her from the Lodge and hide her at St. Rita's. Richter's sure to have us watched."

"Well…it's been a long time. But I'll see what I can do. Only one thing…"

"Yes, Serena?"

"None of that *The devil made me do it* at St. Rita's. At the first whiff of smoke, I'm dropping Ada Richter like a hot potato right back on your doorstep."

"Understood. I'll put the fear of the goddess into her."

"Whatever," said Serena Dove. "

Fiona suggested that she and I visit Tranquility Lodge between three and four in the afternoon when "everyone's blood sugar would be at a low ebb." I would drive and she would penetrate the facility under a glamour.

I might have had my doubts, if I hadn't seen Fiona pull off that trick before, a plump little middle-aged lady who could blend into any background. Fiona claimed that women become more invisible with age which makes it that much easier to sidle through unnoticed. And she seemed dressed for the part, in a very uncharacteristic outfit—no rainbow-striped skirt, no multi-colored coat sweater, no tartan cloak. Just a plain pale green suit looking as if it had been closeted for a decade. And her ever-present reticule, of course. I noticed, too, that the familiar tinkle of bangles was absent.

We left at two-thirty, allowing an hour and a half, which was just about on the button. Meanwhile, I was thinking up alternative routes for our trip home. In case…

Even though I trusted Fiona's glamour magic implicitly, I had to ask, "I know you can probably get into Tranquility, but how in the world do you plan to get Ada out of there. She doesn't even know you."

"I'll mention your name and Patty's, but I don't think she'll demur for a moment. I rather think she'll want to escape."

We arrived at Tranquility Lodge at quarter to four. I intended to park in the most inconspicuous spot. "No, no," Fiona said. "Drive into one of those reserved places."

"They're reserved for hospital personnel."

"Exactly," Fiona said. "Take that one over there by the pine trees."

Could the woman make my RAV4 invisible, too?

Fiona got out of the car, removed a clipboard from her reticule, and strode purposefully toward the entrance, which was centered in a kind of rotunda veranda out front of the building. The reticule was hanging over her arm like a handbag. It may have been my imagination, but she seemed to blend with the columns as she walked up the broad stairs. How I wished I could have gone with her!

Time crawled like a snail across my consciousness as I waited and waited. It seemed like hours but was actually only a half hour before I noticed a pale green shadow emerging from the side of the building. And there was someone by her side! It was Ada, dressed in a doctor's white coat and carrying a black bag. They wasted no time in jumping into the car, and I wasted no time in wheeling out of there with a splat of pebbles.

"You didn't forget your reticule?" I asked as I zipped onto Coolidge Road.

In the back seat, Ada withdrew Fiona's reticule from the black bag and handed it to her over the seat.

"That was amazing," Ada breathed. "Fiona appeared in the day room like an angel from heaven, sort of wispy and unreal. I was at the window trying to get over feeling woozy from the afternoon pills. Some of the others were watching Oprah. The orderly was in the corner reading a magazine. Fiona leaned over and whispered that you and Patty Peacedale had sent her to get me out of there and that we should duck into the ladies room without delay. I thought we'd be stopped, but the orderly never even looked up when we left. In the ladies room, Fiona pulled this white coat out of her green tote. Look, it even has a name tag on it!"

"And the black bag?"

"Fiona just picked that up on our way out. It was on a chair just inside Dr. Wacker's office. I thought Wacker would see her, but he just gazed right through us and kept talking on the phone."

"My friend is very talented that way," I said. "What's in it?"

"A stack of medication forms, a bunch of different pills shrink wrapped in plastic sheets, a Robin Cook novel, and the remains of his lunch. I think it was corned beef." Ada leaned over the front seat. She looked even thinner than the last time we'd met, a keyed up, worried expression in her dark eyes. "Cass, this will never work. Jerry will come after us. Me they'll just drag back to the Lodge—because Jerry's got himself named my conservator and a commitment form signed by a psychiatrist and our family doctor. So he can make all the changes he wishes in our joint ownership of properties. But I'm afraid that both of you will be charged with something. Surely this isn't quite legal."

So...not a voluntary commitment, then! Ceres save us. "Don't worry, Ada. No one in the Lodge really saw Fiona, and we're bringing you to a sort of safe house for runaway wives. Just until we can have you declared sane." While reassuring Ada, I was driving south by a different route than the way we had come. I had no idea if the hospital would notify the police that Ada was missing, but I didn't think that anyone had seen us leave and could identify my car. Just as a precaution, I headed back to Plymouth through Salem and Lynn; it would take longer but might be safer.

"Now, Ada, I really would like to know the details of the incident that got you in trouble in the first place," I said.

"Oh, you mean that thing with the police, Jerry's *excuse* for having me locked up. It was just a smoldering cushion on Jerry's chair in his study. He must have dropped his cigar or something like that. He could have just poured a bucket of water on it, but instead he called the fire department and the cops." Suddenly Ada's voice had lost the note of nervous excitement and gone vague. "He claimed I'd set the chair on fire. Maybe, but I don't think so. Abbadon hadn't talked to me that day at all. He always said that Monday was the devil's holiday."

"The place we're bringing you—the director is going to help you send Abbadon on a permanent holiday. But you have to promise me one thing," I looked into the rear view mirror meaningfully. "No practicing your new skill, or she'll send you right back to Jerry."

"Maybe I can't help it," Ada wailed.

"Help it, Ada," I declared firmly.

Ada leaned back and shut her eyes. We drove the rest of the way in silence, except for Fiona's humming.

The iron fence and locked gate that had once sheltered nuns from the world now protected the abused women and children who had sought refuge at St. Rita's. We presented ourselves to the electronic monitor and were permitted to drive into the interior courtyard. Serena Dove herself welcomed us at the door of the former convent. With a sigh of relief, I consigned Ada to Serena's spiritual care.

"Well, that should be the last of our involvement with the Richters," I said as I drove Fiona to her cottage in Plymouth center. "I thought maybe you were humming a spell back there to deflect Jerry Richter."

"Yes, but I doubt that we've heard the last of him," Fiona said. "Magic is all well and good, but you'd better contact your daughter at Katz and Kinder in case we need legal help."

CHAPTER FIVE

You've got to jump off cliffs
and build your wings on the way down.
Ray Bradbury

The four of us went to the airport to see Deidre and Conor off on their Roman adventure. Conor seemed entirely relaxed and nonchalant, a seasoned traveler with a minimum of luggage. For his *Nat Geo* photography assignment, he'd brought only his Nikon. It would be easier, he said, to rent all the other equipment he'd need from an Italian shop rather than to have to shepherd the lot through Security and Customs. Deidre's luggage, however, more than made up for Conor's Spartan travel gear, with her carry-on doubling as a work bag and several suitcases which had to be checked through.

Mother Ryan had decided it was best if the children said their good-byes on home turf, so Deidre was footloose and fancy-free for the first time in many years. And she looked it!

She was wearing a casual shirt, a khaki vest, and seasoned jeans just like Conor's. Her vest pockets, however, were filled with sewing notions and embroidery accoutrements instead of filters and lenses. They carried matching leather jackets, and Deidre sported a Travel Smith shoulder bag. "I feel as if I've forgotten something or someone important," she confessed to us, blue eyes sparkling. "Because this can't be me, flying off with no responsibilities."

"Do you a world of good!" Phillipa declared. "But I wish you'd have let me pack you a decent lunch. All you're going to get on Alitalia is some nuked pizza, you know."

"Be sure to check out that cat refuge in Rome. It's called Torre Argentina," Heather said. "The volunteers are feeding hundreds of cats who have taken refuge in the oldest Roman ruins. Where did you say you were staying?'

"Conor's rented a small apartment on the Via Capo d'Africa. It's within walking distance of the Colosseum where he'll be working.

"How very cozy," Fiona said, tossing an extra pinch of pollen over our departing friend. "Now don't forget to get in touch with Anna Amici in Benevento. And give me a call if you need any words or anything. Do you have a BlackBerry?"

"Conor has one."

Fiona reached into her reticule and brought out a small notebook and pen. "Just write down the number for me, would you? You never can tell…"

"Here…take this for the plane. Lavender and sage, very soothing." I pushed a small dream pillow into her work basket. "We'll miss you, you lucky girl. Throw a coin in the Trevi fountain for me."

Not a glimpse did I have, as we all hugged Deidre at the security gate, that I would be tossing that coin myself in a few days time.

Conor was already through, urgently motioning to Deidre. "Oops! Gotta go, girls." Deidre's face was alight with joy as she ran to join Conor.

༺༄

Feeling a tad guilty about just dropping Ada Richter in Serena's lap, I called my daughter Becky, a family law attorney, and filled her in on the situation. "So there you have it, honey. Ada may need a lawyer somewhere along the line."

Becky whistled. "Jerry Richter. You couldn't have crossed a more ruthless bastard if you'd tried. He's going to find where his wife is hiding, and he's going to raise merry hell."

"By that time, we'll have had two psychiatrists declare that she's *compos mentis*. There's an incident report at the police station in Plymouth, but Richter decided not to file a complaint."

"What kind of incident?"

"A fire in his study. A chair cushion. Richter claims that his wife is into pyrokinesis—firestarting."

"*Is she*, Mom?"

"He has no proof of that."

"Oh, good heavens. Okay, I'll have a look at the incident report, and I'll drop over to St. Rita's to meet my new client. I just don't know where you find these weird needy women, Mom."

"They find me, Becky. In this case, Patty Peacedale asked me to help Ada. What else could I do? Be sure to call Serena first. The gate is kept locked."

"Sure, Mom. I know the drill. I'm also going to keep a weather eye out for some hulking, skulking private eye. Richter has some beauts who work for him, you know."

"I leave it all in your capable hands," I said. And that was truer than I could imagine at the time

Because three days later, Fiona got the panic call from Deidre.

Conor had been kidnapped!

∽

"Dee was at the borderline of a full hysteria. She could hardly talk between little spurts of panicky screams," Fiona said. "We said some words together on the phone, invoked the appropriate goddesses and guardians, and I think she became somewhat calmer. There was a young man from *Nat Geo* there with her, and a woman officer named Carmela from the Polizia di Stato, so she isn't alone at the apartment."

We were clustered in Fiona's living room for an emergency meeting. On the scarred cherry coffee table, there was a steaming pot of lapsang souchon and a bottle of Glenlivet, even though it was only ten in the morning. Phillipa and I drank tea in thistle mugs; Heather and Fiona sipped restorative glasses of Scotch.

Between sobs, Deidre had told Fiona that *National Geographic* was being instructed to pay 500,000 Euros for the return of their photographer. That was about $650,000 in US currency. The kidnappers would be in touch later with delivery instructions.

Commissario Russo from the Polizia di Stato, who seemed to be taking charge of the case, suspected that the 'Ndrangheta was responsible, a gang of criminals from Calabria, similar to the Sicilian Mafia. The kidnapping of a foreign national also involved the Guardia di Finanza, financial police. Since the Italian government had passed a law forbidding the payment of ransom and immediately freezing the assets of victims' families, the number of incidents had dropped off considerably. But an American firm could find ways to bypass Italian banks and the Guardia di Finanza, as the resourceful mobsters knew very well.

"Dee begged me to fly to Rome at once and do a finding. She said in recent incidents, kidnappers had sent the families pieces of the victims' ears as 'proof of life'. She's desperate for me to locate the place where Conor's being held before they start hacking him up," Fiona said. "Although their apartment is on the small side, Dee said, the living room is a generous size, with an alcove where she'll have a cot put up for me."

"Oh, to Hades with that. *we'll all go*. Everyone's passports in order?" demanded Heather. She tossed her long chestnut braid back resolutely. Her hazel eyes shone with determination.

"Oh, goodie." Fiona sighed with relief. "I feel I could really use the back-up this time—it seems a dangerous and chancy situation." She took a tiny bottle of sage oil out of her reticule and dabbed a drop on her wrists, offering it around to the rest of us like a package of Tic-Tacs. "I've arranged for Laura Belle to spend a few days, or however long it takes, with her grandparents, Don and Viv MacDonald, in Boston. They're a tad nervous about my darling's little penchant for truth-telling, but as she doesn't speak very often, I assured them there would be little or no occasion for embarrassment. So, I'm ready to go as soon as possible."

"But if the apartment is really small..." Phillipa protested.

"Not to worry," Heather said. "I'll make reservations for us elsewhere. For you, too, Fiona. Just leave all the travel preparations to me."

With the Morgan family fortune in hand, Heather was prone to grand gestures.

"We did that when we all cruised to Bermuda," Phillipa said, "and you went overboard as usual. So to speak. Could I ask that you keep it simple this time? Because I insist on paying my share, so no rental at the Taj Mahal."

"Of course, Phil. That's in India, anyway. Just the bare necessities. Because the important thing is that we do all we can to rescue poor Conor. Oh, to think that Dee finds love at long last only to have him snatched away in this cruel, cruel way," Heather said, casting her arms wide dramatically. "We'll have to use candles. I'll bring my psychic power purples. And we'll need incense and herbs. Cass, you bring your herbal first aid kit."

"Do you want Cass to be detained by the airport police for trying to smuggle in controlled substances?" Phillipa asked tartly. "I doubt those guys can tell one herb from another. And you'd better take care that your potent purples don't appear to be suspicious either. "

"Whatever herbs are needed I will get for Cass in Benevento," Fiona said.

"Joe's still in Indonesia," I said faintly. I had longed and *spelled* for an exciting trip, *but not this way*, with grave peril to someone we cared about. We could use some psychic help with search and rescue, of course. Should I take my prototype visionary pillow, the one that I kept hiding for myself to avoid the trances it invoked? No, it was stuffed with herbs and quite redolent. Suppose some officious security person questioned the contents? "Will I be able to leave Scruffy and Raffles with Dick. Or if not with Dick, at the Animal Lovers Sanctuary?"

"Yes, and you'll have to take Boadicea back to home base, too," Phillipa said with feigned regret. "Stone sometimes has to work long hours, and that's not fair to the poor dear." Despite every protest, Heather had sicced the fierce old boxer onto the Stern household to guard against the thieving O'Reillys, and Phillipa was jumping at this opportunity to restore her peaceful, cat-centered household.

"Well, don't blame me, Phil, if your light-fingered neighbors walk off with the store. A good guard dog is better than any alarm system ever devised by humans," Heather declared, and not for the first time. "Holy Hecate! In all the excitement, I forgot to tell you! I finally hired a couple to help us out. So the thing is, Cass, your two can stay right at the house with my crew, where they'll be ever so much more comfy."

Who? who? who? We sounded like a chorus of owls, eager for a bright note in an otherwise black morning.

"You know them, Cass. I believe you ran into them once or twice. The Kitcheners, Max and Elsa. You remember— the couple who found Madame de Rochemont's body in the cistern? They're British, you know. Oh, you'll love Max. He's a real old-fashioned butler. But it's okay—they're cool with the dogs. Elsa used to have Corgis 'just like the queen's', she said."

"Your very own Jeeves. How cool is that!" Phillipa said. "Maybe your luck in domestic matters has changed."

Heather's news flash hadn't come as a revelation to me, but I'd mastered the art of the flabbergasted face. The psychic glimpse I'd had of Heather's new houseman, however, had been along the lines of *My Man Godfrey*. A kind of high class butler imposter, who solves all the household problems with perfect aplomb and *then reveals his true identity as a gentleman*. But one thing a clairvoyant should never do is to claim unrevealed prior knowledge. So I did not say, *That's what I saw, but I didn't tell you.*

"I met Kitchener under adverse circumstances," I said. "In defense of his employer, he was threatening me with a French rolling pin that looked a lot like a baseball bat. I can certainly vouch for his protectiveness. How did you find each other?"

"The long arm of coincidence, otherwise known as *the Cosmos' answer to a maiden's prayer*. I happened to run into Rosalie Boyd Idelicato in Bartie Bangs' office. In fact, she introduced herself. She's one of the executors of the de Rochemont estate, and Bartie is her attorney, as well as mine. She knew all about our infamous circle of five and our involvement in solving the disappearance of Madame. Since I happened to mention my housekeeping problems, she told me that she was going to have to let the Kitcheners go now that the estate was being sold. She gave them a wonderful recommendation. Loyal, reliable, and efficient."

"Well, *mazel tov!*" Phillipa exclaimed. "It certainly sounds as if you've found the perfect couple for the Morgan-Devlin menagerie."

I joined the general chorus of congratulations but I did have some private reservations. For some reason, I felt there was more to the Kitchener history than was written in their resume.

But I would say a few good words for the new arrangement and hope for a blessing.

Meanwhile Heather was on her cell phone explaining the situation to Dick, the quintessential understanding husband and all-around teddy bear. She admonished all of us to go right home and pack for "however long it takes," because she would have tickets for us on Alitalia by tomorrow or the next day at the latest.

"I'll tell Stone about this little jaunt in person," Phillipa said. "I don't think he's going to be wild about the idea of our taking off without notice and discussion to track down a gang of ruthless kidnappers in a foreign country. Oh well, I'll just have to be very reassuring that we will stay strictly in the background and let the Italian police handle all the rough stuff. I wonder if Stone has any contacts with Interpol or the Polizia di Stato?"

My plan was to send an email to Joe on board the Gaia in Indonesia, and hope that it reached him after the fact, to spare myself the lecture that Phillipa was going to get. The worst part, though, would be explaining to my canine companions that they were about to be shunted off to Heather's place for an undetermined stay. Raffles enjoyed the "doggie day care" atmosphere of the place, but Scruffy would not be amused.

֍

Caged for a week with that mangy, flea-bitten crew? No way, Toots! It's a zoo, not a place for a savvy canine with all his marbles and gonads intact. And I don't fancy being stuck in that garage-kennel with the big guys who snore all night. Sleep deprivation, kennel cough, ticks, hookworm, parasites, and a nasty case of the trots with that diet of twigs and bark they give us. There's a law against animal abuse, you know. I think I'm feeling sick already. Ack Ack Ack. It's not fair!.

Not fair! Not fair! Raffles adopted a dejected air that was quite foreign to his exuberant nature.

"You'll get to see Honeycomb—won't that be nice!" One more ploy to mollify the dissenters—Raffles was the offspring of an unsanctioned liaison between Scruffy and Honeycomb.

That grumpy blonde bitch? Never know whether she'll be in the mood for a nip or a nuzzle.

Nuzzle! Nuzzle!

"Stop complaining—you'll probably have a grand time, you old dog!"

I set about packing my so-called travel clothes, most of which had been purchased from the LL Bean online catalog. But just to placate Heather, I added a few of the upscale outfits that she'd made me buy for the Bermuda cruise. And my visions pillow, which I finally found hidden in a built-in blanket chest under the eaves.

When something is lost, Grandma had taught me, I should simply walk through all the rooms saying to myself *nothing is lost in spirit, nothing is lost in spirit*, and I would be directed to the place where the missing item could be found. Most of the time this worked pretty well, if the lost article was still in the house and not donated to Good Will or the church fair. And it worked again this time, miraculously. Who would have thought of looking in that old storage chest for a visions pillow? Probably I'd been hoping its efficacy would be defused by all the herbal moth-away satchets I'd layered between wool blankets. The darned thing was a little too powerful for my sensitive psyche.

But this wasn't a cruise, and I didn't fancy lugging a lot of excess baggage around a foreign city, so I settled on one quite large suitcase and a neat carry-on, both on wheels, a resolve that caused some painful decision-making, particularly pertaining to shoes. Why did every outfit seem to call for a different pair? How I wished I could throw just a few clothes into a duffle like

Joe's and not worry about what I would need for occasions I couldn't anticipate!

While I was going through this soul-searching, with every stitch of clothing I owned out on the bed or hanging off chairs, Joe called from ship's phone on the *Gaia*.

"Hi, Sweetheart. I got your *uninformative* message. '*Going away with the girls. Back in about two weeks.*' Going where? Why? What's happening there? Are you all right?"

"I am fine, but we have a situation here. You know that Dee went to Rome with Conor O'Donnell on a photography shoot?" I proceeded to fill him in on the entire troubling events of the past week from the send-off at the airport to Deidre's desperate call from the apartment in Rome. "She begged Fiona to fly over and help with a finding, and Heather thought... we decided...the thing would be for all of us to go. We won't actually be involved with this criminal gang in any way—we'll simply see if we can help with information from the sources that have always worked well for us. We plan to stay strictly on the side lines."

"*Jesu Christos!* These are some ruthless gangsters you're talking about. I don't like this *at all*." Joe's voice had taken on a particular edge I knew. Angry as hell but controlled. "But if you insist on going, I hope you really mean 'the sidelines'."

"Of course, honey. Trust me." I really wasn't certain if I was lying or not. But there are times when a lie is kinder than the truth, particularly with angry men.

"*Yeah, yeah.* Listen, I want you to call the ship and leave a message for me when you get settled in Rome, you hear? Where will you be staying?"

"I don't know yet. Heather's making all the reservations—she's good at that."

"Sure, sweetheart, if you like all that first-class, five-star stuff. Listen, I love you very much, every last part of you, and I need you to promise you'll stay safe."

"On my honor as a devout coward, I will stay safe." After all, with friends like mine to watch my back, I felt secure enough.

Meanwhile, Scruffy was nosing around the open suitcase with a suspicious expression. *You smell that big bag thing there? Disgusting, isn't it? When she takes that one out of the closet, it always means trouble and neglect for us canines.* Scruffy educated his offspring on life with human companions. *Toots is leaving, she's going away.*

Going away. Going away.

They lay together under the big window in our bedroom and gazed at me disconsolately with their noses on their paws. Can anything make a person feel guiltier than the reproachful silence of one's loyal dogs?

CHAPTER SIX

Rome is the city of echoes, the city of illusions, and the city of yearning.
Giotto di Bondone

Our Alitalia tickets were *Magnifica* first class—no surprises there—which Heather claimed was simply an upgrade from her frequent flyer miles and would not cost us a penny extra. We were pampered with good Italian wines with every course: antipasto, ravioli, and delectable veal entrees, followed by pastry and espresso. Faced with the possibility of consuming crate-raised veal, Heather, of course, had opted for the vegetarian plate which at least featured some excellent eggplant and lasagna. Lulled with soft pillows and comfy blankets, we hardly noticed that we were, after all, flying over the remorseless Atlantic Ocean and several time zones that would rob us of half a night's sleep.

It was morning in Rome when we landed, groggy and distinctly overfed. Fiona was limping on swollen ankles. She leaned heavily on her walking stick topped with a silver coyote head. Coyote, wily shapeshifter, was one of her totem animals. She saw me looking and winked. "Don't worry. Just an old lady's walking aid."

We were excited and in high spirits, as high as they could be considering our desperate and distressing mission. But really,

Italy! Drenched in romance and antiquities! Who would have thought last week when we were slogging around Plymouth that some strange quirk of fate would whisk us away to an Italian adventure today! If only this trip didn't involve dire peril to Deidre's Conor, I would have been thrilled.

A uniformed driver awaited us with a sign that read "Ciao, Circle of Plymouth! Welcome to Roma." After an interminable wait getting through Customs, we were guided to a shiny black limousine with shaded windows in which all of our luggage and ourselves fit nicely. Heather sat up front with the driver, practicing the few words of Italian she remembered from courses at Vassar. He replied in English.

With faces pressed against the glass, we were agog at our first glimpse of the Eternal City, especially the ruins of temples left intact while the city was built up around them, craning our necks to view the Colosseum as the driver expertly maneuvered through a maze of reckless drivers. We finally drew up in front of a grand hotel in the city's center, which was appropriately named The Grand Hotel Plaza.

"Just the bare necessities," Phillipa murmured."

"Travel with Heather is always a marvelous experience," Fiona said. "I feel we'll be that much stronger psychically if we're physically comfortable, don't you?"

"So must it be! And I bet we're going to be supremely comfortable in this little place," I said as I unfolded myself and stepped out of the door that the driver had opened for us. Several smartly uniformed porters dashed out to handle our luggage, while we trailed after Heather to the front desk. Looking around me, I felt noticeably underdressed in my LL Bean chinos, turtleneck, and blazer.

Heather had booked us into two suites, each with double bedrooms and a sitting room between them, on one of the top floors. Her balcony opened to a gorgeous view of Rome, whose skyline is considered to be a national treasure; no high rises were allowed to obscure its historic beauty. "I'll watch out for Fiona. Sometimes she needs a hand," Heather said quietly. "The bellboy brought your cases to the other suite."

"This is likely costing a fortune," Phillipa said, looking around at Heather's opulent sitting room. "Are you going to let us pay our share?"

"The Goddess provides—blessed be her thousand names," Heather said. "My broker, Reginald Standeven, is one of those old-fashioned guys who buys low, sells high, and doesn't constantly churn the portfolio to make more commissions for himself. A couple of weeks ago, he found an opportunity for me to gain a substantial profit by selling some stock that was falling off the green bandwagon I prefer. Two birds with one stone. I was reinvested in a more environmentally-sensitive company and still made a considerable profit. The hand of Fortuna the Roman goddess of good luck was clearly in evidence. I wouldn't want to spit in her eye by divvying up."

"Nicely rationalized," Phillipa said. "But one of these days, you're going to have to see reason."

Heather smiled a Mona Lisa smile. "Right. One of these days."

I didn't bother to interrupt this exchange, which I knew to be fruitless when Heather and her trust income were involved. "Oh for Ceres' sake, let's unpack and freshen up so that we can get together with Dee as soon as possible." I really wanted a long, long nap, but Deidre was more important.

Our suite was just as luxurious, two indulgent bedrooms with Persian blinds and a glorious marble bathroom. The sitting room was furnished with sumptuous chairs and sofa, an accommodating desk with Internet access for Phillipa's laptop, and a buffet with fresh flowers, fruits, biscotti, and a coffeemaker. Our balcony overlooked a lemon tree garden. The scent was divine.

"I could get used to this," Phillipa said, wheeling her suitcase into one of the bedrooms. She began taking out her clothes and hanging them in the closet. They would be mostly black, of course—her signature color.

Curious, I turned on the TV set. *Little Women* was playing, the 1949 version. June Allyson and Peter Lawford were conversing in passionate Italian. It seemed a whole different film than the one I remembered, but I tore myself away.

A half hour later, Phillipa and I knocked on the door to the other suite. The four of us were soon speeding down the Via del Corso. Heather barely had time to point out the street adjoining the hotel where every internationally known, upscale name brand had a store. *Later, later!* We whizzed by the Spanish Steps and the Trevi Fountain with our *pazzo* taxi driver. Minutes later we had arrived at Dee and Conor's on the Via Capo d'Africa. Phillipa insisted on settling the fare, saying she needed practice handling Euros.

We met halfway up the stairs with screams of surprise, cries of distress, and exclamations of joy. Seeing Deidre again was a revelation of what stress can do—or undo. Our petite, neat blonde friend was an unkempt wreck! No longer a radiant young woman in the rapture of a new romantic love; her face was lined and drawn, her curls oily and limp, and her eyes full of acute misery. I'm not a fan of group hugs but I soon found myself to be part of a Circle-of-five huddle inside her living room.

"Holy Mother," Deidre said when we broke free. "I thought you'd never get here. I'm out of my mind with worry about Conor." A handsome woman in uniform seated by a window overlooking the street was introduced as Carmela DeCosta from the Polizia di Stato. She had the expressive eyes, dark curls, and square jaw that are so distinctly Italian, but she spoke very good English. As we were soon to find out, most Italians who had regular dealings with Americans did speak our language, and if Heather tried to converse in her halting Vassar Italian, they steered her away to English.

Leaving Carmela to hold the fort—mainly to wait for a call or letter from the kidnappers that would give instructions of delivering the ransom—we whisked away our tear-stained little friend for a private conference in Heather's suite. It was there that Fiona laid out our maps of Italy and Rome and took out her dowsing crystal from the moss green reticule to which she'd fastened a cameo brooch with the profile of a Roman matron. She polished the pendant against her new garden tapestry blazer. Fiona was ever a fan of flamboyant color.

While Heather ordered what passed for American coffee and a bottle of Sambuca from Room Service, Fiona began her dowsing journey though the provinces of *Italia.* The crystal pendant behaved so erratically that, if it were mine, I might have been tempted to throw the cursed thing right off their picturesque balcony.

"They must have followed an evasive route," Fiona said. "A canny bunch of gangsters." She rested her arm for a moment and took a sip from her cup of well-laced coffee. After a minute, she sighed, stood up, and walked to the window, quietly observing the suite's view of the magnificent Roman skyline. When she turned back to the sitting room where we were all gathered around the map-strewn coffee table, we could see her drawing herself up into a full-fledged glamour, a shapechanging we delighted in watching and grievously envied. Our plump little mentor suddenly appeared to grow taller and younger. Her coronet of carroty-gray braids shone in the nimbus of sunlight from the window, and the vivid colors of her jacket gleamed like heavy silk in more muted and richer shades.

"Amazing," breathed Heather, echoing all our thoughts.

"The goddess lives in every woman," Fiona said with an enigmatic smile.

"It's the *calling her forth* part that confounds me," Phillipa said wryly.

"Now I will try again, I will zero in on the place where dear Conor is being held," Fiona said, striding to the coffee table and purposefully taking her crystal pendant in hand. It swung obediently in lazy circles of smaller and smaller circumference until it came to a halting stop. I even thought I saw a tiny beam of light touching the name of a particular town. We all leaned over to examine the place closely—it was called Campobasso, south of Rome, in the center of the "boot" of Italy, surrounded by mountains.

"Of all the towns in all of Italy, how in Hades are we going to get the Polizia di Stato to search this one!" Deidre was exasperated and near to tears again. "It's always the same dilemma with us. *We know*, and no one believes us."

"Tell us how they grabbed Conor," I suggested. "Were you a witness? Could you pretend to suddenly remember a careless word that might have been spoken at the time, a phrase leading to Campobasso?"

"Oh, yeah. Like one of those bastards just happened to say, All aboard for Campo...Campo..whatever." Deidre paced up and down the sitting room, more agitated now that we had a vision of Conor's whereabouts than she'd been when we knew nothing. It was the profound frustration of psychic knowledge that we had all experienced from time to time.

"We were walking back from the Colosseum." Deidre collapsed onto the sofa, closed her eyes, and sighed wearily. I realized that she'd already told this story many times. "Conor insisted on carrying all the photography equipment except his beloved Nikon, which he generously allowed me to hang around my neck. As we passed some small shops, I said I would just pop into the bakery and pick up a loaf of fresh bread for our lunch. What a merry mood he was in! 'And I must have some pastries, too, for my Irish sweet tooth,' he cried out as

I entered the bakery. I half-noticed a black car slowing down and pulling to a stop at the curb. A man leaned out and spoke to Conor by name. I thought it must be someone he knew from the Colosseum staff. But when I heard Conor cry out only moments later, I ran out of the shop just in time to witness two thugs hauling Conor into the back seat, leaving all his borrowed equipment strewn over the street. Before I could scream for help, the car had raced down the street and disappeared. I thought I would die on the spot. I demanded that the woman in the bakery call the police at once, but she drew back as if she were afraid and made me do it instead. Me! I don't know a word of Italian. Well, just a few words, now. I could hardly talk, but I did my best. The dispatcher passed me on to someone who apparently understood hysterical English screaming, and a squad car arrived a few minutes later. Much too late, of course."

"And Commissario Russo?" Fiona asked. "When did he become involved? And what kind of man do you judge him to be?"

"He'll be around. You'll see for yourselves. As soon as I described the abduction to the officers who responded to my panic call, the commissario was contacted. My sense of Russo is that he's dedicated to his work but somewhat cynical and pessimistic about wringing ultimate justice out of the Italian justice system. That's just my quick impression, of course. How in the world are we going to convince him that Conor is probably being held in Campobasso? He will think we are all *strega*."

"Well," Phillipa said, "aren't we?"

"Let Fiona tell him," Heather suggested.

"Yes, Fiona by all means," I agreed. "Isn't there some *believe-me* spell you can put on this commissario guy?" I turned to Fiona who had thrown herself into a soft plush chair with glamour fast fading.

"As a matter of fact, that kind of thing comes rather naturally to a Pisces person like myself," she said thoughtfully. "Let me have another cup of that good strong coffee to clear my head." This was followed by a small ladylike *hic*. I glanced at the Sambuca. It was surprising how fast the liquid level had descended in that bottle.

"You could tell him you saw the place in a dream," Deidre suggested eagerly. "Oh, do we really truly believe that's where the thugs are hiding him?"

"Fiona has always been our true finder," I reassured Deidre. "I would bet the ranch on her."

"No, I will simply talk to him with map in hand. He's a man, after all, and men can be suggestible. What I mean is, a man can sometimes be diverted into thinking a course of action was his own idea. How old is the commissario?"

"Old enough to take on an avuncular tone, which just drives me nutty," Deidre said. "A sort of *just-leave-this-to-us-professionals,-little-lady* attitude."

"Let me see..." Fiona ruminated. "What is the most hypnotic of fragrances?'

"Jasmine. Rose geranium. Chamomile," I rattled off. "They've all been used successfully to intensify medical hypnosis in research on epilepsy. The thing is, though, we'd have to buy them. You remember that Phil warned me off trying to bring any of my herbal first aid through airport security?"

"Oh, good. I have jasmine and chamomile right here." Fiona reached into her reticule and took out two small bottles.

Phillipa raised her winged black eyebrows and rolled her eyes upward at me. "You should have given your Wiccan kit to Fiona. Apparently she and her little bottles of essential oils magicked Security."

"Does anyone have rose geranium oil?" Fiona inquired. She took out a large handkerchief embroidered with *ansuz*, the rune of connection and sacred knowledge, saturating it with the two scents. "No? Well, I think these will work as well, especially with a touch of the old glamour." She chuckled, that rich dark chuckle that is so infectious. Commissario Russo wouldn't stand a chance.

"The thing about aromatherapy," I said, "is that it travels to the brain by the most direct route."

"*Nose to brain, nose to brain,*" Phillipa intoned. "Don't even try to resist this woman's wiles."

"Well, Phil, haven't you always said that if you feed a man the herbs of his youth he will instinctively trust you?" Heather reminded her.

"Oregano!" Fiona exclaimed. "I'll add a little oregano oil as well."

∽

Somewhat out of breath after climbing the three flights of stairs, Fiona settled herself in Deidre and Conor's apartment where she would await Commissario Russo. Deidre had said he often dropped by in the afternoon with more questions. As soon as we arrived, Carmela left to make her report, cautioning Deidre again about how to answer the phone if the kidnappers called.

Although the place was small, it had a pretty little wrought-iron balcony with pots of red geraniums and fragrant rosemary, and the view of the street with its ancient stucco walls was delightful—a postcard of Rome. The apartment itself was quaintly furnished with various pieces of oak furniture, burnished and timeless, a few small cushioned chairs and a faded green sofa; Deidre's crafty touches had made it homey and comfortable, but an understandable disarray was taking over. In order to sit down, we had to move untidy piles of newspapers, correspondence torn open and abandoned, cast-off sweaters, and the like.

Deidre's hands were shaky, so Phillipa took over the French coffee press. An aura of uneasy quiet came over us as we shared the strong brew—it seemed as if we were all waiting for a call to break the spell. Fiona sat on the little sofa, her arm around Deidre.

Deidre gazed at the phone as intently as if it were the new household god. "I'll have to delay for three rings before answering. Any calls will be monitored by the police, you know. Although usually Carmela stays with me to advise and so forth. Maybe they're losing interest in Conor—do you think?"

"The police will not lose interest—I'll see to that," Fiona declared. "I expect that Russo will be along later, and Carmela."

After coffee, Heather insisted that we'd just be in the way of Fiona's campaign to steer the investigation to Campobasso, so she shanghaied Phillipa and me for a shopping tour of the Via del Condotti, just steps from our hotel. "Gucci, Armani, Prada, Versace, Chanel, Tiffany." As we clattered down the stairs, she recited the names with the ardor ordinarily reserved for a litany of goddesses. "It's the Rodeo Drive of Rome, only more so."

"I'm rather fond of Versace," Phillipa admitted. "You remember that I lost a Versace gown on that blasted cruise?"

"Do I ever! Your own fault, too," I murmured. "Almost got *me* killed as well."

"Let's spruce up Cass with an Armani jacket, what do you say?" Heather conspired with Phillipa to bankrupt me. *What was wrong with my L.L.Bean blazer?* I wanted to know. That must have been a joke line, because the two of them fell over each other in raucous laughter.

So we trekked forth on the buy-till-you-die expedition. At the Georgio Armani flagship store, I went immediately to the discreet *saldi!* rack, where I was attracted to a stylish cashmere blazer—a rich shade of green, always a good color for me. Seeing my interest, Heather grabbed it off the rack and insisted I try it on for size. It was a gorgeous jacket, and the fit was perfection. But one look at the price ticket, and I dropped it like a burning brand. The day that I'd pay $700 for a jacket (on sale!) would never dawn. Heather fussed, and Phillipa pulled me away for a hit of espresso at a nearby bar before she could be embarrassed by our heated exchange of views. We drank our bitter espresso standing up like true Italians. It was a bit like main-lining caffeine.

From Armani's we moved along to Versace—"*Mala fortuna,*" Phillipa muttered, and kept her American Express in her pocket. Then it was Prada where Heather bought a shutter-pleat dress in a lovely shade of blue for Deidre, and on to Gucci for handbags and scarves. Phillipa purchased a black messenger bag and an elegant black and white printed silk scarf, which at least was not *unrelieved* black. Heather wondered aloud if Fiona would use a new reticule. "Don't mess with a good magickal thing," was Phillipa's advice. They chose a ravishing scarf of peacock design instead. I bought a dark coffee briefcase for Becky and a small gold hobo bag for my daughter-in-law. Both were on sale, but I felt overcome with the particular kind of exhaustion that comes of spending an unaccustomed amount of money. At that point I insisted on another espresso break to rest my aching feet and a panini to soothe my jetlagged nerves. Heather soldiered on without us and caught up later swinging an armful of swank shopping bags. Apparently she'd popped back to Armani, Versace, and Chanel.

When we had limped back to our rooms, I discovered that Heather had, of course, purchased the blazer for me. I was too tired to make a really sincere fuss. When we got home, I would make a sizeable donation to Animal Lovers, her special sanctuary for forsaken pets.

Meanwhile, it appeared that I would be given the chance to donate what would have been my naptime to accompany Heather on her pilgrimage to *Largo di Torre Argentina* in the *Campo Martius,* where there was a cat sanctuary whose website she had been visiting from home. What a yowl! There must have been a couple of hundred homeless cats there, given food, shelter, and veterinary care by a dedicated crew of volunteers, who had started out with only a damp, unlit cave to house their operation.

Roman cats "of no fixed abode" had traditionally inhabited Roman ruins. It was a common sight to see a cat perched on a broken column or peering out of fallen masonry. So while Heather studied every aspect of the rescue operation, largely dependent on the donations of tourists, I reveled in the surrounding ruins. The square where the homeless cats had found sustenance was the site of four Republican Roman temples, the most ancient being devoted to Feronia, a fertility goddess, and to the remains of Pompey's theater. After their meeting house, the Curia, had been burned down, the Senate convened in the spacious portico of Pompey's theater, and it was there that Julius Caesar was assassinated.

It may be that the imagination of clairvoyants is more vivid than ordinary; I have no way of comparing, having always been just myself. But when I imagined the scene, I felt the horror of Caesar's last thoughts. To be done to death by friends and colleagues! They would drag his body back to the steps of the capitol like a sack of bones, then try to pass off their butchery as an act of patriotism. If it weren't for Marc Antony...

By the time I brought myself back from my time travels, Heather was writing a check and pressing it into the hands of the sanctuary manager, who looked somewhat flabbergasted. Heather hadn't told her the story of broker Reggie Standeven's coup and the necessity of spending a stock market killing credited to Fortuna the Roman goddess of good luck as fast as possible.

It was only at dinner later, Sabatini's in the Piazza Santa Maria, that we learned from Deidre of Fiona's encounter with Russo.

Still no word from the kidnappers, but Carmela was on duty at the apartment and would contact Deidre immediately if there were any developments—which is the only way we could drag her away from her obsessive vigil at the phone. By then it was nearly eight, which is "Early Bird Specials" in Rome, where everyone dines at nine or ten.

Heather ordered two bottles of Prosecco to cheer us on, plus bottles of Frascati and the house Chianti. Already Deidre was weepy into her *Pollo con Pepperoni* and no wonder. "How can I enjoy this beautiful chicken when I don't know how poor Conor is faring?" She pushed her dish away.

"The *Nat Geo* people were at the apartment today, two Banana Republic types, neatly pressed chinos and blazers with leather elbow-patches, Fred and George," Fiona said, teasing one of her grilled prawns off the skewer. We were all relieved that she'd not insisted on dowsing the food for wholesomeness, as she often did in restaurants. Wearing with aplomb (and a hint of glamour) the peacock scarf over a brilliant turquoise tunic, Fiona looked elegant and perfectly at home in the Roman scene. "Very supportive, they were. Promised that the publisher would pay the $500,000, regardless of proof...well, you know."

"Proof *of life*," Deidre said with a tragic little squeak. "Like an ear or a finger!"

"Commissario Russo arrived just as Fred and George were leaving," Fiona said, taking dainty but steady sips of the sparkling white wine. "Of course, there was no mention of ransom in Russo's presence. Italian law forbids it. But, what the *Polizia* don't know...some things are better left *obscura,* as we *strega* well know."

"So, tell all...did you manage to impress Russo with your findings?" Phillipa asked. The new Gucci scarf was swirled handsomely around her shoulders. Truffled spaghetti had been prepared tableside for her on a huge round of cheese, slivers of which became part of the finished dish, the truffles freshly sliced on top; now she was expertly twirling strands of pasta with a flourish. "What a presentation! I just love to order a dish I'm not likely to make at home. But I wish one of you had taken the Steak Florentine. I did want to taste that, too."

"A bloody big slab of a dead animal," Heather said. "It's early in the evening, but I was hoping that trio of musicians would play for the diners."

"Let us all remember that the human species is naturally carnivorous," Phillipa said.

"Oh, enough with the food fights, you two. I want to hear about Fiona's campaign," I said. "But I think your wish is about to be granted, Heather."

Two men and a girl threaded through the sparsely-filled tables singing *Santa Lucia* and *Funiculi, Funicula* to the accompaniment of a guitar and a mandolin. More diners wandered in from the bar.

"You never saw anything like Fiona this afternoon." Deidre waved away the musicians, the better to relate her story. "Well, maybe you have. Just another Fiona phenomenon. And in a rather different glamour, too. I don't know what to call it, but it's the persona that inspires Italian men to write songs about *Mama*. The commissario was quite *charmed*, of course."

Fiona smiled modestly and swiped a piece of bread in the prawns' brandy sauce. The musicians were drawn back to our table and played softly near her, *Sorrento* and *Core 'ngrato*. Fiona nodded to them appreciatively; they wandered off to serenade another table. "Not entirely a *Mama* persona, my dear. He *is* a rather attractive man. *Sympatico*."

"And all the time she's chatting on about the eternal beauty of Rome and where did he imagine the 'Ndrangheta were holding dear Conor?" Deidre continued. "Meanwhile, she's also unfolding one of those tourist's maps of Italy and wafting that jasmine and goddess-knows-what hankie under his nose. Silver bangles tinkling, her finger pointing casually toward the center of the map, in the general vicinity of Campobasso, of course. The commissario's eyes just kept following the musical bracelets, the fragrance, Fiona's hand. He gazed at the map. Fiona hummed. You know how she does. You could literally see the light of Fiona's vision dawning in the poor man's eyes."

Deidre's own eyes threatened to fill with tears again. "Then Russo leaned over and peered more closely at the map. He said that the 'Ndrangheta are rumored to have a stronghold in those hills right there, pointing right at the squiggles above Campobasso, muttering '*È possible, possible.*' He also said that they *could* send in the Carabinieri, but the risk would be great for all. I think that was the commissario's way of warning to me that Conor would be in the most danger." She put down her fork and pushed away the plate of *pollo.*

"This is not good," Phillipa said. "We have to dream up a safer method of rescue than relying on the Polizia di Stato. I mean, I'm sure they're efficient and dedicated and all, but..."

"...They're not the Massachusetts State Police and the FBI," I finished her thought. "I know that's very chauvinistic, but having Stone in the family, so to speak, has spoiled us. Anyway, what about a simple spell to keep Conor safe and bring him back to Rome? It's not as if we've had great success in working with law enforcement in the past."

"But how can we call Conor home when he's locked up somewhere?" Deidre wailed. "And why have we not received ransom instructions yet?"

Heather patted her hand. "If magic works at all, and we know it does, there is a divine energy that we can connect with—we've done it before. *Anything* is possible."

"With some occasionally weird results," Phillipa commented. "Collateral damage, I think you've called it in some of our past screw-ups."

"Now, now," Fiona said, drawing herself up into a Wise Woman glamour. "Let's have no negativity, ladies. Cass's idea makes sense on many levels. *If you want something done right…*"

"Thank you," I said. I'd been gazing at the candle centerpiece on the table, and I got a quick glimpse (in my mind's eye) of a swarthy man leaning on a motorcycle with snakeskin handle-grips and talking on a mobile phone; some kind of assault weapon was strapped to his shoulder. His face was deeply pock-marked, and there was a scimitar scar across his forehead. Fortunately, not much nausea accompanied this instant vision. My grilled fish was too good to waste. "Dee, I believe you'll hear from the kidnappers really soon, perhaps tomorrow. They've been moving about and now they're more settled, their plans ready. There will be a call."

"If we're going to spell Conor out of those hills, we're going to need a little help," Fiona said. "I have this contact in Benevento—Anna Amici—and I believe that she and her friends can be of assistance. The Italian *strega* will have some home court advantage."

"How exactly will you manage a trip now, Fiona?" Phillipa asked.

"I have a plan, if you agree, Phil. I thought that you might stay right here with Dee tomorrow in case there's news, as Cass thinks there will be. Your steadiness will be much needed. Both you and Heather have Blackberries, so you two can keep in close touch. Heather and Cass and I will pay a visit to Benevento and see what can be arranged. The trip is a long one so we may have to stay overnight."

"Yes, yes—I'll hire a car and driver!" Heather exclaimed. "I wonder what the hotels are like?"

"Ceres save us—please Heather, let's try not to be too ostentatious," I said.

"What, *moi?* You worry too much, Cass. It must be that New England puritan streak. I have in mind something practically invisible. An unpretentious gray sedan. And by the way, that jacket was simply *made for you.*"

"Apparently," I said dryly.

CHAPTER SEVEN

Let each woman find in herself her own goddess.
That should be the meaning of these rites.
Thornton Wilder

The unpretentious, practically invisible gray sedan that Heather had arranged for us was a Rolls Royce Ghost with a darkly handsome driver who could speak English, barely. Heather sat up front with the young man, practicing her Vassar Italian, Fiona and I in back, as we drove south on poplar-lined roads and gazed at the neat patterns made by farms and vineyards. It took a few miles to realize that the beauty of the countryside owed something to the absence of billboards, fast food joints, and strip malls. The brilliance of the sun and the lulling motion of the sleek car would have been enough to mesmerize me, only needing Fiona's melodic voice to complete the trance. She related the history of the city of Benevento and its association with the goddess Diana, described the ruins of a temple of Isis unearthed there and a sacred site where the magical walnut tree had once stood. I was sure, in my impressionable trance, I would memorize everything. I almost thought I was there in that matriarchal past, snaking through the cool depths of the temple of Isis in a sinuous line of women. And there, on a high moonlit hill, invoking the virgin huntress Diana. And there, dancing madly around an enormous branching walnut tree with other *strega*. I shook my head to clear it of the little film running behind my eyes.

"I've arranged for us to stay over at the Villa de Noce, an inn run by the Amici family," Fiona said at the close of her absorbing dissertation. That woman was a walking library. Phillipa had often declared that she should be bound in volumes.

"How delightfully rustic," Heather said, "but I thought perhaps the Hotel Villa Traiano…"

"Fu-ghedda-boutit," Fiona said with a distinct *Sopranos* accent.

∽

It was late afternoon when we arrived at the Villa de Noce, a rambling two-story yellow stucco building surrounded by olive groves. A stone patio encircled the building, offering tables and chairs shaded by trees rather than umbrellas, interspersed with fig and lemon trees in pots placed where they could enjoy the sunshine.

"This is, like, way beyond picturesque," I said. "Reminds me of a TV ad for some imported extra virgin olive oil."

"Let's hope they have hot water as well as pastoral views," Heather muttered.

We dropped our overnight bags on the slate floor inside the inn and looked around at the whitewashed walls and dark walnut beams of the cool sprawling lobby. Coppery urns held huge bunches of dried herbs, sage and lavender. The wall sconces, dancing nymphs, held up aromatic candles. A trio of imperious cats eyed us from the shaft of sunlight cascading across the floor where they had enthroned themselves. Immediately, I felt right at home, and I heard Heather let slip a sigh of contentment.

A small round woman with a broad Italian smile bustled out of the back rooms, uttering cries of delight as she rushed forward to meet Fiona with a hug and a kiss on each cheek. "Welcome, Fiona! I was so excited when we talked on Skype. Welcome to Benevento, dear ladies of America." Introduced to us by Fiona as her "internet pen pal," Anna wore a dark dress that nearly reached her dark laced shoes, and over it, a chef's apron, the ties wrapped around twice. Her hair was mostly hidden by a bright paisley scarf, a few white curls escaping their confinement. The scent of herbs wafted around her: rosemary, oregano, basil. Whatever she was cooking, I looked forward to the dish being served for our dinner.

Our hostess insisted that we must all have a glass of homemade wine to toast the occasion before being taken to our rooms. She poured from a decanter into rough little glasses on a polished but distressed walnut table; the wine was a powerful red that seemed to please Heather's knowledgeable palette a great deal. As we were escorted to our quarters by another of those darkly handsome, slim young men that Italy apparently had in abundance, she murmured, "I suppose there isn't a chance in Hades of buying a case of that excellent red and having it shipped home."

"I would guess *not*," I said. "Some pleasures can only be enjoyed *in situ*."

We were lodged in three single rooms, each as white and pure as a nun's cell, but with a snug single bed, good lighting, a discrete little desk, a soft bedside chair, and a sturdy armoire. And no crucifix over the bed. Paintings of an ancient walnut tree in many aspects adorned the rooms; bowls of apples, walnuts, and nut-crackers shaped like woodsmen (possibly an Italian version of the Green Man?) were placed on night tables.

"Comfortable," was Heather's verdict. When our hostess had bustled off to the kitchen, we compared rooms. "The Hotel Villa Traiano, however, would have been…"

"Completely conventional," Fiona said firmly.

"But we're sharing a bathroom," Heather complained. "And there are no phones. *Ergo*, no room service."

"It's a large bathroom," I pointed out. "And that marble bathtub looks divine."

"No shower, either, my dear." Heather said. "Oh well, I suppose it won't hurt to rough it for once." No room service and a shared bathroom was Heather's idea of roughing it.

"I'm going to confer with our hostess before dinner," Fiona said. "Why don't you two sit out on that patio and enjoy the afternoon rays, while I see about the business of the evening. Perhaps the young server will bring you an espresso." She hurried off to what was probably the kitchen as if she knew the place well.

"Or more of the delectable homemade wine," Heather said as we obediently went outside. "Whatever they're cooking in that kitchen, the aroma is heavenly. Dare I hope it's not veal or rabbit or goat?"

"You would, perhaps, prefer manna from heaven? Just close your eyes and open your mouth," was my advice. "And whatever the entrée may be, observe this countryside...the entrée was free-range for sure."

Heather sighed. "I do rather miss veal. Don't ever tell Dick."

The server appeared with two tiny cups of espresso and two glasses of red wine. He looked like a clone of the good-looking porter.

"Let's not tell Phillipa either," I said. "She'll be bummed out to have missed the country cuisine, the homemade wine, and the attractive young men."

"This spell to rescue Conor—what form do you suppose it's going to take?" Heather wondered. "Are you going to drink that wine?"

"Not a clue. But I feel strangely relaxed, as if we're in good hands." I passed her my glass of wine and drank the two coffees myself. I would need a clear head for...whatever.

We dined outdoors at one long table on the back patio overlooking the olive groves. We were joined by Anna Amici's sister, Gloria, an earthy, younger version of our hostess with ravishing dark curls, and her brother Giovanni, who smiled broadly under a lavish mustache and murmured *"Bene, bene,"* at everything that was said, convincing me that he understood very little English. Anna had doffed the apron and the scarf, revealing her abundant white hair, an attractive contrast to her smooth olive skin.

"We will meet with the other *streghe* as soon as the moon rises," Anna said in English. "There is a small private lake and a secluded grove of walnut trees. No one from Benevento would ever intrude. Sometimes a tourist, but…they are soon frightened away. The ceremony is all arranged. We will invoke the Goddess Diana."

Dinner was to die for. An antipasto of fresh mozzarella, roasted red peppers, and a savory local salami. The first course was polenta with grilled fresh porcini. Then, a savory ragout of meat and vegetables that was indecipherable but delectable. I guessed rabbit and sausage but said nothing. A sharply dressed green salad followed. Then ripe peaches in red wine and pine-nut encrusted macaroons. Espressos, *de rigueur*. A decanter of yellow liqueur which I knew to be *strega* made right here in Benevento. I thought I would be too stuffed to romp around in the moonlight, but when we set out at nine, I felt bright and clear-headed, and my toes were in dancing mode.

Anna and Gloria had tied rope belts around their dark dresses. The braids were blue, red and black, with thirteen knots and two sheathes, one for the ritual knife with which we were familiar, the athame, and the other for a silver handled scissors. *A trifle ominous? No more than our athames would be to a mundane.*

We drove to their grove in a gaily painted cart powered by two handsomely outfitted mules. We probably could have walked faster, but the mule cart seemed perfect for the time and place. Gloria drove the team, her dark skirt hiked up over shapely tanned legs.

At the lake's edge, with a bronze moon just clearing the trees, we met eight other women, all darkly dressed and loose-haired. *Ciao! Ciao! Comé sta?* Kisses were exchanged all around. They were several ages, and each one wore a similar rope belt with two sheaths. Three of the women carried brooms of birch twigs. Others carried bunches of rosemary, fennel, and rue.

Counting the five of us, we numbered thirteen, *so a perfect coven!* As it rose, the lady moon grew brighter and lighter, her expression sad and compassionate. Despite the dire circumstances, somehow I felt deeply blessed to be here beside a lake (albeit, a tiny one) in Italy under a benevolent moon. A week ago, this would all have seemed an impossible dream. *Best never forget that the goddess Fortuna, without warning, may take your life in an amazing new direction,, always on a day when you're thinking, nothing will ever change.*

The broom ladies swept clean the area in the grove for our ritual. Eyeing the bare feet of the other celebrants, Fiona, Heather, and I took off our shoes. *When in Benevento, do as the strega do.* One of the brooms was fixed into the earth, brush side up. "Symbol of the feminine spirit," Fiona whispered to us. *Would a broom with the handle up symbolize the male?* Elemental symbols, so beloved of Freud.

After Anna Amici cast the circle, a stone bowl was set on one of three flat stones at the center of the sacred area. One of the women poured strega into it and lit the liqueur; the alcohol content burned blue for a short time which was observed in reverent silence. Sandlewood incense in a small iron cauldron mingled with a scent of the walnut trees to perfume the air. Chanting in Italian, the women seemed to be drawing down the moon into the person of Anna. Holding the scissors in one hand and the dagger in the other, the women made circular motions in the air. Gloria leaned over to say, "This is our gesture of power."

Fiona produced a picture of Conor which I didn't even know she had. I recognized it as having been taken at Ostera last year, at our own outdoor celebration. Conor was caught dancing a merry step for the entertainment of the children, his eyes bright and his smile sweet. It was perfect.

Heather and I glanced at each other. "Fiona must have taken this. She never told us about using Conor's image," Heather mouthed silently.

"We've used photos many times in bringing home spells," I reminded her.

The photo was passed around the circle where it elicited murmurs of approval. When it returned to Fiona, she proceeded to wrap the photo loosely in red thread handed to her by one of the other women until it was completely covered. This she gave to Anna, who placed it on the second stone altar.

One of the women, Theresa, pulled her dress off over her head and went down to the lake with a silver ewer. *No underwear.* A pale naked body in the moonlight.

"Uh-oh," Heather whispered. "I hope to Hecate that this ceremony isn't going to be skyclad."

Gloria leaned over and said, *"No, no signora.* Theresa doesn't want to get her good wool skirt wet. She has to wade way out to where the moonlight streams across the lake. There she will fill the ewer."

Another woman, Fiametta, placed a silver basin on the third stone pillar in front of Anna. Theresa came splashing out of the lake, handing the ewer to Fiametta, who filled the basin. Caterina added a few drops of oil. Anna gazed at the oil in silence for some moments, then took out her silver scissors and broke up the drops with silent intent.

"She is cutting through the *malocchio*," Gloria whispered.

The thread-wrapped photo of Conor was passed around the circle again, and each of the celebrants cut one of the threads with her scissors. Gloria passed her scissors to us so that we could do the same. "We are freeing the prisoner now. We say, *the power of love breaks all locks*," she explained. "We will burn the bonds." This was done in the small cauldron that held the incense.

"Now we will dance the boy home," Gloria said. The women sang a litany of Italian goddesses—*Aradia, Diana, Fortuna, Vesta*...and we began to clap hands and dance around the sacred circle, lightly and joyously, faster and faster. The energy we raised grew more and more intense until, at a signal from Anna, we threw out hands upward to the lady moon.

Breathless, we sat on the brushed ground with the Italian witches as a bottle of wine and a basket of wine biscuits were passed around. "Cakes and ale," Heather whispered. "Spell-work always makes me *so* thirsty."

"I've noticed that," I said. "Will this ceremony bring about results—free Conor with no harm—do you think?"

"I have every faith in Anna and her friends," Fiona said. She sat with her back against a walnut tree, smiling benignly at us all and rubbing her arthritic legs. When it was time to leave, Heather helped her into the cart. Suddenly she appeared to be quite exhausted. "Magic can be tiring," she whispered, "if you put your whole spirit into it."

As soon as we returned to our rooms that night, Heather got an excited call from Phillipa. "A good thing I was here with Dee," she said. As I'd predicted, the gangsters had called Deidre. Not to tell her how the money was to be paid, but to up the demand from 500,000 Euros to 750,000, nearly a million in American dollars.

Shortly after the new ransom demand, a messenger had arrived with a small parcel for Deidre. Inside the box was what appeared to be a blackened portion of a little finger nested in cotton, and accompanying the grisly object was the Roman gargoyle amulet that Deidre had made for Conor. Commissario Russo questioned the messenger extensively. The boy could only describe the sender as an elderly woman who met him on the street a few blocks away from the apartment with the package, the address, and the fee for delivery.

Deidre had been hysterical with fear and anger, Phillipa said, and it had been all she and Carmela could do to calm her with cold cloths and an herbal tisane that the policewoman had recommended.

Fiona took the phone, and with a wisp of glamour about her shoulders, firmly declared, "Phil, I want you to tell Dee that the finger does *not* belong to Conor. Tell her we performed a ritual tonight that will free Conor from his captors—unharmed."

We promised to start back the first thing in the morning. "Also, Phil, stress to Dee that the Benevento ladies evoked a most impressive spell," I said. "Fiona is very hopeful." In truth, I wasn't absolutely convinced that this evening's work would bring forth the needed miracle, but I always feel that an optimistic outlook is a charm in itself. Optimists live happier lives, except for that occasional nasty shock when things go wrong.

After good-byes and hugs and promises to keep in touch with Anna Amici, the driver sped us out of Benevento in the early morning, past houses advertising tarot and palm-reading and shops offering magical ingredients. Unlike the charming locale of the Villa de Noce, the town itself was as commercial as Salem back home.

But our driver, as if embarrassed by all this commercial enterprise, took the time to point out two outstanding ruins, Trajan's arch, one of the best preserved victory arches in Italy, and the Teatro Romano, a Roman theater that, in its time, could seat an audience of twenty thousand. Soothed into trance by the motion of the car, it was easy for me to imagine myself in that crowd, weeping over one of Seneca's plays.

Fiona slept all the way back to Rome, snoring lightly, and Heather and I drowsed in and out—the whole experience had been exhausting but illuminating. Italian magic! This whole evening would be just the experience to write up in my traveler's grimoire. So far, the blank pages of that lovely little book had seemed too pristine to desecrate with mere travel notes. But *this*! Never could tell when a bit of strega know-how might come in handy.

"Do you think we ought to carry silver scissors?" I whispered to Heather.

"Sure. Good for cutting coupons, opening plastic packages, and scaring the crap out of bad guys," was her conclusion. "A woman armed with a scissors—who knows what she will want to snip?"

CHAPTER EIGHT

Nor shall my love avail you in your hour.
In spite of all my love, you will arise
Upon that day and wander down the air
Obscurely as the unattended flower...
Edna St. Vincent Millay

Deidre met us with screams and cries—who could blame her? Phillipa was standing by with a lacy shawl (her own, black of course) and a cup of tea, looking essentially helpless to deal with the escalating crisis. The small parcel containing an anonymous finger had been taken away to the lab by Carmela, but Commissario Russo was still there. Fiona had already met him, but Heather and I had not. His warm brown eyes and sympathetic expression made him a reassuring figure, and, as Fiona had observed, he was handsome in a rugged, compact way that reminded me of Joe. Abundant gray hair, full lips, a cleft chin. *Yes!*

Obviously, he was still enchanted by Fiona, whose hand he kissed in a lingering way. "Nothing is known yet, I'm afraid," he told us gently. "We will compare DNA of this *thing* we've been sent with what we can find on Signor O'Donnell's hairbrush, but that may take some time. The laboratory..." Russo spread his hands in a wide gesture of helplessness. His *telefonino* chimed and he began speaking into it urgently and quietly.

"It's not Conor's finger, Dee." Bangles softly chiming, Fiona put her arms around the little figure huddled on the sofa. "What do the guys from *Nat Geo* say about the new ransom demand?"

Deidre sobbed afresh. Phillipa motioned us all toward the bedroom, delegating tasks like a general. "Dee needs to lie down for a while. Cass, turn down the coverlet. Fiona, you hold her hand. Heather, get a cold cloth from the bathroom."

As soon as we were alone together in the bedroom, Phillipa whispered, "Fred and George are referring the matter to company headquarters in Washington, D.C. My sense of it— *Nat Geo* will cooperate if the deal can be trusted. Not a word to Russo, however."

"He's no fool, but he is accommodating," Fiona said. "He'll look the other way, if it comes to that. I've even talked to him about our special skills and our trip to Benevento, and he did not demur. The Italians are not conflicted about their beliefs. Any man who can be a good Catholic and a loyal member of the Communist Party at the same time, not to mention a devoted family man and still..."

"You have faith that the Benevento magic will help us?" Deidre sat up and let the cold cloth fall into her lap.

"I have faith, with all my heart and soul," Fiona said ardently.

"Me, too. Absolutely," Heather declared. "And now, since poor Phil hasn't been out of this apartment since we dashed off to Benevento, why don't Cass and I take her out for lunch, while you hold the fort, Fiona?" Then she practically pushed the two of us out onto the stairs. "There's a bar down the street where we can grab a panini and a glass of *vino*. Really, I think we should confer somewhere far away from the commissario, who may not be as accommodating as Fiona supposes. Now, Phillipa, tell us *everything!*"

"Fred and George as much as guaranteed that the *Nat Geo* organization will pay the new ransom demand. You know it's almost a million in US dollars?" Phillipa said as we walked to the corner. "*Nat Geo* assumes we will soon receive directions for wiring the money to a Swiss bank account of the gang's choosing. But the top men at *Nat Geo* are not happy campers. Apparently there's an insurance policy that companies working overseas can carry to cover this kind of thing, but *Nat Geo* never thought it would happen to their guys who are usually trekking through rain forests after rare orchids or following Bedouin tribes through the desert. The money is going to have to come out of the corporation's pockets. Well, not entirely. Do you know anything about Conor's family?"

"I didn't even know he has a family," Heather said. "I sincerely hope you are not referring to a wife and children?"

I shook my head before Phillipa could answer. "No, I would have got that kind of deception when he first shook hands with me. What about the O'Donnells, then?"

"Golly, Cass. What a treasure you are—you should be screening dates for single women looking for decent prospects," Phillipa said. "Dermot O'Donnell, Conor's grandfather, my dears, is a big wheel in The Irish Technology Group, developing the next generation of smartphones, handhelds, and something else beyond my understanding—don't ask me! Bottom line is, the O'Donnells have made a fortune in Silcone Valley and are now poised to bring their latest and greatest technology to Ireland. Fred and George told us that *Nat Geo* contacted the family, who have been 'very cooperative'. I suppose that means they are going to ante up some of the cash."

"Was Dee surprised? I mean, about Conor coming from a wealthy family," I asked.

"She hardly took any notice except to say that she had no idea. All she cares about is getting Conor back in one piece."

We arrived at the place Heather had spotted. *Il Caffè Pazzesco*. Most patrons were standing at the bar, eating and drinking. We ordered panini, a carafe of white wine, and espresso, paid, and carried our lunch to one of two little unoccupied tables in the dark corner.

Phillipa took apart her grilled sandwich and peered inside suspiciously. "Looks okay. Tomato, fresh basil, asiago, and prosciutto. A little olive oil. I could make this myself. I think I'll buy a panini press when we get home." She took a cautious bite.

Heather drank deeply of her wine. "Not bad for a house wine," she pronounced, refilling her glass.

I wasn't facing the door, but a mirror on the wall, none too clean but still reflective, showed me an image that made me push away my half-eaten sandwich and grab Phillipa's arm. The gangster with the pock-marked face and scimitar scar whom I'd seen in my vision a couple of days ago had just entered the café and was looking around. He glanced at our table casually, then sauntered toward the bar.

"We've got to get out of here," I whispered urgently.

"But we haven't finished eating…" Phillipa complained.

Heather drained her glass.

"No, wait a minute." The swarthy man turned his back to order a grappa " *Now!*" I insisted and practically dragged them out the door from the gloom of the café into the brilliant sunshine. A motorcycle was parked beside the lamppost. *His* motorcycle, the same as in my vision. I recognized the handlebar grips which were figured like snakeskin. Well, at least he wasn't packing that assault weapon, whatever it was. Probably something that cut a person to ribbons in three seconds.

"Try to memorize that number," I said as I hurried us back to the apartment.

"Hecate, preserve us!" Heather exclaimed. "What has got into you, Cass?"

"That man who just came in, the ugly guy—he's *one of them*. He must be watching the apartment. Probably followed us to the café."

"And you know this...how?" Phillipa asked.

"She's had a vision, Phil—what else?" Heather declared. "AG01824. The commissario will want to trace that."

"Oops!" Phil said, looking back. "The ugly one has just come out of the café and is surveying the street"

Grabbing their hands, I pulled them into an alley. "I think this leads to a back entrance to Dee's place."

"Worth a try," Heather said. With her long limber stride, bronze braid swinging as she ran, she outdistanced us in no time, then jogged back to tell us she'd found the rear entrance but it was locked.

"Let's try it again," I suggested. My sixth sense was still kicking in.

This time the door was not only unlocked but also being opened by Fiona. "I saw you from the balcony," she explained. "And I saw the creep tailing you. I gave him a good jolt, my dears. My best psychic whammy."

Making a mental note to pin her down later on the exact nature of the whammy, I asked breathlessly, "Is the commissario still here? We have a motorcycle license plate for him to trace."

"He's one of them, isn't he, the heartless *bastardo*? No the commissario is gone but Carmela is here," Fiona said.

Heather ran up the stairs two at a time to brief Carmela without being too specific as to how she knew the ugly man was 'Ndrangheta. The policewoman dashed down the front way, hoping to apprehend the gang member, but all she saw was the back of his motorcycle racing down the street and a black helmeted driver.

Carmela returned in a fairly exhausted state and collapsed onto a chair. I got her a glass of mineral water from the refrigerator, which she drank with a grateful smile. A minute later, she was using her *telefonino* to contact Russo with the license plate number. "How do you know he's part of the gang?" she relayed the commissario's question to us.

"He was following us," I said. "Why else?"

"The commissario says that Italian men frequently follow good-looking American women," Carmela repeated. "Nevertheless, he will check out the plate and see if the owner of the motorcycle comes from Calabria or has 'Ndrangheta connections."

It would be no use explaining to the commissario about my vision. No matter how Fiona had brainwashed him about our talents, that sort of thing was not considered evidence in the mundane world. I only hoped the license plate would confirm what I already knew.

∽

We stayed at the apartment for the rest of the afternoon. Phillipa made coffee—real American coffee—and found some biscotti to serve with it. Deidre alternately cried and slept in the bedroom. Carmela made a number of calls on her *telefonino*, speaking in Italian which none of us understood.

"Let's try to take Dee out for a bite," Heather suggested about seven o'clock. Just then her BlackBerry played its merry tune and she turned away to answer. When she turned back, she passed the phone to me. "It's your sailor, Penelope," she said.

There wasn't much privacy in the apartment, but it was still light and warm, so I took the cell phone out onto the balcony. "*Ciao*, honey! Now don't you worry about us. We're just fine. But tell me fast, how are you?" I rather assumed it was bad news. So many times in the past Joe had called to tell me he was in custody for breaking some law in an environmentally good cause, or that he had injured himself playing the hero with the younger Greenpeace volunteers.

But such was not the case this time. "I've finished the Indonesia assignment, sweetheart, so I thought I'd fly in to Rome tomorrow to join you. No point going home if you aren't there. I'll just be missing you, not eating right, and forgetting to take care of myself properly."

"Right. So like a helpless male creature," I agreed. "And as it happens, we are staying in lavish suites at the Grand Hotel of Rome, and I have a private bedroom with a queen-size bed."

"Perfect. Maybe when this situation is resolved, you and I can have some time together for sightseeing? There are so many things I'd like to show you..."

I sighed, thinking of all the fun, romantic things a couple could do in Rome if not on the trail of cold-blooded, finger-chopping gangsters.

"Any news of Conor? Instructions for paying the ransom? If you need someone to deliver the goods..." Joe, as always, craved being part of the action.

"It's been very weird, Joe. There was only one call after the first, raising the ransom from 500,000 Euros to 750,000—which is an awful lot in US dollars. But no follow-up with instructions on how to pay the money. The general thinking here is that, since paying ransom is illegal in Italy, *Nat Geo* will be asked to make some kind of bank transfer from the US to a foreign bank, Switzerland or the Caymans."

"Dee must be going crazy," Joe said.

"She's been through so much, poor little gal," I said. "And that's not all." I told him about the finger in the box and the amulet. "Fiona insists that the awful thing doesn't belong to Conor. I sure hope she's right. Because the amulet was...is... his."

"Maybe there will be something I can do to help," Joe said. "Anyway, I'm leaving tonight, so I should be there sometime late tomorrow, if the different times zones don't screw everything up. I'll call again as soon as I have a confirmed flight. I just wanted to be sure that you weren't on your way home."

"*Ships that pass in the night, and speak each other in passing,*" I recited with suitable drama. "Here I am on a balcony in Rome, and there you are in some environmentally-threatened forest in Indonesia."

"Sweetheart, if you flew to the ends of the earth, I would find you…"

"Oops! Hold that thought, honey. Heather is waving to me wildly, so I think there's been some news. I'll have to go now. Call me!" I ended the call abruptly because of the obvious excitement going on in the apartment living room.

"What's up?" I asked as soon as I stepped in from the balcony.

"Oh, Cass!" Phillipa said. "It's Conor!"

"Conor's escaped his captors and walked into a Carabinieri training camp near Campobasso," Heather said.

"He'll need protection," Carmela said. "The Carabinieri are bringing him back to Rome. They are well armed to protect him from any threat of recapture."

"I've seen them standing around Rome with assault rifles strapped to their backs," Phillipa said. "Talk about overkill."

"He's safe! He's safe!" Dee cried fresh tears.

"This is as it should be," Fiona said. "I'll send an email to Anna. A bit of *strega* reinforcement might be a wise idea."

We danced around the room laughing and crying until we were exhausted. Carmela watched us with a wary eye, talking from time to time on her *telefonino*, probably to Russo. "It's confirmed by the officer in charge at the training camp," she said to us while still on the phone. "They have Signor O'Donnell in their custody. But Commissario Russo is concerned about secrecy. He's warned them to keep tight security in bringing him back to Rome, that the 'Ndrangheta will make every attempt to grab him again…or…."

"Don't say it," Fiona commanded. "Banish the thought."

"We can't go out, then," I said. "Dee will want to stay right here, and she'll need us to stay with her. Moral and psychic support."

"Fine," Phillipa said. "I'll order pizzas."

Heather laughed. "How typically American," she scoffed.

"*Pizza Trasporto*," Carmela said, looking into a small leather notebook. "063340190. You can order pasta or salad, too."

And so we did. Heather found some red wine in the kitchen, and we had a take-out feast, still in an ebullient mood. Conor's escape was pure magic, and we all knew it. All except Carmela, of course. She refused wine and nibbled her pizza with a worried frown.

"I've called for back-up," she said. "We'll have some one here soon. They will be armed, of course." She patted her own holstered weapon affectionately. Both the Polizia di Stato and the Carabinieri were always seen to be packing plenty of gun power.

It seemed almost anti-climatic when I shared my own news over the remains of pizza crusts, that Joe had finished his Indonesia assignment and was on this way to join us. Joe thought the trip itself would be about nine hours, but he had no idea what flight he would catch and when he would actually arrive. I glanced at my Timex. "If he got a direct flight right away, he might even be here tomorrow. He can stay with me in my room, can't he, Heather?

"Of course he can! *Let not the marriage of true minds admit impediments.* I'll alert the desk later."

The two police officers (wearing those macho uniforms we'd all eyed covertly) arrived shortly afterward with serious-looking side arms, leading us naturally to wonder what sort of trouble we were being guarded against. With two more bodies crowded into that small apartment, however, it was decided that Fiona, Heather, Phillipa, and I would return to our hotel. Carmela and other officers would take care of Deidre, who was to call us the minute there was more news of Conor. The Carabinieri escort was in the process of driving him back to Rome, and we wanted to know when he arrived safely.

"Yes, you guys get some rest. I won't sleep a wink until Conor's here in the flesh," Deidre declared. She took up the embroidery that Heather had bought for her in at an exclusive needlework store near the Via del Condotti and savagely stuck a blue-threaded needle into the Madonna's robe.

"That girl needs her handwork for stress relief," Heather had said. "It's not like Dee to sit and wring her hands."

Fiona and I were fairly exhausted and went right upstairs to our rooms to relax while waiting for news. Phillipa and Heather went to the piano bar, where Heather swore she was going to order nothing but a double espresso to keep her awake and alert.

"A wise move," Fiona said. "Call us on the house phone if you hear any news. We won't care what time it is."

I was in bed, half-asleep, when I heard Phillipa return to our suite about midnight. She leaned into my room and said, "Joe called on my BlackBerry. He was just boarding his flight and will be in Rome sometime tomorrow No news yet on Conor. I'm going to bed, too."

Comforted as I was by the prospect of Joe's reassuring presence, it was an uneasy and restless night for me and for all of us. At six in the morning Carmela finally called Heather.

Conor was home!

"How is Deidre? What about Conor's hand?" Heather had wanted to know. Deidre was mildly hysterical and overjoyed, of course. Fiona had been right; the finger that had arrived by messenger had probably been chopped off a corpse. Conon's dear hands were intact.

"Oh, thank the Good Goddess," Fiona exclaimed when we met for an early room service breakfast in Heather's suite. "One says these things out of some sure inner knowledge, and then immediately one's conscious mind comes up with a thousand pesky doubts."

"I know just what you mean," I said.

CHAPTER NINE

Whom neither shape of danger can dismay
Nor thought of tender happiness betray...
This is the happy warrior.
William Wordsworth

We gathered at the Via Capo d'Africa apartment about ten; it felt a little crowded with us five, plus Conor, and three armed officers, counting Carmela. But it was a huge satisfaction to hug Conor and to see Deidre beaming with joy and love, although the marks of anxiety still showed in the dark circles under her eyes and listless curls. Conor, too, although freshly showered and dressed in clean jeans and shirt, showed the effects of his ordeal even more. A bruised cheek, a black eye now fading to yellow, and slight limp from a gashed leg told their own story of captivity and escape.

"So wonderful that you got away, Conor! Please tell us how you managed to escape," Heather urged. "Was that a miracle or what?"

"The girls have been saying prayers and whatnot for your safe return," Deidre said, winking at us and tucking her arms though Conor's as they squeezed into the one chair big enough to hold them both.

"A miracle worthy of St. Jude!" Conor declared. "Those devils had me secured in a kind of shed behind the main villa. From what the Carabiniere told me, I was being held in the 'Ndrangheta mountain stronghold. They chained me up by my ankle to an iron ring in the wall and padlocked the door from the outside. I didn't think I had an icicle's chance in hell to free myself, but for want of anything else to do, I worried and worked on that ring in the wall, as well as the ankle cuff. You'll notice that my feet are narrow enough for an Irish elf."

Conor stuck out one of his feet for our examination; it was, indeed, very slender for a man. It was also bruised and scraped an ugly red. Now that our attention was drawn to it, we could see that both of his shoeless feet were raw and sore.

"Well, time passes slowly when you're chained to a wall, but finally the girl brought me some muck of stew for supper and a wee bowl of olive oil for dipping the bread. I surely did yearn for a bit of butter, but the oil worked as well for greasing my foot. I wriggled and waggled most of the night and finally got the foot out of the cuff. So it was either get away then or get found out and beaten up in the morning."

Two tears slid down Deidre's cheeks; she wiped them away with the back of her hand and smiled at Conor.

"The door wouldn't give an inch—and besides, throwing my shoulder against it would have made a fearful racket. But I was, after all, in a shed, and as is usual with sheds, there were a few old tools and things. I found a putty knife stuck to a tub of putty on some shelf on the back wall. So I used that to pry around the small barred window until I could lift it right out of the wall. By then it was just coming to daybreak, but there'd been quite a party going on the night before and it looked as if things were going to get off to a slow start that morning. I eased myself out the window and sprinted down the hillside as if the fiend of hell himself was chasing me. Bare-footed, you know, but I hardly gave that a thought. After a while, maybe a half hour, I could hear the faint sounds of men and dogs on my trail, but I splashed myself through a brook to kill the scent and just kept on running. Finally I got onto a road which made it easier going. I have no idea how far I ran. Whenever I heard the motor of a truck or motorcycle, I'd throw myself off the road into the brush. Then one of the trucks stopped and my heart nearly stopped with it. But the driver only paused to take a leak by the side of the road and climbed right back behind the wheel. I could see it was a farm truck loaded with vegetables, so I jumped onto the back and hid between the boxes and bushels. After we'd gone quite a distance and the roofs of a town rose ahead of us, I figured the driver would pull in there, so I hopped off and kept running. The wind was surely at my back, because, lucky for me, I stumbled straight into this training camp. The Carabiniere."

"You were lucky, all the way," I said. "Maybe you two should get out of here now, in case the 'Ndrangheta are offended by your escape."

"Oh, barking mad they'll be," Conor said. "There's nothing noble or colorful about those gangsters, no matter how they're painted by romantic journalists. A bunch of dumb, coarse soldiers, except for the top men, the money men. But I'm going to finish the assignment I came here to do, and be damned to them."

Carmela, who had been talking on her *telefonino*, appeared to be only half-listening, jerked to attention at this remark. "Signor O'Donnell, please reconsider," she said. "We can try to protect you, of course, but these men are going to be looking for you. When they're crossed, no one knows what they may do. The safest thing for you would be to pack up yourself and Signora Ryan, and go home."

Conor smiled in his agreeable way, but I could see his jaw was firmly set, and his mind as well.

"What does *Nat Geo* say?" Phillipa asked.

"Delighted as they are not to be shelling out a million dollars, give or take, they've offered to spend whatever is needed on bodyguards and such while I finish my job. Also to pay for the damage to the rental equipment that got spilled on the street and so forth. Lucky me again, my Nikon was hanging around Dee's neck when those thugs invited me into their car, so that's still in good shape. I think we'll be fine."

I did not have a good feeling about this. I glanced at Fiona who was looking at me and shaking her head. Carmela on the other side of the room was shaking her head, too.

"If you insist on continuing your Roman adventure, we'll have to assign two officers to work in shifts guarding you," she said. "That's a great deal of man power to protect one civilian."

Unperturbed, Conor continued, "Think of it as protecting the safety of tourists in your beautiful, historic city. Also, I promised Dee a Roman holiday, and here we are in Rome, so we're going to do some sightseeing as well, as soon as I send the work to *Nat Geo's* editor."

"Conor, you'll be the death of me," Deidre said, but she was grinning at him, not at all displeased with the prospect of a little more time in Rome. I thought of the long days she'd spent working at her shop at the mall, Deidre's Faeryland, then home to care for the four youngsters, and how she'd more or less lived the life of an overworked young nun ever since she'd lost Will. And I remembered how she'd always wanted to be included in our most daring escapades. Cute little blonde she might be, but a woman warrior at heart.

"We're going to hold hands now and say a little prayer for the two of you," Fiona said. "Think of it as a spiritual shield." She nodded to Carmela, who smiled and nodded back.

And so we did, without conferring, surround the couple with our best blue-white light of blessing and protection. And Fiona performed her sprinkle of corn pollen thing as well.

Carmela had quietly slipped into the kitchen for a glass of mineral water.

We left at lunch time, as did Carmela, who we learned was going home to her two boys, ages ten and twelve, cared for by their grandmother while the policewoman worked her varying shifts. She and Deidre, it had turned out, had much in common and had compared family pictures and experiences during the past few harrowing days, which had helped to keep Deidre sane during the ordeal of Conor's absence.

One of the officers stayed at the apartment to guard Conor; the other would take over at four and Carmela would look in later as well.

There was a lunch buffet daily at our hotel, with an appetizing spread of Italian ham, salamis, cheeses, olives, vegetables, and fruits, like a lavish antipasto. "Ah, braised fennel," Phillipa said with satisfaction. I could see her mind ticking off the ingredients of the dish in that cookbook she kept in her head.

After feasting on all that delectable salty stuff, we went up to our rooms to nap like true Romans, last night's rest having been interrupted by the drama of Conor's return.

"Will they be all right, do you think, Fiona?" I asked, yawning over a cup of cappuccino in Heather's suite.

"We'll stay, I think. In case," Fiona said.

"But do you think that Conor's escape really was the result of our spell-work in Benevento?" Heather asked. "Or just a fortunate coincidence?"

"Patty Peacedale often says that coincidence is just the Lord's way of remaining anonymous," I said. "Substitute any deity of your choosing for 'Lord,' and I think she's on to something."

"We'll never know for sure," Phillipa said, "but we have had more than our share of happy 'coincidences.' We must be doing something right."

"*Intention*," Fiona declared. "Focusing on intention with ritual and incense, summoning energy with chanting and dancing, and actively sending our good thoughts out to the Cosmos—that's what we do, and I believe it works. And now, ladies, It's my intention to have a wee lie-down."

And so did we all.

ﹸ

Later that afternoon, we'd only been back at Conor and Deidre's apartment for a few minutes when Phillipa's BlackBerry rang. She listened for a moment, then handed it to me.

It was Joe!

He was on his way to the hotel, he said. No, I said, we're all at Conor's apartment, and I gave him the address. I went out onto the balcony to watch for him.

Then I could see him sauntering down the street from a taxi, the duffle over his shoulder. At last! Just to see his muscular walk and jaunty Greek cap was to realize how much I had been missing him. I ran down stairs and onto the street.

The pleasure in his smile matched mine as we hurried to meet. Then something strange happened. His expression changed from a look of love to a look of horror. He seemed to be fixed on something behind me. I could hear a motor roaring. Joe began to run. Two moments later, I was in his arms, but he was pushing me down to the street, covering me with his body.

A motorcycle roared past us. The man driving it was wielding an assault weapon. A stutter of shots rang out in the street. On the balcony where only few minutes ago I had been watching for Joe, geranium and herb pots shattered in the blast of bullets. I heard screams inside the apartment. The motorcycle never slowed down and was lost around the corner before the officer on guard could get down the stairs. He began talking in rapid, excited tones on his *telefonino*.

"*Jesu Christos!* Welcome to Rome," Joe said. "Are you all right, sweetheart?"

He helped me struggle to my feet, and without taking time to greet my lover or make a decent reply, I raced up the stairs, Joe following.

"*We're all right*, we're all right," Fiona exclaimed the moment I came into view. "Well, most of us. Carmela has a flesh wound in her arm. Ernesto is calling for an ambulance."

The apartment was still smoking from the burst of gunfire that had come through the doors that opened to the balcony. A line of bullet holes marking the back wall had destroyed whatever lay in their path, a bookcase, several pictures on the wall, an easy chair and one of Deidre's pillows, embroidered with the legend, *Amor Is My Armor*.

CHAPTER TEN

Speak softly and carry a big stick.
Theodore Roosevelt

"What the hell is going on here?" Joe surveyed the chaos with a worried frown. "I thought you gals and Conor were being guarded by the Polizia di Stato." The wall looked like it had been marked by Zorro, everyone in the room was still in a state of shock, except for Fiona, who was intent on tending to Carmela.

"We were. We are. Carmela, the girl who got shot, is a police officer. So is the man who just ran by us on the stairs." I put a calming hand on Joe's arm. "But as you see, Conor escaped the hornets' nest, and the hornets are not taking it kindly."

Soon I got busy administering hugs, asking questions, and assessing the damage to everyone's person and spirit. Surprisingly philosophical about the ruin of her pied-a-terre, Deidre said, "Thank the Holy Mother we're alive. That's all I care about. Wasn't it a blessing that you weren't still on the balcony, Cass! Oh, poor Carmela—how bad is that?"

"*You were on that balcony?*" Joe was incredulous, looking out at the mess of broken pottery shards.

"I was looking out for you," I explained. "So it was a good thing you got out of the taxi when you did, because that's when I ran downstairs."

Joe's face registered worry and anger in equal measure. I would hear about this later, but really, we hadn't planned on putting ourselves in harm's way, only in helping our Deidre through a time of trouble.

Fiona was wrapping a towel around Carmela's arm and administering the smelling salts she always carried in her reticule like a proper Victorian lady. She also managed an unobtrusive sprinkle of pollen over Carmela's head. Carmela was biting her lip bravely and worrying about her boys. After all the times she had told them that being a policewoman in Rome was not dangerous, how would she explain a bullet hole in her arm?

"They will be the envy of all their schoolmates," Heather assured her. "A brave mother injured in the line of duty. You'll be their heroine. The teacher will beg you to talk to the class, to dazzle the boys and encourage the girls."

Carmela's wan smile rewarded Heather for her flight of fancy.

Shortly afterward the screaming ambulance arrived and bore the policewoman away for proper medical attention. Then came Commissario Russo, who, if not screaming, had lost his usually calm demeanor, as he talked volubly in Italian (and with his hands, as well!) to the two officers he'd brought with him. There was nothing to be seen or collected, however, but a few casings on the floor or embedded in the wall. Soon the commissario turned his attention to lecturing us, echoing Carmela's advice that all of us go back to America at once.

Apparently, Conor had some Italian, because the two of them argued, Russo at top voice, like an angry general, and Conor quietly, placatingly, reasonably, like a wily diplomat. Although we couldn't follow the heated exchange, we could see that Conor had won his point as the commissario stalked off shaking his head and complaining about *Americani pazzi*.

"Are you ready to go home, then?" Joe asked me quietly. "Now that Conor's back safe and sound."

"Are you kidding? Here I am in Rome and I haven't even seen the Parthenon or the Spanish Steps. Wow! You really hit me like a ton of Roman cobblestones." I was rubbing my elbows and my rear end, which had taken the brunt of my fall.

"Want me to rub that for you?" he asked. "I've been told I have healing hands."

"Later, honey," I promised.

༄

The apartment on Via Capo d'Africa was a disaster, and the landlady was screaming blue murder (in spitting Italian) that Conor was *mala fortuna*. She wanted them evicted as of yesterday, and insisted on being paid for the damage they had attracted. When Conor took her aside, however, whatever settlement he made quietly and privately appeared to mollify her. But she was still sternly opposed to his continued tenancy.

"Oh well," Conor said, "I suppose you'll be happier surrounded by your friends, Dee darling," and he booked himself and Deidre into a double room at The Grand Hotel Plaza one floor below our own.

Although Conor still appeared to be careless in matters of security, there was no doubt that the couple would be safer lodged in the bosom of a major hotel than off by themselves in an easily-accessed apartment. Commissario Russo was better pleased by this new arrangement. An officer in plainclothes was posted to loiter outside Conor's door, and *Nat Geo*'s bodyguard awaited Conor in the lobby, to accompany every excursion.

༄

How delicious it was to have Joe with me in an unfamiliar and luxurious bed that night. Making love in a hotel room always has that extra fillip to it, an aura of sinfulness, as if we were two lovers having an affair and not a staid married couple. *The thrill of the unknown and the charm of the familiar.* Although, with Joe's job, we were apart so often that every time he came home, it was like another honeymoon.

I admired the new bruises, cuts, and welts Joe had acquired, as he always did on every Greenpeace sortie, and he admired, so he said, my voluptuous whiteness, like a Tintoretto goddess. Flattery like that will get a guy everywhere. But we tried to be very, very quiet, conscious that Phillipa's room was just on the other side of the suite's sitting room. But the feel of Joe, the smell of him, the taste of him was so arousing to me—inevitably we had to laugh at the failure of our own best efforts to be discreet.

The next day, nothing would do but Heather would have us all troop over to Trevi Square to throw coins in the fountain, an excursion I'll always remember as one of the highlights of our Roman adventure. I insisted that Joe carry my camera so that he could take photos of us five in this romantic setting. Conor had decided to take a break from photographing the bowels of the Colosseum and accompany Deidre, since he'd promised her a "Roman holiday," after all. So we had to be escorted by a police officer (heavily shadowed face, wearing the showy Italian uniform with red-striped pants and a side-arm strapped to his belt) and a bodyguard, one of two burly young men supplied by *Nat Geo* (very low key in faded jeans and a worn jacket suitable for hiding a shoulder holster.) Working in shifts, both the officers and the bodyguards were under their separate orders to stay glued to Conor's side for the duration of his stay in Rome.

The fountain was not as we imagined it, or as it had appeared in the *Three Coins* movie in Cinemascope. Although the water gushed with a gusto that quite lived up to its fame, the square wasn't spacious and picturesque; it was crowded on all sides by a motley crew of tourists who filled the plaza to overflowing, some of them pressed up against the iron railing that surrounded the fountain. Almost everyone seemed to be taking photos of Neptune and the horses, one calm and one restive to symbolize the changing moods of the ocean.

Fiona moved slowly, leaning on Heather's arm and using her walking stick for balance. The events of this morning, I reflected, must have been quite unnerving for a senior citizen, and I vowed to myself to be more protective of the oldest member of our circle for the rest of our trip.

Like a Roman legion, we formed a wedge and pushed ourselves up to the railing that surrounds the roiling water, and each of us threw a coin over her shoulder into the fountain. The coins had been pressed into our hands by Heather; they were of ancient Roman origin but not particularly valuable. Theodosius, Constantine the Great, and Julius II made their historic splashes. Phillipa hummed *which one will the fountain bless* and remarked "how corny is this!" But she didn't miss her turn to toss in Agrippa.

Conor stood aside, good-humored but not a party to such superstitious folklore. And it was Joe, not Conor the professional photographer, who stepped back to snap the five us tossing our coins and laughing.

At that moment, standing beside me, looking up through the crowd, Fiona saw someone she didn't like the looks of moving toward Conor. I felt her bristle; her elbow dug me in the ribs as she pushed forward, making a path through the crowd by swinging her stick back and forth until she reached Conor's side. The police officer was lighting a cigarette. The bodyguard was leaning against a wall, gazing down at the water. Joe had the camera up in front of his face, snapping pictures.

A short rough man strode purposefully toward Conor and drew something out of his belt. I saw the gleam of a knife and screamed. Following my gaze, Deidre screamed, too, at an even higher octave.

People turned to look at the two of us screamers, our aghast expressions, our bodies still plastered against the fountain's guard rail, but no one seemed to see the real drama. While I watched, frozen in place, Fiona took a fencer's stance and drew something out of her walking stick. *It was that rapier she'd promised she wouldn't bring!* Tall and lithe Heather was already shoving through the mass of people to join in whatever melee was about to happen.

"Holy Hecate!" Phillipa swore. "What in Hades is going on over there?"

Fiona lunged with the rapier. The assassin, if that's what he was, leapt back. Fiona thrust forward again, aiming at his middle. He doubled over to protect himself, slicing through the air ineffectually with his blade. The crush of people around them pressed away with startled cries. Fiona stepped back, then forward again with another lunge, this one aimed higher. With an ugly oath none of us could understand, the dark man jumped to the left and plunged through the mass of tourists.

It had all happened so quickly, it was over in the blink of an eye.

Heather reached Fiona just as she was putting away her weapon. Hearing the commotion at last, the police officer dropped his cigarette and drew his pistol. The bodyguard came out of his blue study, pushed through the crowd, and tried to tackle the dark man, who hurdled clear and rapidly melded into the crowd. Joe dropped the camera (fortunately, it was hanging by a strap around his neck), and pressed through the tourists to get to my side, while Deidre pushed the other way toward Conor. People close enough to witness our dramatic little scene pulled away, and a little murmur ran through the crowd in waves, but it weakened when it reached those farthest from the action who had seen nothing. Presently the crowd closed over the event like water over a dropped stone.

Conor, his arm around Deidre, looked at Fiona in some surprise. "Glory be to God," he said. "How did you get that little darling through the airport?"

"I discovered that swords are perfectly legal when shipped through checked-in luggage," Fiona said in a dignified tone, returning the rapier to its sheath. She glanced at the two chagrined guards. "The less said about my part in this incident, the better, don't you think, gentlemen?" She resumed leaning on the walking stick with the silver coyote head, the very image of an arthritic senior.

"Oh, will they never give up and leave us in peace?" wailed Deidre.

"Well, at least we've thrown our coins in the fountain, assuring that we will return someday to the exciting city of Rome," Phillipa said. "Although I doubt it will ever be this exciting again. Say, Fiona, have you been taking fencing lessons, or what?"

Fiona smiled modestly. "An old friend, retired stunt man, taught me a few moves in my younger days when I was at Berkeley. Haven't had too much chance to practice lately, though, because it upsets Omar, poor sensitive fellow. Took me half a day to coax him out from under the sofa."

"Holy Hecate!" Phillipa said for the second time, but softly, shaking her head in disbelief.

Leaning on Joe's shoulder, I closed my eyes against the gleam of the sun on the statue of Neptune, feeling dizzy and a little nauseous. "We'll be all right, Dee," I said. "It's over for now. These wise guys have made their macho point, and they're going to be pretty busy this week anyway." I felt justified in offering this comfort because at the moment I'd closed my eyes, I'd seen that little film that sometimes plays through my mind. It appeared to be a company of Carabiniere attacking the

'Ndrangheta stronghold where Conor had been imprisoned. I recognized the uniforms of the Carabiniere who had returned Conor to Rome, and who had probably debriefed him on the way back about the route of his escape.

Later, we discovered that the last photo Joe had inadvertently snapped was of Fiona poised with her rapier like D'Artagnan of the Musketeers. Heather had a poster made of it, which she hung in her conservatory at home where we often feasted after Sabbats and Esbats.

CHAPTER ELEVEN

Tourists don't know where they've been,
travelers don't know where they're going.
Paul Theroux

Dinner that night was at Piperno in the Jewish Ghetto, recommended by Phillipa, who was making a study of Roman restaurants. It was the kind of decision we naturally left in her capable, short-nailed cook's hands.

A police officer in plain clothes and one of the tough guys hired by *Nat Geo* were sitting together at a small table by the door, drinking wine which, judging by their expressions, must have been sour. They appeared not to have ordered any food. *Perhaps a requirement of bodyguarding?*

I asked Deidre how she had liked touring the Colosseum with Conor.

She shuddered and grinned ruefully, digging into her deep-fried artichoke. "You may say *I told you so* if you wish, Cass. That place gives me the willies. Especially down in those mosaic tunnels where Conor is working. But he was very understanding, weren't you, sweetie?"

Conor smiled at Deidre. "The poor thing has a touch of the Banshee, and she flees from her own shadows. Dee could hardly wait to get out into the sunshine, could you, little darling?"

"Plenty of sunshine at the Trevi fountain today, " Phillipa commented. "I bet the Colosseum looked harmless by comparison. *Ouch!*"

"Oh, sorry, Phil," Heather said innocently. "Well, here we are in historic Rome, one of the most celebrated cities in the world. So why don't we ladies do some sight-seeing, while Conor finishes his assignment? Keep Dee out of the haunted corridors."

"Oh," Deidre breathed. "I would so like to do the Vatican tour!"

"Ah, your Catholic roots are calling. But we'll have to stand in line for three hours for tickets," Phillipa complained.

"Not a bit of it," Heather said. "I know how to get us the kind of reservations that bypass the multitudes. It's too late, though, for the tour that culminates in a papal audience. That one has to be booked weeks in advance."

"*Ché disappunto!*" Phillipa said. "But let the Vatican be my treat. I have my laptop. I'll book the tour online for tomorrow at whatever decent hour I can arrange. If Heather will just be kind enough to part with the particulars. And by the way, these stuffed squash blossoms are superb. So easy in sunny Italy to harvest these lovely things all summer. Fat chance of that in New England. Perhaps if one contacts the farmer directly…" She made a note in the small brown leather notebook she carried in her new Gucci handbag.

"You must decide what you'd like to see most in the Vatican—other than the Pope, of course, "Heather said. "Everyone says there's much too much to take in on one visit. It would take a week to do the place justice."

"The Madonna of Raphael and the Sistine Chapel," Deidre said. "And *La Pietà*." Her radiant smile was more than enough reason to visit the *de rigueur* religious attractions.

"The Vatican Library is still closed for repairs, so…the Etruscan Museum is my second choice," Fiona said. "If there's time after Dee's Sistine Chapel. Did you know that Michelangelo painted the face of one of his critics into The Last Judgment on the altar wall? A cardinal who objected to the nude figures he felt more suitable to a tavern than a chapel. Michelangelo portrayed him as a judge of the underworld, with donkey ears and a coiled snake covering his genitals."

"How appropriate! I'll go along with the Etruscan stuff," I said. "Possibly the origin of Italian magic."

"I'd like to tour the Swiss Guards," Phillipa said. When Heather and I looked at her with raised eyebrows, she added, "Best trained army in the world. Cute uniforms, too."

"What about you, honey?" I asked Joe, who was working on his osso buco and listening quietly, as he tended to do when we five were in high gear. "I suppose you've already seen everything."

"I've seen a lot but I'm sure it will be a whole different experience touring the Vatican with you gals. All that psychic energy—I wonder if you'll set off any alarms?"

"Ha ha. I think we can get you through tomorrow's expedition without being nabbed by the Inquisition." I said. "Then you can relax, honey. Because after that we're planning to visit the Pantheon with its comforting Pagan roots, and Phil wants to bask in the Keat-Shelley memorial, her poetic pilgrimage."

෮

The next day's Vatican tour proved to be arduous indeed, and we were all a little footsore afterwards. Heather had commandeered a transport chair to spare Fiona from the miles of walking, and Joe obligingly pushed it from masterpiece to masterpiece. She'd not brought her walking stick, having been warned by Phillipa that all visitors had to pass through a metal detector. No brief tops or shorts, either. Not to worry—

we were staid Plymouth matrons with covered shoulders and sensible shoes. Well, we were witches, too, but it's been a long time since there was a working witch-detector at the Vatican. And we wore our silver pentagrams *inside* our shirts.

We walked those sensible shoes for what seemed like several miles of art treasures, stopping now and then for an invigorating spritz from the atomizer in Fiona's reticule.

"What is that stuff?" Joe asked.

"Mostly lavender," I said. "Goddess knows what else. It's very refreshing. Want a splash?"

"No, thanks. If you get arrested for misbehaving in the Vatican, someone with a clear head will have to bail you out."

༄

"If I never see another priceless Renaissance fresco again, it will be too soon," Phillipa said in a faint tone as we limped out through the magnificent Bernini colonnade to the Piazzo di Pietra, looking for the nearest café where we could rest our weary bones and savor a pick-me-up. Phillipa had not been too tired, however, to ask Joe to take her picture with a member of the Swiss Guard, who remained expressionless throughout the ordeal.

It was a great photo. Phillipa with her wings of shining black hair and black outfit from top to toe, leaning suggestively toward the sternly impassive Guard in his colorful striped uniform and cocky beret.

Heather had a poster made of that one, too.

༄

Joe warned us, but do you think we listened? *Don't go to the Pantheon on a rainy day.* Turned out there is a 28-foot hole in the center of the dome allowing "the gentle rain from heaven" to drop like mercy on all intrepid sightseers like ourselves. Also, the dim light from the oculus was mighty gloomy on an overcast day. Joe, proving once again that he was an exemplary mature male, only whispered "told you so!" once.

The report from Commissario Russo was another splash of cold water. He had tracked us down through Heather's BlackBerry, the number we had given him to contact us for emergencies.

The good news was that, as I had foreseen, the military arm of the police had raided the 'Ndrangheta stronghold where Conor had been held for ransom. The bad news was that, by the time the Carabiniere burst in, the place was cleaned out and deserted except for one ancient, very deaf caretaker. It appeared that someone had tipped off the Calabrian *mafiosa*. Maybe even someone in the training camp where the Carabiniere force had prepared for the assault. The 'Ndrangheta routinely paid informants in all branches of law enforcement.

"The commissario gave a mighty sigh," Heather reported. "Apparently he confronts this kind of frustrating result all too often. He wanted to alert us that we should continue to be very careful and to assure us that he had assigned two officers to take turns guarding Conor day and night—not Carmela, she's on sick leave. And, again, he pleaded with us to go home to the States. I said we'd go when Dee went and not a day before."

That vow was to return to haunt us later as our Italian sojourn kept adding days and destinations. But at that point, we figured Conor's assignment would be completed in a day or two, and all of us would soon be winging our way home.

The unsatisfactory raid was a case in point about clairvoyant visions. Sure, I'd seen the stronghold being penetrated by the Carabiniere, but I'd been clueless about what a fiasco the attack would be. It was bitterly disappointing to realize that Conor might still be in danger from resentful mobsters. The escape of a kidnap victim must have been a grave insult to their macho façade.

No transport chairs being available at the Pantheon, Fiona was leaning heavily on Joe's arm as we viewed the final resting places of Raphael and a royal flush of Italian nobility, whose tombs were watched over by an honor guard. The interior was immense and impressive in the beauty of its concept. Originally built by Marcus Agrippa before the birth of Jesus, the Pantheon was the best preserved building of ancient Rome, and had been an inspiration to generations of architects thereafter.

Fiona reminded us that "Its original purpose was to honor *all the gods* and only in the seventh century was it sanctified by Pope Boniface IV, and looted of its precious metals by later popes. Those magnificent bronze doors were once covered in gold. Pity. Still, becoming a Christian church probably helped to keep the place intact. I think we should hold hands and say words of power in honor of all the gods, as was originally intended." She hummed a few bars of "Give me that old time religion..." and motioned us into a circle.

Joe coughed or choked or something. I patted him on the back. "This is what happens when you travel with a coven, honey," I reminded him. "Spontaneous rituals at the drop of a peaked black hat. Why don't you go admire those splendid doors more closely for a few minutes while we humor Fiona." I took Fiona's arm and released him from his charge.

We formed our circle, attracting a few curious glances from tourists and a couple of security people who probably figured we were holding hands for some kind of prayer ritual, which actually it was.

"All right, but no dancing," Deidre said. "Phil, do you have some appropriate words?"

Phillipa's glance from under dark arched eyebrows suggested that she was never at a loss for an appropriate ritual. She closed her eyes and thought for a moment while we waited expectantly. Already I could feel the energy building up in our hands.

Dear Juno watch over our traveling days, Diana the huntress stand guard through our nights Athena share wisdom to guide us always, and Venus inspire romance and delight.

That sounded like a Phillipa incantation, always on the lookout for romance. *May the pantheon of gods and goddesses keep her safe from folly!* Phillipa was the tarot reader of our circle, but a card called The Fool flashed upon my inner eye—a traveler skipping along the edge of a cliff, oblivious to the danger of a misstep.

After repeating such a musical rhyme a couple of times, we could hardly help ourselves from tripping a little light fantastic around our circle. Even Deidre who had commanded *No dancing.* Nothing too obvious, though. Some tourists paused to watch, a nun grasped for her cross, and one of the security people held his *telefonino* at the ready. From the corner of my eye, I saw Joe slip out of the immense doors and lean against one of the marble columns. The rain had let up and the September sun was golden on the old stucco buildings around the square.

"Watch out, Rome…here come the darling dancing witches of Plymouth," Phillipa sang out, leading us in a soft shoe shuffle out to the Piazza del Popolo and across the street, breathless with laughter, to a promising outdoor café. We found a dry table under an umbrella. The delicious smell of freshly ground coffee wafted out from the bar. We ordered espressos and do-it-yourself pizza sandwiches from a selection of meats, vegetables, cheeses, and sauces. Heather insisted that we add a bottle of *Trebbiano d'Abruzzo*, and I must admit it did complement the smoky mozzarella and hot capocollo admirably.

"What about the Spanish Steps and the Keats thing?" Deidre asked, propping her little feet on an empty chair.

"We don't have to crush everything into one day," Heather said, "like ordinary tourists."

"No one who knows you ladies would call you ordinary tourists," Joe said firmly. "Adventurers maybe. Travelers certainly. In several dimensions. But I think Fiona could do with an afternoon rest right about now."

Fiona smiled at Joe gratefully, not denying it. To see her now, huddled in her coat sweater of many colors, her crown of carroty-gray braids somewhat unraveled, who would imagine that she had nearly skewered an assassin on her rapier the day before? Now that I thought of it, hadn't there been a hint of warrior-queen glamour in her instant response to danger? Perhaps there was something inherently exhausting about that transformation into power. Like my clairvoyant visions that generally left me faint and nauseous.

"You're right, Joe," Heather said. "Maybe we could all do with a lie-down this afternoon.

Joe moved his leg nearer mine under the table. I became aware of his warmth pressing against me, and I wondered how much self-interest had been at the root of his solicitous advice.

"What if we meet around four this afternoon in the lemon tree garden. There would still be time to take in the Spanish Steps if we feel like it. Or not," Phillipa suggested.

A nap with Joe is not necessarily a restful siesta—but refreshing in its own way. "Ah, love in a shaded room on a Roman afternoon," Joe said, stroking my bare belly, which I was pleased to see looked flatter when I was lying down with no clothes on. I'm not what you would call a poster child for taut abs. On the other hand, Joe is, and I admired his compact muscular body, the broad chest and waves of dark hair that led downward to his groin. After a while, we actually did sleep.

Then it was more espresso in the lemon tree garden. The cups were so miniscule, it's no wonder the Italians quaffed up so much of the stuff. Conor had rejoined us after his day spent capturing the frescoed escape tunnels at the Colosseum. That meant we had to be accompanied by the spiffy uniformed police officer and the casually-attired hired gun *Nat Geo* had commissioned as we walked to the Spanish Steps in the Piazza di Spagna, where Phillipa was incensed to spot a MacDonald's with a very discreet exterior tucked away to the left of the stairs.

"Oh, goodie," Diedre said, squeezing Conor's arm. "Wouldn't you just love a good old American hamburger with dill pickles instead of garlic and tomato sauce?"

"Oh, *delizioso,* Dee." Philipa said with undisguised sarcasm, making the sign of the pentagram in mid-air. "Not on your life!"

Looking just a little hurt, Deidre said gamely, "Well, Conor and I enjoy them. But the place does tend to get really mobbed. Italians don't seem to form orderly lines the way we do. It must be some cultural thing."

Joe laughed at our squabbles and, to change the subject, pointed out some unique features of the church, Trinita dei Monti, that dominated the top of the stairs.

"Blessed are the peacemakers," I said.

Phillipa was already wandering away to her heart's goal, the Keats House at the foot of the Spanish Steps, where the poet had lived the last few days of his life. The restored pensione, now dedicated not only to Keats but also to Shelley, Byron, and other romantic poets, was filled with portraits, prints, memorabilia as well as rare first editions and manuscripts, including those of Mary Shelley (my particular heroine) as well. Deidre and Conor sat outside the historic site on the stairs, their heads together, whispering like two teen-agers, while the rest of us followed Phillipa from one deep sigh to another. Fiona had her walking stick to assist her balance, so I put my arm through Joe's as we admired the displays. As is usual with me in such places, I became somewhat bemused with the abundance of sensations and after a while could take nothing more into my brain. Sort of like a circuit overload, I had to quit before I frizzled up entirely, so I went into a kind of walking sleep, nodding and smiling.

Didn't fool Joe, though. "Had enough, have you?" he said. "Just lean on me, sweetheart, and snooze away."

By the time we reached the room overlooking the piazza where Keats had died, Deidre and Conor had caught up with us, accompanied by the bored police officer. The bodyguard stayed outside watching with suspicion every visitor who entered.

But as soon as Deidre put her little foot on the threshold of Keat's bedroom, her face turned ashen and she backed right up into Conor's arms. "You'd think all these visitors would wash away any lingering spirit, wouldn't you?" she said, her tone faint and fearful. "But there's a kind of wisp in the corner. Not the bed—that's not the real deal. *He could feel the flowers growing over his grave*, you know. When he was dying. Let's get out of here. I could use a shot of the Irish right about now."

Phillipa looked at Deidre with a rare envy. "What I would give to see and hear a 'wisp' of Keats. *Silent, upon a peak in Darien.*"

"No, you wouldn't, Phil. It gives me the shivers," Deidre said.

"Me, too," said Conor with an elfish grin. "Just when I think the two of us are on our own, suddenly it's a *ménage à trois.*"

Nevertheless, we had to drag Phillipa away, still reciting, *When I have fears that I may cease to be...* and could only shake her out of her romantic depression by asking where we should go to dinner that night. Immediately, she brightened. "I made reservations at the *Sapori del Lord Byron* in the Lord Byron Hotel. Seemed appropriate somehow, considering today's itinerary. The cuisine is supposed to be outstanding, even for Rome. It's a bit far, though, the Parioli district, near the Villa Borghese. We're a party of seven, and that's not counting the dynamic duo of guards—I'll see what our hotel will do for us in the way of a van or something like that."

"This will be our treat, then," Joe said in a brook-no-opposition tone. Heather started to protest but thought better of it.

The brilliant Italian sun was setting, its final powerful gleams hitting some gilded tower that reflected directly into my eyes. Momentarily blinded, I grabbed Joe's arm. "There's someone watching us. I can feel it."

Fiona, leaning on Joe's other arm, suddenly stood taller and flexed her walking stick. Trying not to be too obvious, I scanned the crowd of tourists, sitting on the steps and milling around the shops and cafés. If ever I had wished for COD, clairvoyance-on-demand, it was now, but my so-called *third power of the witch* was unreliable. (One of the Thirteen Powers, according to Fiona.)

Seeing my expression, Phillipa nudged the police officer who had been sent to keep an eye on us and gestured toward the crowd. The Roman cop, a robust young man with dark glasses and a rakish tilt to his cap, wearing a short navy blue jacket, well-fitted, light blue pants with a red stripe down the sides, and brown boots, had already attracted her interest. Now he put his hand on his side arm and looked where I was looking. *There was something, someone…*an aura of evil intent, although admittedly, I don't see auras.

But all this sudden attention in one direction had made that *someone* nervous. A short, middle-aged, bearded man sitting at the foot of the stairs, rose from his obscure place among tourists in various postures of fatigue, and jumped onto the bicycle by his side. He cast one malevolent look our way and sped off, weaving expertly through the milling tourists.

"We're still being watched," I said.

"Now, don't get yourself and the girls in a tizzy—we're very well guarded," Conor said easily. But he put his arm around Deidre's shoulders protectively. If he'd stopped to analyze the situation, he might have realized that, the farther away from him she was, the safer Deidre would be. "And if all goes well, I should be finished up at the Colosseum tomorrow, so no more worries. We can book our flights to the U.S."

"Oh good, we'll be home for Samhain," I said. Actually, I was also thinking that we would be home for my birthday, the 21st, but it did seem a bit self-serving to mention that.

"And your birthday," Joe said immediately, bless him.

"My Good Goddess, this has been one eventful month between Mabon and Samhain," Phillipa said. "What else can possibly happen?"

CHAPTER TWELVE

If I am fancy free
and love to wander,
It's just the gypsy in my soul.
Clay Boland and Moe Jaffe

Almost as weary as we had been after the Vatican tour, our little party trudged along back to the Grand Hotel with the uniformed officer on one side and the jeans-clad bodyguard on the other, and Joe, as well, jaunty and alert, keeping a weather eye on everyone we passed. I noted that he could out-swagger the best of them in his own mature macho way.

It was six when we got back to our suites. Plenty of time, Phillipa said. Our reservation had been made for eight-thirty, early by Italian standards but late for us. "This place is *molto elegante*," she warned us, "so dress up to the nines!" She appeared to be looking most meaningfully at me and Fiona. We ignored her.

Nevertheless, when the time came to leave for the Hotel Lord Byron, Fiona was in full glamour, resplendent in her new peacock scarf and turquoise tunic, to which she'd added a Navajo squash blossom necklace of silver and turquoise stones. A turquoise badger-claw belt buckle dressed up the reticule on her arm. And she wore silver bangles, of course. One always knew where Fiona was from the tinkle of her bracelets. I had slipped into my beige Donna Ricco cap sleeve cocktail dress (originally purchased for our ill-fated Bermuda cruise) and over that, wore a deep fringed silk shawl, the border embroidered with leaves in vivid shades of green, a gift from Joe. The card had read, "Something to go with your lovely green eyes," so I couldn't help smiling every time I wrapped myself in it.

Phillipa looked us over critically. "Okay," she said without notable enthusiasm.

She herself was in black, or course, a fabulous satin sheath and evening coat, but the latter was lined in vivid scarlet. Deidre was wearing her new blue shutter-pleat dress with a silver jacket and silver shoes (more cruise leftovers), and Heather wore a russet velvet evening suit with satin lapels. Conor had donned what was probably the only jacket in his wardrobe, a navy blue blazer, with gray trousers and a red-striped tie, and Joe wore a charcoal pin-stripe dress suit in the Roman style that I didn't even know he owned (*had that come out of his duffle bag?*) with a light gray silk turtle neck.

"I think we cleaned up rather well, don't you?" Deidre said, smiling mischievously at Conor. "What about the two guards? The *Nat Geo* guy never wears anything but old jeans."

"The *Sapori* has arranged for our guards to sit at a little table in the lobby near the door, not in the dining rooms," Phillipa explained with satisfaction. "The officer will be in plain clothes so as not to be overly conspicuous. They won't be dining but will be served espresso."

A bodyguard's lot is not a happy one.

∽

Although initially subdued by our ultra-formal, spacious surroundings, all that mahogany and spotless heavy linen, as the dinner progressed, and the wine flowed like, well, wine, we became more jovially ourselves and had quite a merry time. Heather was already talking about booking our flight home when Conor got a call on his BlackBerry and excused himself to answer it, not to put a damper on our frivolity, and also to be able to hear the caller. He went out into the lobby where our two bored guards were slouched at a table the size of a pizza pan.

When Conor came back he was half-smiling. "Well, darlings, *the best laid schemes of mice'n men gang aft agley....* That was *Nat Geo* headquarters, where it's only the close of their business day. And..." he paused dramatically. In truth, we were all hanging on this next pronouncement. I even had time to imagine my joyous reunion with Scruffy (although he would be plenty pissed off) and Raffles.

"And?" Deidre said impatiently.

"*And*...the boss wants me to go immediately to Venice," Conor said, with no little pleasure at our expressions of dismay. "It seems there's been a discovery of finely worked gold reliquaries, processional crosses, chalices and what-have-you, hidden away since 1913 in a glory hole at the *Scuola Grande di San Rocco*. Black as ebony wood they were, but now that they've been cleaned up and polished to a rare gleam, the gold artworks are on display by appointment at the *Sala del Tesoro* in the *Scuola*. Since I'm here on assignment in Italy already, the boss sees no reason why I cannot pop over to the *Scuola* and take a few photos of the loot."

"Oh, Conor, what about your guards?" Deidre looked apprehensive and worried, but no less so than the rest of us.

"*Nat Geo* will inform them that they're no longer needed, since I will now be safe, the boss believes, once I'm clear of Rome." Conor explained coolly, but I could sense the unease under his unruffled appearance.

"*Jesu Christos*, you won't even have the protection of the Roman Polizia di Stato," Joe said. "Doesn't this editor realize that these mafia types have long arms?"

Our ebullient mood somewhat deflated, we progressed in silent thoughtfulness to espresso and dessert—an elaborate, artistic presentation, much admired by Philippa. Fiona was the first to snap out of the doldrums.

"Apparently our fate is fixed, my dears. Do you remember the bronze image of the Goddess of Fate driving an implacable nail that we saw at the Etruscan museum? I've always dreamed of seeing Venice," she said. "And of course, we couldn't possibly leave Deidre on her own without psychic protection for her and Conor. And I will speak to Guido—Commissarion Russo— about safeguarding these dear children in Venice. We're going to have lunch together tomorrow."

Heather, Phillipa, and I gazed at each other knowingly. Phillipa gave a barely discernable shrug.

"Don't worry, ladies. I won't tell him any more than is useful for him to know," Fiona said. "But I've found the commissario to be very accepting of the intuitive arts. Surely he will speak a good word for us in Venice. But for the most part, we'll rely on our own psychic defense."

Conor looked cheerfully resigned to being the Pied Piper of our little company, leading us ever onward into uncertain adventures. "It appears that you have your own bodyguards, Dee. And a fey lot they are."

"I suppose you believe we can keep on pulling miracles out of our conical caps, like Conor's escape?" Phillipa's tone was skeptical.

Deidre looked at her warningly, "Conor's escape was entirely due to his own resourcefulness, Phil."

"Of course, of course," Heather said soothingly. But her knowing smile transported me back to our mysterious rituals at Benevento. *Who knows what works?* "Has the company arranged for your accommodations in Venice?"

"Yes, we're booked into a pleasant *pensione*, just the two of us," Conor replied cautiously.

"Fine," Heather said. "I'll make hotel reservations for us four, not to worry. Oh, and Joe, too, of course."

And that's how we found ourselves installed in the fabulous Danieli Hotel, overlooking the lagoon and its myriad islands, only steps from the Piazzo San Marco.

CHAPTER THIRTEEN

I stood in Venice on the Bridge of Sighs,
A palace and a prison on each hand.
Lord Byron

I wouldn't have missed this for the world, I decided. *No matter how Buona Fortuna got me here.* Bouncing into Venice over choppy waves, the spray splashing us and the windows of our motor boat transport with salt, seeing the city rise out of the sea like an enchanting Renaissance vision, was one of the most breathtaking experiences of my sheltered life. Every one of us was thrilled; our enraptured expressions said it all. Even Joe and Conor, world travelers, each in his own way, were energized by the view and our enthusiasm for it.

The motor boat made its first stop at the Danieli, then continued on to the *pensione* with Conor and Deidre. Waving goodbye from the hotel dock, I marveled at how fresh and enthusiastic Deidre appeared (ah, the adrenaline boost of a new love!)—and Conor, too, the camera of his imagination always ready to capture the next vista.

Tired and soggy, the rest of us looked a motley crew as we waited for Heather to confirm our reservations at the Danieli. Rooms not suites this time. Heather and Fiona sharing. But the accommodations were "Deluxe Doubles."

"You've got a whole room to yourself" I remarked to Phillipa, who was looking around the lobby and eyeing a slim, handsome Italian man who appeared to be checking in. "Any chance of Stone jumping on a plane and joining you?"

"I've considered that," Phillipa said thoughtfully. "I believe he could find some way to bring in a hand gun, since he's licensed. A little extra protection, and maybe an interface with the local *polizia*." Her tone suggested that this was a sensible, not necessarily desirable possibility."But on the other hand, I don't think we'll be here more than a few days. I mean, how long could it take Conor to snap away at those lost treasures? A day? A day and a half?"

"Ah, but to see Venice with the one you love!" Ever the romantic, that's me.

"I do love Stone deeply," Phillipa said. Perhaps catching my thought that Stone's presence would have had a steadying influence. "But I don't need to have him glued to my side to enjoy the scenery." The impeccably tailored, dark-eyed Italian was gazing back at Phillipa.

I let the subject drop in order to immerse myself in the remarkable hand-carved marble columns and sparkling Murano glass elegance of the lobby. The hotel had been created out of three Venetian palazzos of the 14th, 19th, and 20th centuries. Looking as if it were a period production set, the Danieli lobby had indeed figured in many movies filmed in Venice. We ladies from Plymouth, with its Puritan tradition of austere virtues, were naturally in awe of such sumptuous surroundings and a little bit titillated by its opulence. Except Heather, of course, who had probably done the Grand Tour with her Vassar pals and one or more of her husbands—several times.

"I think you'll be comfortable enough here," said our unflappable travel agent. "I booked us all on the second and third floors in rooms overlooking the lagoon. I wanted all the same floor, but some Arab sheik has taken over the best rooms with his wives and entourage."

"We ought to make this evening's dinner reservations in the Terrazza Danieli," Phillipa, our restaurant advisor, said. "It's supposed to be superb, and it's located on the top floor with that magnificent view."

"It's out of our hands," I whispered to Joe. "Let's just go with the flow."

"Okay," he murmured back, "but as soon as we're settled in our room, I'd like to take you over to the Piazza San Marco for an espresso or something at one of the outdoor cafés. Just us two."

"Sounds like a plan," I said. All this sparkle and dazzle was making me dizzy. I needed to get somewhere quiet and shady.

After we'd accompanied our bags to our room and checked out its luxurious appointments, Joe and I strolled arm in arm over to the Piazza San Marco, only a short distance. The smell of wetness was everywhere, but not unpleasantly. It was like being on some huge cruise liner. The Piazza, so often photographed, was therefore both familiar and unreal. It could have been a hologram of a Renaissance square. One almost expected to see gentlemen in colorful doublet and hose, daggers in jeweled sheathes at their waists, instead of tourists in wrinkled parkas, weighed down with cameras.

The sky was overcast, the air rapidly cooling, and in the long shadows of the late afternoon, the moored gondolas struck dramatic angles. A winged creature supposed to be the lion of St. Mark loomed over us, and we were surrounded by the doge's palace and the Basilica San Marco. Other sight-seers were scattering, seeking warmer places. A single violinist, somewhere out of sight, was playing a Vivaldi concerto with great ardor. We had our espressos at the nearly deserted outdoor café with October leaves blowing across the stone piazza and pigeons settling down to a soft murmur. The moment was heaven, or as near it as I ever hope to be. The tourist is tempted to record such an enchanted experience in an array of photos. *Stifle that impulse!* Magic is meant to be ephemeral.

Sauntering back to the hotel an hour later, I noticed a short, brutish man in a black leather jacket leaning against one of the picturesque lamp poles. It was too chilly for outdoor leisure and too gray for the dark glasses he was wearing, I thought, and looked at him more closely, but obliquely. I pinched Joe's arm and whispered, "See that guy over there? *No, don't look straight at him!* Does he look familiar to you, or am I just being paranoid?"

Joe leaned over and said, "I haven't seen him before, but he's armed. Bulge under his jacket. Let's put it down to an over-zealous bodyguard in the sheik's entourage. Did you see the armed Arabs hanging around the grand entrance?"

"Well, yes, but after Rome and the over-gunned Carabiniere, it didn't seem that unusual." The natural exuberance of Italy seems to blend in with extravagant uniforms and weaponry. "But still…"

"But still, *the better part of valor* is suspicion" Joe finished my thought. "Much as I enjoy being in Venice with you, I hope to hell that Conor gets finished with this business before he gets finished altogether."

Banish that thought. "Maybe it *is* time to go home, after all," I said. "But by Ceres, I want my gondola serenade first." I walked faster, because I was getting chilled, for whatever reason.

"As our resident Cassandra, can't you read this guy's intent?" Joe asked.

"It doesn't work that way," I said. "And I'm glad of it."

It was good to get back to our Deluxe Double and warm up with a shot of grappa. Strong but effective. Joe turned on the TV and managed to find a nature show, which, although the voice over was Italian, lost nothing of its gritty realism of creatures snacking on other creatures. I thought about getting ready for tonight's culinary adventure. Maybe a bath in that seductive marble bathtub first.

There was a quiet knock at the door. Joe opened it. Phillipa stood there, BlackBerry in hand. "It's Serena Dove for you, Cass."

Joe turned off the TV and said, "Ah, news from home. Must be important. Why don't I go check with the concierge about hiring a gondola for tomorrow while you gals take your call." He slipped out of the room before I could tell him it was okay to stay.

"Serena? This can't be good news." I took the phone from Phillipa's hand and motioned her into the room.

It wasn't.

"Cass, dear," Serena said. "We're having a bit of a problem here concerning Ada. And I thought I should give you a *heads up* before you come home. And when exactly will that be, dear?"

"Problem?" I asked weakly.

"Yes. Ada's been arrested for the murder of her husband Jerry.'

"Good Goddess!"

"Yes, dear. The evidence seems to be entirely circumstantial, though, and personally I believe she's innocent. Also, I've retained an excellent criminal defense attorney to represent her. Former nun, Sister Jude, now Magdalene de Santos, Esquire. Do female lawyers get to use that honorific, I wonder? We were novices together, Mag and I, years before I got drummed out of the Church for turning a blind eye to some poor abused woman's abortion. But I mustn't digress on long distance. Mag will work *pro bono* until we can shake some dollars out of the Richter property."

"If de Santos needs a colleague, have her get in touch with my daughter Becky at Katz and Kinder. She, too, will work *pro bono*, I'm sure, and because she's in family law, she knows a great deal about the machinations of Jerry Richter."

"We hope to get Ada released on bail, although that's a tricky proposition in a murder case. We will plead Ada's uncertain mental health, which her late husband established for us. Much too fragile for the rough-and-tumble of the county jail. She should be held more humanely on house arrest, with an ankle monitor."

"Yes, I'm familiar with that sort of thing. I will be surprised if the Judge agrees," I said. "There's been a recent case we were involved in...a murderer who also pleaded health problems and then engineered his escape by sawing off the monitor. Well, keep the good thought."

"Then if need be, we can play the insanity card later," Serena continued on her train of thought."

"What about motive? What does the prosecution think that Ada had to gain?"I asked. "Richter surely left a will? Have you seen it?"

"Yes and yes. Leave it to Richter to find a legal way to avoid spousal rights. His brother Burt and sister Clare are the sole beneficiaries, but there's the matter of those real estate holdings Richter transferred to Ada's name for his own nefarious purpose, taxes probably. As you know, he was moving to divorce Ada, but first, he wanted her declared incompetent and himself named as conservator so he could sign the properties back to himself. You gals foiled that plan by getting Ada out of the funny farm, and I hid her for a few days. Until he found us out. Well, I knew that would happen. Didn't I tell you about that sleazy thug from Providence who does his detective work? But by then, I'd already had Ada declared *compos mentis* by Sister Mary Joseph. Jerry would have found a way around that eventually, of course. Because Mary's only a psychologist, not a psychiatrist. If he hadn't been murdered, that is."

It was a lot to take in from a faraway hotel room in Venice. After I was quiet for awhile, Serena said, "Cass...Cass...are you still there?"

"Yes," I said. "I'm trying to process all this information. I think it's blowing fuses in my brain. But what I'm wondering is, how did he die, Serena?"

Now it was Serena's turn to hesitate. Finally, she said, "Yes, it was a fire, Cass. Started in a pile of trash in the cellar. Burned its way up the stairs into the kitchen. He died of smoke inhalation. Thank the good Lord."

I thought Serena meant, *good that Richter hadn't burned alive* not *good that he was dead.* "He wasn't a popular attorney," I said. "There were a lot of financially ruined husbands and destitute, custody denied wives who might have been angry enough to seek revenge."

"The Plymouth detectives are looking at Ada because one of them remembered the previous fire complaint that never got filed," Serena said. "And the fire marshal has declared the fire's origin to be suspicious."

"Stone Stern. Phil's husband, is a Plymouth detective. We'll call him. Perhaps he can help, or at least encourage continued investigation of other possible suspects."

"Wonderful. But, *when are you coming home, Cass?*

"A few days, I think. We have a situation here. It's a long story." I said.

"I'm not surprised. You are always in a situation, and it's always a long story. I'll pray for you, dear."

"As soon as I get home, I'll see what I can do about Ada. I'm glad she has a good attorney. Will you keep me posted?"

Serena promised she would, and we ended our conversation with mutual assurances that we would find a way to exonerate Ada.

Meanwhile, Phillipa, who had been sitting in one of our very comfortable chairs and listening to my end of the conversation, said "Do you think that Ada Richter is a bona fide fire-starter?"

"It's possible. But Serena seems confident that she's innocent of any involvement in Richter's death." I filled her in on the rest of the story. "Will you call Stone and ask him to look into Ada's case?"

"Of course. I'm sure the hours are creeping by slowly for Stone without us and our crazy quests. He'll probably be grateful to have things back to abnormal," Phillipa said. "And it's reassuring to know there's another crime waiting for us at home. Life in Plymouth might have seemed dull after our brush with the Calabrian mafia. Well...time to get gorgeous. See you at dinner, Cass."

As soon as Joe returned to our room, I told him about Serena's call. "Would it be selfish of me to be glad that we're here and not there?" Joe said. "Give the defense attorneys time to sort things out. Doesn't seem to me that the cops have much real hard evidence against Richter's wife."

"Yeah, maybe. Serena's a very capable woman," I said, flipping through some of the brochures on our lovely little desk. Although I'm not particularly adept at converting Euros into dollars, a quick survey of the Danieli's rates made me wonder how I would ever pay Heather back...if she would allow me to do so. The generous donation I'd planned for her "pet" project, the Animal Lovers Sanctuary had now escalated and would probably require a mortgage on Grandma's cottage. I held up the brochure for future bookings with its exorbitant prices in front of Joe's eyes.

"Don't sweat it," Joe reassured me. "I'll take care of our hotel bill when it's time to check out. No more of Heather's nonsense, however generous and well-intentioned."

"Maybe we should have stayed at the *pensione* with Conor and Dee," I said doubtfully.

"No, sweetheart. If I were planning this trip, the Danieli is just the place I would have chosen for us."

"Hey, big spender! You guys at Greenpeace locate a sunken treasure ship on this trip?" I asked, secretly quite pleased.

"With all your clairvoyant skills, Cass, you'll never know everything there is to know about me." Joe's grin was infuriating.

"Ditto," I said, remembering some of the off-the-wall spells we'd been casting at our recent gatherings. Fiona was right. A husband should never be burdened with the small details of a witch's magical life.

And besides, I'd already seen the healthy bottom line of his personal account, in the bank book he kept in the secret pocket of his duffle, a disreputable bag made from recycled canvas hand-sewn by Brazilian villagers. It was a wonder that they let us into the Danieli with that thing in tow. *No, I hadn't been snooping*, I told myself…just looking for a good place to hide a Navajo medicine bag I'd got from Fiona to keep Joe safe. In the end, I'd had to settle for another little zippered pocket. Fortuitously, it was empty except for a kind of hook for hanging the duffle over a door, which Joe would never use.

I had my own personal bank account, too, of course—which doubled as my business account. *Cassandra Shipton, Earthlore Herbal Preparations and Cruelty-Free Cosmetics,* potions and notions for sale from my online catalog. *Once divorced, twice shy.* Every woman needs to have money for which she need never report to anyone. Of course Joe and I also had a respectable middle-class couple's joint account as well, to take care of our household finances and living expenses.

"Here's what I'd really like to know…" I said, watching Joe hang his suit on the shower rod to benefit from the steam of the baths we were going to take. "When did you buy that handsome Italian suit, and how could you possibly pack it in your duffle?"

"Answer one: from a men's shop at the airport in Rome. Answer two: rolled in towels. Just one of the many areas of my expertise. Would you like to learn about others?"

"Will they be more exciting than riding in a gondola with a well set up gondolier singing *Come Back to Sorrento* ?" I added my new Armani jacket to the shower rod.

"You'll tell me," Joe said, drawing the elaborate drapes. "You know what I wonder about? Why are there no Venetian blinds in Venice?"

By the time we got around to dressing for dinner, Joe suggested we take our baths together to save time. A self-defeating proposition.

"Would it be too much to ask for the moon to be rising over the Grand Canal tonight?" I wondered as I fixed my hair in the slightly Greek style that Joe liked.

Not too much at all.

The Lady Moon, in all her magnificence, presided over *La Serenissima* and conferred her blessings upon us. I definitely thought she was smiling. And the cuisine was outstanding, too, so we were assured by Phillipa.

Deidre and Conor had joined us just as we were digging into the traditional Danieli antipasti with its variety of appetizers from black cuttlefish to spider-crab salad. A bit bizarre but tasty. Phillipa was in culinary heaven.

Conor told us that his work was going well but he needed one more day. Heather wanted to know if it would be safe, then, to book our flights home. Sure, Conor said, but he and Deidre wouldn't be leaving until the weekend. There was a charter plane taking *Nat Geo* personnel back to the States, and seats had been reserved on it for himself and Deidre.

"A lieutenant of the *Polizia di Stato* was waiting for us at the *pensione*," Deidre said. "Plain clothes, I was glad to see. Evidentally Commissario Russo requested that the Venice police contact us in case we had need of continued protection."

"Which is exactly why we are going to stay here until the weekend as well," Fiona said firmly, patting Deidre's hand to the tune of tinkling silver bangles. "In case you need *our* kind of protection."

"Would that be your faery powers or your remarkable walking stick?" Conor asked. That endearing grin of his took the sting out of any wise crack. He was reacting, as any sensible man would, to our force of five, but he'd get over that in time. Joe had never been fazed, Heather's husband hardly noticed, and Stone had become resigned to our odd talents.

So we had a little more time to enjoy Venice. I can't say I felt sorry about that. But paying the sky-high Danieli rates was another matter. I glanced at Joe. He appeared cool and unruffled. Also quite handsome in his new Italian suit. *An entirely objective opinion.*

"I've made arrangements for us to take a gondola ride tomorrow," he said. "With music accompaniment. I think that means an accordion and singing gondoliers. Dee, you should come with us, if you've seen enough of the church treasures."

"Oh," Deidre clapped her hands. "But will there be room?"

"Room for six, so I'm told," Joe said gallantly.

"What time tomorrow?" Conor asked.

"Eleven. He'll call for us at the Danieli's private dock. Does that mean you can join us?" Joe asked.

"No, no. Press of work and all that, saints preserve us. Absolutely have to finish the treasures of the *Scuola Grande di San Rocco* today. Because tomorrow night, Dee and I are going to take the night train to Pompeii. As long as we have a couple of extra days before the charter takes off, *Nat Geo* suggested I shoot some new excavations. We'll be staying at the Hotel Forum. Classy 4-stars, compared to the *pensione*. Not that we're complaining, dear friends. We were very snug and well fed."

The entrees arrived. Deidre looked down at her bucatini with bacon and tomato sauce, a small smile playing on her lips. "I was going to tell you this evening myself. But you don't have to come with us, you know. The danger is over, and we'll be just fine. And besides, the new excavations are all erotic statues and things like that."

"Nonsense. As long as we're here, we may as well take in the sights," Phillipa said briskly. Her baked sea bass could only be served for two, so she'd roped in Fiona to share. She poked it with her fork, experimentally.

"But I won't be home for my birthday!" I wailed. Then a moment later, *the light dawned over Marblehead*—my dearest friends, who were right here at this table, would be celebrating my birthday with me. I would miss my children, of course, but how alive I would feel, how precious existence would seem to me in that illustrious city of the dead. "But traveling from Venice to Pompeii…what a birthday present that will be!"

"Never mind that we're zig-zagging all over Italy," Joe said.

"Who cares, honey. Point A to Point B makes for a dull tour," I said.

He shrugged an Italian shrug, the quintessential resignation to craziness.

"Enjoy the night train, kids, but I think we older bodies will choose air travel," Heather said. "We can fly from Venice to Sorrento in an hour and a half and arrange for a car and driver to take us to the Hotel Forum, which is practically next door to Pompeii. Or we could stay at the Ambasciatori in Sorrento, gorgeous views of the Bay of Naples, but perhaps missing the point. Don't worry—I'll take care of everything."

"I agree that the point is to stay close to Dee. We depend on you, Heather," Fiona said. "I never could get my head around reservations. I believe it's a common Pisces problem. But you're a Cancer with moon in Taurus, well organized for an emotional person. This sea bass is quite extraordinary, don't you agree? Who wants a taste?"

I had a moment's sympathy for Conor, who had expected to have his girl all to himself for a delightful Roman holiday, and instead was getting a whirlwind tour of Italy with the weird sisters. He must feel as haunted as Macbeth.

Conor must have read my mind, because he looked directly at me and smiled ruefully. *"Whither thou goest..."* he quoted, then went on to tell us that the Venetian *Polizia di Stata* had assigned an officer to guard him as he took his last photos at the *Scuola*. "A lovely gondola ride is just the thing to keep up your spirits, darlin' Dee. Surely you're tired of hanging around a bunch of moldy antiques, and me with my head in a camera."

"Are you kidding, Conor? I'm loving this—what an adventure! As long as you're safe," Deidre said. "And Pompeii sounds a treat!"

"You'll love it," Joe said. "It may be a city of the dead, but it brings alive that ancient Roman culture. They've even replanted the original gardens, and the villas look like a page out of The Last Days of Pompeii. Consider it a gift from the Cosmos, Cass—isn't that what you believe?"

Yes!

CHAPTER FOURTEEN

The reason firm, the temperate will,
Endurance, foresight, strength, and skill,
A perfect woman, nobly planned,
To warn, to comfort, and command.
William Wordsworth

Our gondola ride the next day was another unforgettable experience, not only because of the kitch romance of it all, gliding along the grand canal as the gondoliers sang Italian folk songs, but also (as I looked back on it later) because of the curious incident of Fiona zapping that man with the camera. Who would have imagined that she had such hidden depths of psychokinesis? My daughter-in-law Freddie was a psychokinetic whiz, of course, who even did occasional jobs for the CIA, and then there was Ada Feuer Richter, who might or might not be a fire-starter, another psychokinetic talent...*but Fiona?* The fourth power of the Thirteen Powers of the Witch, mind over matter, is one of the most difficult to develop—and to restrain once you had it up and running.

The day began with a slight overcast that partly cleared and gave way to a mysterious mist on the canal as we glided away from the Danieli's private dock. The gondola really did hold the six of us comfortably, along with the two gondoliers, who wore the traditional straw hats with a red ribbon hat band. The rotund one with a mop of black curls and a red neckerchief sat behind us with an accordion, playing and singing; the other, slim and brooding, stood up in front, maneuvering us along with a pole, sometimes pushing off from the walls on each side.

By the time we came to the Bridge of Sighs, the sun was full out, illuminating the richly muted shades of ancient stone: ochre, umbra, burnt sienna. A slight breeze made brush strokes of reflected colors on the water. The fellow with the accordion belted out *O Solo Mio* in a rich baritone. The moment was all I had ever imagined Venice to be—pure magic. I used that memory trick of bringing conscious awareness to the scene. *This is me riding in a gondola with Joe and my dearest friends.* Mindfulness freezes the frame perfectly for later viewing. And I would want to remember every detail, even to the slightly rank smell of the canal.

Naturally, Phillipa couldn't resist reciting *One more unfortunate, weary of breath, rashly importunate, gone to her death...* although softly, so as not to drown out *Santa Lucia*, the next selection. It was a toss-up whether our Italian adventure was inspiring her more as a poet or as a cook, for she was constantly scribbling in the black leather notebook (poetic thoughts) or the brown leather notebook (ideas for recipes.)

"Oh, this is heavenly," Deidre sighed, as *Torna a Surriento* gave way to *Que Sera Sera*. Fiona sang along, interpreting the lyrics as "the future *is* ours to see..."

In the midst of this idyllic moment, I looked up and saw the same man I had seen at the Piazza San Marco. I nudged Joe, who had his arm around me, and whispered urgently, "Look, look! Is that the same man in a black leather jacket we noticed near the Piazza San Marco? Is he following us? Why would he be doing that?"

Joe's pleasure in having arranged the quintessential Venetian experience vanished into a grim scowl. "Yes, same bastard," he muttered. "No idea why he would be hanging around. If they're pursuing anyone, it's Conor. Never mind, sweetheart. We'll soon be past him."

Fiona, who so often appeared to be rapt in her own vague thoughts, never really missed anything relevant. I saw she was listening to our exchange intently. Silver bangles tinkled as her hand gripped the coyote walking stick.

"*Fiona, don't!*" I exclaimed.

The man lifted a camera out of his pocket and took several quick shots of our party.

Fiona stood up, pointing her walking stick at him as if it were a wand. Her lips moved as she muttered some imprecation under her breath. The gondola rocked dangerously.

"*Signora, signora! Siede!*" cried the singer with the accordion. The other gondolier standing at the front of our boat turned toward us and saw Fiona drawing a pentagram in the air with her stick. "*Sangue di Cristo!*" he exclaimed, tottering and struggling to maintain his balance.

At that moment, the man with a camera appeared to stagger and lose his footing on the canal's stone wall. He rocked back and forth for a moment, then fell into the murky water with a cry of dismay and a great splash.

Two men in a launch moored nearby dropped the cigarettes they were smoking and leaned out with arms and hands outstretched to haul the sputtering, flailing man up into the boat. He clawed at the launch until he was on board, swearing in an Italian dialect a mere tourist could not follow. Apparently, his camera was now at the bottom of the Laguna. And possibly that gun bulging under his jacket as well.

Fiona sat down again with a soft thud and pulled her tartan shawl more closely around her shoulders. "Bad vibes, that one," she said. "Aiming at Dee, I think. Well, never mind, dear, we'll soon have you out of Venice.

The gondolier frowned at us, grumbled *Maronna,* and turned back to his poling. The accordion player laughed and

muttered, *Americani pazzi*, a term I had heard before. He began
to play and sing *Ò Marie.*

Joe, who had held me tight and close during the rocking
gondola incident, relaxed and whispered, "I'll tip them a little
extra, poor devils. But I can't say I'm sorry that camera went to
the bottom. Or that the bastard got dunked in the canal's fetid
water. Ugh. But what the hell was he after?"

I didn't want to say what I was thinking, as if that would
make it true. *Thoughts are things.* But it occurred to me that,
Conor being so constantly guarded, the irate Calabrian mafia
might want to strike at him through Deidre. *Banish that thought.*
Did these saturnine Mafia types routinely cherish a vendetta
against victims who escaped their clutches? Or was it because
Conor had revealed their hidden stronghold in the hills which
they had then to abandon. Possibly a good hideaway is not easy
to replace. Yes, they must be well and truly pissed.

"It's just as well we're going to Pompeii tomorrow," I said.

∽

While Conor was finishing at the Scuola, guarded by a
Venetian police officer, Deidre went with us to the Murano
Glass Factory where we watched incredible works being blown
into life by the master glassmakers. Imagine a delicate glass
unicorn being shaped from a molten blob right before our eyes!
Heather ordered a set of ruby stemmed glasses to be shipped to
home, declaring that we would toast with them on Samhain,
if we and they arrived at the States in time for the Sabbat and
Conor wasn't sent elsewhere on some new *Nat Geo* whim. *No
way*, Deidre said. Their seats were reserved on the charter, and
that was that. As a birthday gift, Joe bought two exquisite wine
glasses for us, in shades of blue and green, the colors of the
Atlantic on a mild summer day. They, too, would be shipped
to the States.

We couldn't leave Venice without a trip to Harry's Bar, even Phillipa agreed. We met there for an early dinner (late lunch for Italians) so that Deidre and Conor could catch their night train without any hassle. Despite its reputation as a haunt for the loaded and literary, a fabulous view was obscured by glazed windows and the place itself was somewhat unprepossessing. But it didn't matter, we were so impressed to find ourselves in Papa Hemingway's favorite bar! The famous Bellini cocktail, made with a puree of fresh white peaches, was out of season, but the equally famous 10-to-1 martini filled in nicely.

Deidre was thrilled to find an American hamburger, fries, and Coke on the menu. Phillipa shrugged and ordered beef Carpaccio and polenta with grilled porcini. The rest of us had various scampi dishes and risottos, and many Prosecco toasts in my honor. The dining room with its multi-cultural crush of merry tourists seemed to me to have an especially festive air, as if everyone knew it was my birthday. And to think that even a month ago, if anyone were to tell me that I would celebrating at Harry's Bar in Venice, I would have thought her to be *pazza*. I had to pinch myself—and Joe, too—to believe it. After several days of miniature draughts of caffeine, Joe was reveling in his man-sized cup of real American coffee, not (as many bars counterfeited it) a cup of espresso dumped into a larger cup and filled with hot water. Despite the astronomical prices, he insisted on paying the tab for my party.

I'd seen no sign of our brutish stalker in the black leather jacket since Fiona had zapped him into the canal (maybe—or possibly he'd just lost his balance at the moment she was waving a pentagram at him with her walking stick?) But still, despite our jovial mood, I was secretly uneasy about something that hadn't yet taken shape in my consciousness. No sense ruining our last afternoon in this magical city! I said nothing, not even to Joe.

CHAPTER FIFTEEN

They fade like echo in a shell,
Where are the cities of old time?
Edmund Gosse

The flight to Sorrento was a "trip" in itself, with dramatic views of the Amalfi coast and the Bay of Naples. As I looked down on the treacherous road that ran along the mountainous shore, an "engineering marvel," I was glad to be flying above it and not careening along those narrow roads below in a bus driven by an Italian driver like those I had observed in Rome who took traffic lights and speed limits as suggestions subject to interpretation. I said a little blessing for Deidre and Conor who were probably bouncing along down there this very minute. Not for the faint of heart or those with a touch of vertigo, we'd been warned. But Conor was probably unfazed by high adventures, and it appeared that Deidre, as women in love tend to do, had taken on a persona that complemented his—the intrepid helpmeet, the Energizer Bunny hand-maiden.

When we landed in Sorrento, however, we got a brief but sufficient taste of the hair-raising Amalfi road for ourselves as we were driven to Pompeii by another of Heather's hired drivers. He blew his horn impatiently at every inscrutable mirrored turn and inevitable slowdown. I was relieved when we turned inland toward that most famous of dead cities.

The Hotel Forum, when we met there later, was more like a Comfort Inn than the Ritz, especially after a few nights at the Danieli, but Heather, to her credit, did not complain. "It's clean and functional," she said, "and we can keep an eye on Deidre, which is the main thing. I wonder if a sage-smudging ceremony would set off the smoke detectors—what do you think?"

"I think we should settle for a white light meditation and a sprinkle of Fiona's corn pollen," I said. "Possibly we have finally lost those frustrated gangsters. Wouldn't you think they'd be satisfied to go back to their regular drug-dealing and loan-sharking and forget all about having let Conor slip through their fingers."

∽

The next morning, after a breakfast of blood orange juice, Sicilian poached eggs, perfectly ripe melon, fresh brioche, and *molto* cappuccino, we set out to explore Pompeii.

Leaving Conor to set up his lights and paraphernalia to shoot the newly restored frescos on the Via 'dell Abbondanza, Deidre had joined us, looking adorable in her world traveler outfit that matched Conor's casual style right down to the many-pocketed vest.

"Does Conor have a guard with him?" Fiona asked. "Perhaps I should…"

"He says he feels perfectly safe now," Deidre said hastily, seeing that Fiona was gripping her walking stick. "And he does have one of the guides assisting him who's a burly fellow named Fiorello. I think it will be all right."

"Little flower," Fiona said. "With a name like that, he's probably done more than his share of street fighting. Very well then, *Andiamo!"* Waving her stick in mid-air, she gestured us forward to the intriguing ruins.

What an extraordinary experience Pompeii was for a clairvoyant with the hot sun in her eyes! I kept slipping in and out of time present and time past, glimpsing vague misty images of Romans in togas milling about the streets, the vision fading into real gaggles of tourists in jeans and baseball caps, then back again—an encounter with the weird (or wyrd), *things that have been and will be*, a meeting with the Fates, daughters of the Goddess of Necessity to whom all creatures must submit.

Well, you can see how spacey I was! But Deidre, with her newfound talent for seeing dead people, was also affected.

Our guide, Guido, a wiry rapscallion in an artist's beret, who lingered with obvious pleasure over the more erotic mosaics and sighed with impatience whenever Deidre or Fiona were too overcome (Deidre by ghostly vapors, Fiona by arthritic fatigue) to continue at the brisk pace he preferred through the less scandalous sights.

I was particularly intrigued by a Roman garden replanted to represent the aromatic original. Roses in abundance (*Rosa damascena*), feathery fennel (*Foeniculum vulgare*), myrrh (*Commiphora myrrha*), laurel (*Laurus nobilis*), myrtle (*Myrtus communis*) and lily (*Lilium*). The volcanic ash that had sifted down from Vesuvius for generations before the disaster had made the soil incredibly rich in ancient Pompeii. Fig, pear, and chestnut trees had flourished.

"I found a cool cookbook in the gift shop," Phillipa enthused. "A re-creation of Apicius' Roman fare. I suppose one could approximate *garum* with the judicious use of anchovies. It appears that they flavored practically everything with the stuff, a liquid they extracted from fermented fish entrails and salt. Possibly it was tastier than it sounds. They preserved figs and pears in barrels of honey, you know. Bacteria cannot live in honey. I don't know about sautéed lark tongues, though—a thousand larks are a lot for one dinner—and dolphin meatballs. Like high class fish-cakes, one assumes."

"Ugh, Phil," Heather said succinctly. "Sounds like a gourmet dinner of endangered species for the rich and repulsive."

"Well, dear, I've made a reservation for our dinner tonight at *Il Principe Pompeii,* where several Apician re-creations are offered, but you may stick with pasta *ordinario* if you're not feeling adventurous. The ancients didn't have tomatoes or even noodles yet, just some sheets of wheaty stuff. No one really knows if proper pasta came from the Chinese culture or the Arabs."

"Apicius? Good call—does that mean sautéed lark tongues will be on the menu? What about stuffed dormice?" Joe inquired innocently. "A Pompeian delicacy, according to Guido." I supposed he was entitled to enjoy a quiet chuckle from time to time. Being the constant companion of our unorthodox sight-seeing ventures would have driven most men off the Amalfi cliffs.

"Maybe I'll try the lasagna, if they offer anything that plebian," Heather said. "There's not much chance of tucking some nasty Pompeian treat into a nice lasagna. Oh, look at those poor babies!"

Three dogs ranging from dirty white to mangy yellow were smiling at us hopefully. I was glad to see that they did not appear vicious. When Guido crossly shooed them along, they loped away quite docilely. Heather scowled at him.

"Well, there goes *his* tip," Phillipa whispered to me.

We were surprised and somewhat alarmed by the number of stray dogs that had made their home in the ruins. Heather was particularly incensed at how hungry and dirty they appeared, but our guide became quite excited and lapsed into Italian invective when she proposed buying enough *tramezzini* at the miserable snack bar to feed them all. This was most unlike Heather, with her firm convictions about proper and balanced dog food, and a measure of how desperate the canine situation appeared to be. Guido assured us that the dogs had been rounded up, examined by vets, spayed, and released, as noted by their red collars, and that volunteers saw to it that they were adequately fed from time to time. An adoption program was underway, as well, if anyone wanted one of those ugly curs, Guido said helpfully. Heather demanded to know where she could contact the volunteers so that she could donate to the cause, but agreed that regular dog food would be a better choice than soggy sandwiches, as long as they were actually getting it.

"Isn't it amazing! Dogs occupying Pompeian ruins just as cats have found themselves a refuge in Roman ruins," she exclaimed, as we admired the mosaic we found in one villa's entry, depicting a fierce dog with the warning *Cave Canem*!

"Homes for the homeless," Fiona said. "So many cozy crannies among the walls and columns."

Joe declared that his education would be incomplete if we didn't view the painted walls in the brothel that depicted the various services available. Our voluble and enthusiastic guide agreed.

"Dearie me," Fiona mused, examining the garish painting more closely through her granny glasses. "Now there's a position you don't see very often!" We all peered at the graphic display, an exercise in acrobatic imagination. "However did he get his leg *over there?*"

Deidre, the shopkeeper, reveled in the street of little shops where the Pompeians had bought everything from wool and glass to wine and bread, Phillipa hovered over the bakery with its raised oven and various clay utensils—and all of us marveled at road ruts cut into the stone pavement by centuries of chariots in the narrow streets of the city. But Deidre shied away from the glass-encased plaster casts of fallen citizens, caught in their last anguished moments. As the hot ashes in which they had been trapped cooled over the years, their bodies had melted away leaving hollow shapes containing only bones. After the excavation, plaster had been poured into those hollows to recreate their forms in twisted agony. One was a cast of a dog, feet in air, body curled painfully; it was believed that he'd been chained in front of his master's house.

"Fido the faithful," Heather said mournfully. "I hope he wasn't left here while his master fled to safety. I can never understand people who rush away from a disaster leaving their animals to perish."

I had a pang of lonesomeness right then for my own faithful canines, but I shook it off by imagining that Scruffles and Raffles were probably enjoying a raucous vacation in Heather's dog pack. Didn't all the animal psychologists claim that roving in a pack was the ideal life for a canine?

"You're missing the mutts right now, aren't you," Joe spoke softly into my ear, his arm sympathetically curved around my shoulders. "But you know very well they're just fine"

"Hey, you don't suppose you're catching my clairvoyance, do you?"

"I'd rather get fleas. I just want you to relax and enjoy yourself, Cass, this is what we call a once-in-a-lifetime thing, sweetheart. And besides, it's all part of your birthday fete. Didn't you tell me that birthdays over forty should be celebrated for a week, at least?"

"Right. And what a party this is turning out to be!"

It was late when we finished our explorations, and we'd bypassed the dispirited snack bar in favor of the bottles of water we carried and a few biscotti from the hotel. Fiona unearthed several nut bars from her reticule, and we munched on those. "Nuts and seeds," she declared, "Nature's most nourishing and concentrated foods."

By afternoon, she was leaning heavily on her stick and Heather's arm, reminding me that we had really been walking for hours, losing our sense of time among the timeless surroundings. We rested on a stone wall at the Villa of the Faun gathering our strength while the impatient Guido absconded with Joe to view yet more mosaics in excavated rooms nearby.

"Guido didn't want me to miss the three graces," Joe said as we trekked to the hotel. "Naked and quite beautiful. It's amazing what can be created with tiny pieces of colored stone."

"Good old Guido. I hope you tipped him handsomely." How peaceful it was to contemplate the eroticism of Pompeii rather than the evil machinations of Conor's pursuers. "I wonder how Conor fared today? Perhaps he finished his project and we can all go home now."

Back at the hotel, we propped up our feet in the lounge and drank many cups of espresso to revive ourselves. Conor joined us, flushed with the satisfactions of his day's work, and he assured us he'd seen neither hide nor hair of his pursuers. "An inept bunch of devils, at best," he said. "I think we've seen the last of them."

As luck would have it, I had been lightly dozing over my second espresso, and opening my eyes to a ray of four o'clock sunlight hitting the shining brass of the bar and reflecting directly into my eyes. "Oh no, not now!" I exclaimed.

"What is it? What are you seeing, Cass," Deidre demanded.

"Oh, it's nothing to worry about, dear. Just a glimpse of a battered green box being loaded onto a plane somewhere. Not Alitalia, though."

"Well, can't you get a clearer picture!" she demanded "What's the use of being a clairvoyant if you can't get the facts straight?"

Something I'd often wondered myself.

"Too much knowledge is a dangerous thing," Fiona said enigmatically.

"Better write that one down in your grimoire," Phillipa smirked. "You are keeping notes on Fiona, aren't you?"

"Of course. Especially the Benevento stuff."

ᑖᓕ

Just before dinner that evening at *Il Principe Pompeii*—late, as was the Italian custom—Phillipa took a call from Serena. She came into our room and handed me her BlackBerry. "Your confederate in crime."

"Thanks. No rest for the weary witch. Crime seems to follow me everywhere, doesn't it? What would the Law of Attraction say about that?" Then I spoke into the phone, surprised once again that I didn't have to shout to hear and be heard across the planet. "Serena! What's new?"

"Cass, dear. Just wanted you to know that we have succeeded in getting Ada released on bail in my custody. We had to put up practically all the Richter property to do it, but at least we know now that the deeds that were signed over to Ada are worth a cool million or more."

"Too bad—that's sounding like a proper motive for murdering a conniving husband. Where are you keeping her?"

"Right here at St. Rita's, of course. I'm convinced she's innocent, you know. Absolutely. Or if she isn't, perhaps he deserved it."

"I admire your broadmindedness," I said. "Have there been any *incidents* while Ada's been your guest?"

"No, no—nothing here at St. Rita's. Despite the fact that Ada's been helping in the kitchen. It appears that the woman enjoys working with food. As our diet tends more to lentil soup than cherries flambé, she's not been a hazard. Needlework was her second choice. We don't have much call for needlework, though. No priestly vestments to embroider."

"How is her defense progressing?"

"Mag is optimistic. But then, I've never known her not to be. The prosecution has motive, of course, wronged wife and all, then there's that prior incident, but nothing was ever proved against Ada, and lastly, Ada doesn't appear to have an alibi for the night in question. She had been hiding out with us until Richter's PI found her. She managed to elude him, but where she went then is a mystery. She *says* she just wandered around Massasoit Mall and got herself locked in there for the night. Slept in the Ladies Room."

"I think we'll be home Monday or Tuesday," I said. "Deidre and Conor are booked on a charter flight. The rest of us will follow on Alitalia."

Serena sighed over the waves of the Atlantic. "I'll be glad of your very special talents, Cass. Safe journey!"

"What a mess!" Philipa declared when I filled her in on our conversation. "If not Ada, who?"

"That's what we'll have to find out," I said.

None of us ordered fricassee of lark tongues or stuffed dormice at *Il Principe Pompeii* (which, thank the goddess, were not offered on the menu). The tasting menu included vermicelli in the Pompeian style, game meats and fish, chestnuts, truffles, and some very good wines. The walls of the elegant dining room were illustrated with scenes from the villas of ancient Pompeii, and the food was liberally accented with *garum*, which Phillipa declared was an anchovy approximation, just as she had imagined. Over dinner, we finalized our plans for departure. Heather had booked us for one more night at The Grand Hotel in Rome, since all of us would be leaving from the Rome airport. The next day, Conor and Deidre would leave on a morning flight to Washington where most of the *Nat Geo* executives were headed, then another flight to Boston and a bus to Plymouth. Our Alitalia flight would depart that evening, Rome to Boston. A driver would take us home.

Delightful as it was to have seen (heard, inhaled, touched, and reveled in) Italy (much more of it than originally planned!) *home* was a comforting thought. Despite the problem of Ada, which I couldn't even get my thoughts around yet—like Scarlett O'Hara, I'd think about that tomorrow. First of all, I would rescue Scruffy and Raffles from the rigors of the Devlin doggie camp and then I'd sleep in my own bed again. With my own lovely husband. *Yes!*

That sense of self-satisfaction I was enjoying, having helped Deidre through a devastating crisis and had an exciting, memorable vacation *with Joe* as well, was nagged by a small but persistent worry in the back of my mind. What was that glimpse of a green box that kept needling me?

CHAPTER SIXTEEN

They are not long, the days of wine and roses:
Out of a misty dream
Our path emerges for a while, then closes...
Ernest Dowson

Having convinced Phillipa that we really didn't want to leave Rome without having had a genuine trattoria experience, we spent our last evening in Italy at the Ditirambo on Piazza della Cancelleria. So much more relaxed, not to mention cheaper. Phillipa was mollified by the opportunity to try that classic Roman fare, wild boar. The rest of us resorted to the reliable pasta and *pesce*. The wine was local and heady. The cuisine was fun, fresh, and colorful. And the mood was ebullient.

I woke the next morning in a cold sweating panic. The pale light of early morning filtered through a break in the drapes. I was safe and warm in one of the Grand Hotel's luxurious beds with Joe beside me, the gold cross he wore around his neck rising and falling with gentle, peaceful regularity. Our bags (my suitcases, his duffle) were packed and ready, except for a few last-minute items, and stacked against the wall. Our traveling clothes hung side-by-side in the closet—blue jeans for us both, multi-color hand-woven jacket and cream silk shirt for me, navy pea coat and fisherman's sweater for him. *So what was the problem?*

The dream came flooding back to me in waves of terror. The green box, the *Nat Geo* charter plane...

The mid-air explosion!

What time is it! I wasn't aware that I had screamed those words aloud until Joe sat bolt upright, fully alert to any danger as he always woke.

He looked at his watch, propped up on the night-table. "5:40 AM. What's the matter, sweetheart? Did you have a nightmare?" He was ready to sooth me with a sleep-warm hug. I flung him off.

"Ceres save us! What time is Conor's charter flight leaving?"

"About eight, I think Conor said last night. They're probably on their way to the airport already. Is there some kind of problem?"

"Just a nightmare? I hope so." Almost all my clairvoyant hits came in the form of daydream-visions, but sometimes... sometimes a dream surfaced that was clearly not one of my regular dreams. For one thing, I usually dream in vague shadows and pale hues, barely memorable, but my clairvoyant dreams are different, startlingly vivid and in lurid colors. "No, no... *not* a nightmare. That damned green box I saw before. Started in Pompeii. Kept insinuating itself into my mind ever since. Now I know why. It's carrying an explosive device. Phil! She has a BlackBerry."

I threw on a robe and dashed out the door, careless of how my unkempt, uncombed, crazed appearance might seem to hotel personnel moving about the halls to deliver early breakfast orders. Rushing down the hall to Phillipa's room, I banged on the door like a madwoman.

A moment later, Phillipa opened the door wearing a black silk robe, looking as cool and sane as always. "Cassandra! What now?"

Stumbling over my words, I told her about the dream. "It wasn't a regular dream. It was a sighting. I'm sure of it!" Of course, when anyone says, *I'm sure of it*, a doubt is betrayed right there. But was I sure *enough* to face any embarrassment? "You've got to call Conor immediately. We have to stop that plane!"

It was a tribute to her faith in my visions that she asked no questions but went immediately into the room to retrieve her cell. First she contacted the front desk—*yes the O'Donnell party had checked out*—then rapidly called Conor's number on speed dial. She did it again. And again. And again. *No answer!* It was now 6:00 AM.

"Either he's turned it off for the flight or he hasn't turned it on at all this morning. I'd call the control tower but I can guarantee they'll think I'm a crank making a bomb threat, or a terrorist taking credit. There's still a little time, though. Throw on some clothes and we'll grab a taxi to the airport. Maybe we can reach them before the plane takes off."

Joe was already dressed, looking out of our room door with a thoroughly puzzled expression. I pushed him aside and stumbled into my travel outfit. "Let's go...*let's go...*" Grabbing his arm, I pulled him along to meet Phillipa at the elevator. "We can't reach Conor on his BlackBerry, so we're going straight to the airport. Right now. Maybe we can catch them. I pray we can catch them."

The obliging taxi driver must have thought we were late for a flight, and, like any Italian driver, was happy to dodge through traffic and ignore warning lights to earn the extra Euros that Phillipa promised him. Still, it seemed to take forever. A miserably heavy October rain was slowing everything down, even for Italy. *What time is it? What time is it?* was the question I repeated with every heartbeat.

While I was wringing my hands, literally, Phillipa called the airport to locate the gate from which the charter plane would be leaving, instructing the taxi driver where to deposit us. The National Geographic Charter Flight would be leaving Rome Leonardo da Vinci Flumicino Airport at 8:15 AM from terminal 3, Gate C-7. She also called Heather to brief her and Fiona on what was going on and where we were headed.

The whole ride was a nightmare, but the grinning driver succeeded in shaving five minutes off the forty-five minute drive, happily pocketing his huge tip. It was 7:25 AM.

"Fiona said to look out for a police escort," Phillipa told us breathlessly.

As we ran into the airport like three mad fools, Joe spotted the officer in full regalia holding a placard that read *La Famiglia di Shipton*. Although the officer's command of English was minimal, we heard the magic words Commissario Russo and realized that Fiona must have immediately called her influential friend to have us intercepted.

Speaking in voluble Italian (which none of us understood) and flashing important looking identification, the officer got us whisked through security without the required tickets, only to discover that getting to terminal 3 required a 10-minute trip on the shuttle bus. Our only lucky break was in boarding a bus that was just leaving the main terminal. By the time we flung ourselves off the shuttle, however, it was nearly 8:00 AM.

Joe, being faster, ran ahead of us to Gate C-7. I saw him speak to the smartly uniformed attendant, then turn and look back at us. From his distressed expression, I knew exactly what he would tell us when we caught up with him, gasping for breath. The charter plane was already taxiing down the runway, cleared for take-off.

Only the combined restraint of the police officer on one side and Joe on the other prevented me from running onto the tarmac and shouting at the plane to stop.

I thought this must be the worst moment of my life.

What could we possibly do?

Phillipa had never ceased trying to contact Conor on his BlackBerry, which remained resolutely turned off.

"Are you sure—positive—absolutely—about this?" Joe asked. He meant it as a kindly reassurance that tragedy might not be imminent after all, but it drove me nuts. What clairvoyant is ever sure of anything? But I was sure *enough.*

I paced back and forth holding my arms over my chest as if to keep in the screams. Our police escort and the airport personnel eyed me with trepidation. Phillipa and Joe tried to comfort me and themselves. I don't know how long it was before Heather arrived with Fiona in tow. Perhaps just a few minutes. It was readily apparent that they, too, had thrown on their clothes in great haste. But Heather was waving her BlackBerry. "Fiona convinced Commissario Russo," she called across the waiting area before she had even reached our crestfallen little party. "He's going to call the control tower and the pilot."

A sliver of hope shot through me like an icy spear. "He believed her? A miracle!" I cried.

"Well, you know Fiona. She'd already laid the groundwork, in case." Heather caught up with us and threw her arms around me and Phillipa. Fiona puffed into our circle, bangles tinkling madly.

"Fiona?"

She caught her labored breath. "Russo has seen much of the world and experienced many strange events. Not one to leave any stone unturned. He's even consulted wise women in cases of missing children. He said they work with basins of water and drops of oil, an ancient Etruscan ritual."

"But what will happen now?" Distantly aware that my voice was hysterical and continuing to draw attention from security people, I tried to hold myself in check. Joe's arm around my shoulders was a warm reminder not to panic.

"Now we wait for Russo to contact us," Heather said. "He said the matter would be delicate. He would have to suggest he'd had a tip from a reliable source. That the 'Ndrangheta had planted a bomb on the charter flight carrying the man who'd escaped their clutches and was on his way out of Italy. Russo can refuse to reveal the name of his tipster for fear of retaliation. Worst case, embarrassment all around. Best result, vendetta foiled."

"But will they listen to Russo?" I demanded.

"When a commissario for the Polizia di Stato contacts the control tower concerning a bomb threat, they will have to instruct the pilot to divert the flight to the nearest airport that can receive them. To search the plane." Joe said. "It's a big deal. Russo is sticking his neck way, way out."

"I have to admit I'm surprised—and very thankful—that Russo has taken us seriously," Phillipa said.

"Ditto," Joe said. "I don't know what I would have done, if it were me, though. It isn't as if he knows Cass the way we do. To divert a flight plan...!"

Fiona drew herself up into a mini-glamour. "He knows *me*."

Heather paced the floor back and forth, her fists clenched, her bronze braid swinging with every step

"Faith, ladies. Faith and trust in ourselves, in what we know that can't be explained," Fiona said. "It's a gamble for Guido, but how would he feel if he believed me and did nothing?"

Very reassuring, but I was still sick to my stomach. I doubled-over in my chair and crossed my arms over my midsection. With his arm around me, Joe whispered comfort in my ear.

"We've none of us had breakfast," Phillipa said. "Low blood sugar plays havoc with emotions. We'll deal better with the waiting if we have something to eat." We all shook our heads negatively, but she ignored us.

Despite the language difficulty, Heather managed to sweet-talk the police officer into accompanying her as she strode away in search of a bar. A few minutes later, they were back with coffees, biscotti, and a heap of sandwiches. The intoxicating aroma of strong coffee and savory snacks reminded us of our emptiness, and we all dug in, even me, although I found big tears dripping into my salami sandwich. Some part of my mind registered that it *was* possible to cry and eat at the same time!

Minutes passed. Quarter hours passed. A half hour dragged by. Every little while, Phillipa checked her BlackBerry compulsively, making sure it was up and running. The next flight was posted, another charter. From time to time, the loudspeaker blared departure information in enough languages to remind me that Rome was, after all, an international airport. Travelers began to arrive at the Gate C-7 waiting area, eyeing our distraught group with curiosity and suspicion, speaking rapid French to one another. They all seemed to be carrying matching flight bags with Italian and French flags. Heather whispered, "Fashion bigwigs, I bet. Look at their outfits."

As if I cared for designer suits and extreme hair. It was nearly an hour later that the damned BlackBerry finally rang!

"Yes, yes. Pisa? Oh, thank you, thank you." We clustered around Phillipa, trying to hear the other end of the conversation. I was quite tempted to grab the cell right out of her hands. "Yes, we'll go back to the hotel now. No point hanging around the airport, I guess. Safely on land? Everyone out of the plane? Any chance of our speaking with Deidre Ryan? Okay, then. Later, right."

Phillipa smiled broadly through our cacophony of anxious question. "It's okay, ladies. You can relax and give thanks to all those goddesses we've been invoking. At least we know they're not going to blow up in mid-air. They're at the Pisa airport. Everyone's out of the plane, but since it's a bomb situation, they're all being detained for questioning, even the pilots and flight attendants. The *Nat Geo* executives are fussing and fuming about the delay, not surprisingly. The bomb squad is searching the plane. At this point, I think we should all pray that they actually find something."

Our taxi back to the hotel seemed much faster than the frantic ride to the airport had been, when we had resented every red light and traffic tie-up. Our rooms were all on one floor this time; we clustered in Heather's suite, where Phillipa made espresso at the room's buffet, passing around the tiny cups and constantly brewing more. It seemed as if none of us could get enough caffeine. We waited...and waited. Phillipa slipped out onto the balcony, and we all pretended not to see that she was puffing a cigarette in the rain. I would lecture her later when I felt strong again. If ever. Her BlackBerry rang while she was stubbing out the butt.

Throwing open the sliding door, she said triumphantly, "It's Dee! It's Dee!"

CHAPTER SEVENTEEN

Beseech you sir, be merry; you have cause,
So have we all, of joy; for our escape
Is much beyond our loss.
William Shakespeare

"We're in Pisa. At the airport," Deidre complained to Phillipa while we all hovered around, trying to hear the conversation. "Can you imagine! Some fool phoned in a bomb threat or something, and right now the bomb squad is searching the plane from nose to tail. I just didn't want you all to worry if our flight is delayed or you hear anything scary on the news."

We were giddy with relief, laughing and crying, while Phillipa explained what had happened. "The fool who phoned the control tower at Rome Leonardo da Vinci Flumicino Airport was your old friend Commissario Russo. As for *why* he put himself in the hot seat of official inquiry, it's because Cass 'saw' the bomb, and Fiona convinced Russo that it was the real deal. We owe him a great big vote of thanks for taking a chance on us."

A simple explanation of such an unexpected event is never quite enough. Phillipa was still going through everything that had happened this morning, starting with my nightmare right through Deidre's own call, when Deidre broke off for a minute.

"Hang on," she said. "They're bringing something out of the plane."

"Is it a box? What color?" I'd been hanging over Phillipa's shoulder, and now I pushed her aside to ask the question uppermost in my worries.

"Don't know. They got it in some kind of a shielded container. Holy Mother! Looks as if we'll be delayed here for a while yet. How sure is this?"

Phillipa wrestled the phone back. "You know Cass," she said. "*Adamant* doesn't begin to describe the way she's been about this hit. She was convinced enough to have been going crazy with worry about you two."

"Well, I guess we ought to be thankful. If our kindly commissario believed her, she must have been *molto* persuasive."

"We can thank Fiona for that part. And you know how convincing she can be," Phillipa said. "I don't know what to pray for. If there's no bomb, Russo will be in deep trouble. If there is something—what a close call! Listen, Dee. Go have a nice espresso or something with Conor and call me back the minute you know if they've found an explosive." The call ended and Phillipa tucked her BlackBerry back in its case hooked to the belt of her black slacks.

"Now we wait some more," Heather said. "Might as well finish my packing. We have to check out by noon. I suggest we kill time by enjoying a long lunch somewhere, then head over to the airport. Again. Our Alitalia flight boards around six."

Personally, I couldn't think that far ahead. I must have looked thoroughly haggard, because Joe urged me to go back to our room and rest for a while. It was only ten, and I felt as if I've already lived a lifetime in this one morning.

Still no word when we met in the lobby at noon. What a sober little group we were! The matter of *bomb-or-no-bomb* was hanging over our heads like the sword of Damocles.

After checking out, Phillipa shepherded us to the Da Lucia in the Trastevere district for lunch, where Heather and I soothed ourselves with their homemade gnocchi and Phillipa and Fiona adventurously ordered the cuttlefish with snow peas.

"I feel as if all we've done the past two weeks is eat and dodge gangsters. *Eat, Pray, Run.*" Heather complained.

"Don't forget all the once-in-a-lifetime stuff…the evocative ruins, the matchless art treasures we've viewed," Phillipa reminded her. "And if we've had a few memorable dining experiences along the way, I'm willing to take the entire credit. If it was left to Dee, we'd have all been chomping on Big Macs at the Spanish Steps. "

Just as Heather was refilling our wine glasses with the house white wine for the umpteenth time, as if trying to assure that we would soon be too inebriated to fret, Phillipa's BlackBerry finally rang!

"Holy Mother!" Dee exclaimed. Her voice was so high-pitched and excited, I could hear her when I leaned over Phillipa's shoulder. "There was a device all right! The bomb expert said it was so poorly made that it may never have exploded, unless it got jostled or something like that. It was in the galley, tucked away with the caterer's cart. Now they're going to interrogate the caterers, the guys who loaded the supplies, and just about everyone else who handled baggage."

"Score another one for Cass!" Fiona said, as Phillipa repeated the news. "And Guido, who had faith."

"What time do you think you'll be taking off?" Phillipa asked.

"No one knows. Everyone's in a very bad humor considering their lives have just been saved. Even Conor is out of sorts. Wow, this incident has really made me think that I ought to name a legal guardian for my children, just in case. Mother Ryan is rather old for all that responsibility."

"You're planning to continue traveling the world with your footloose lover?"

"No, no. Just a sensible precaution."

"Yeah, well don't look at me. Maybe Cass…"

I shook my head vehemently.

" Oh, hooray," Dee cried out. "The word has just been passed along that we may anticipate getting out of here around six. The first smiles I've seen all day. *Ciao*, Phil! See you all soon."

By way of celebration, Heather ordered another carafe of wine.

By the time we arrived at the airport for the second time that day, we were feeling no pain. Except Joe, who had stuck with mineral water in order to be what he called the "Designated Ladies' Escort." His guiding hand was firmly under my elbow, and Fiona's as well, when we finally boarded the plane. Phillipa and Heather came giggling after us.

Heather said, "I'm trying to remember. Did we actually throw our dear little Roman coins into the Trevi Fountain? I mean, in all the excitement…"

"Absolutely," Phillipa said, and immediately began humming *Three Coins in the Fountain*.

Heather had booked us into first class, of course. I stretched out my legs, reveling in the spacious seat, leaned my head on Joe's shoulder, and closed my eyes while the plane taxied down the runway. A kaleidoscope of scenes revolved in my brain. It was almost too many sensations to process. The richness, the beauty, the terror, the great pasta!

A flight attendant came by and offered to serve us the beverage of our choice.

"Prosecco," I murmured.

"No prosecco for us, thanks," Joe said firmly. "Just bring us a pot of regular American coffee, please. Black."

Arrivederci, Roma.

CHAPTER EIGHTEEN

Oh give me my lowly thatched cottage again;
The birds singing gayly, that came at my call,
Give me them,
and that peace of mind dearer than all.
J. Howard Payne

Hey, Toots! Sure thought you had abandoned us for good, ack ack.
For several days after we got home, Scruffy literally dogged my
footsteps wherever I went, coughing pathetically from time to
time. *Been abandoned before, you know. I could tell you stories...*
Miserable grub at that place where you left us for weeks and weeks.
Mangy herd that lives there chomps down on dry stuff that's enough to
break a pit bull's jaw. I sure could use some building up with stews and
stuff. Probably been losing muscle mass on that lousy chow. And there's
new people in the kitchen over there, you know. The woman smells okay
but that guy is definitely not simpatico, if you know what I mean. Kept
giving us the brush off, out into the yard for all hours of the day and
night. Very stingy with the biscuits, too. Yes, Honeycomb was there,
that blonde bitch gives me a snarl whenever I make nice with her. Well,
yes, Toots, there were other females, friendly enough but they've been
fixed, and what fun is that?

Fun is that! Fun is that! Raffles romped after, as ebullient as ever. Just being with females, especially Honeycomb his dam, put an extra prance in his gait.

But it was obviously going to take a few good meals and some long walks together to mollify his sire. Between bouts of dusting and catching up on herbal orders, I had to give my furry friends a great deal of special attention. Joe drew the line at pups in the bedroom, however, which was just as well, as their presence did put a damper on romantic interludes.

What an adventure—our Italian jaunt! All the more extraordinary for having been a spontaneous rescue expedition. It would take some time to absorb the variety of impressions and sensations we'd experienced in Italy. There were photos, of course. Joe had taken a slew of those "Kodak moments", and Conor, when he wasn't fulfilling his *Nat Geo* assignments, had surprised us with some unexpected and spectacular candids of our circle of sightseers. But the prize went to Joe's accidental snapshot of Fiona defending Conor with her rapier at the Trevi Fountain!

We were all home, we were all safe, and we were all rejoicing in an anticlimactic way. Deidre embraced us effusively with her affection and thanks for our rescue efforts. Conor still didn't fully realize what we had conjured for him, but he suspected. The days following our homecoming were busy ones for him, finishing up the details of his Italian assignments, and for Deidre, settling back into her family routine and her shop. Mother Ryan, obviously relieved to be released from her role as caregiver-in-chief, promptly took off for a long weekend in Las Vegas with her gambling cronies. Deidre still had loyal Bettikins to mind the home front while she worked.

Heather said that only a banishing-of-bad-vibes ceremony would get us on the right path again, and there was a dark of the moon coming up before Samhain.

Fiona emphatically agreed. "And we ought to have a cleansing before the high holiday!"

The banishing-cleansing ritual was set for Tuesday, at Heather's place. Cold though it might be in late October, that ring of stones on the Morgan mansion hill with its surround of pine had become a place of invisible power that could be felt whenever we entered its magic.

The other matter that wouldn't wait was the murder of Jerry Richter. As soon as I had a chance to take a contemplative breath, I called Serena Dove to check in. Her sigh of relief was audible. "Oh, you're back at last! I've been praying for that. Quite a responsibility you dumped on St. Rita while you were touring sunny Italy. Well, yes, I realize it wasn't exactly a vacation. Still, it must have had its high tourist moments."

I had to admit that was true enough. The Vatican! The arrival in Venice! Pompeii! But we were home now, and I needed to know what was going on with Ada.

Yes, Serena explained, Ada had been arraigned for the murder of her husband the shady divorce lawyer, and yes the attorney that Serena had engaged to defend Richter's wife (former nun, Sister Jude, now Magdalene de Santos. Esquire) got the woman paroled on house arrest due to her weakened mental state. Ada was currently a resident at St.Rita's home for runaway abused wives (which wasn't any too far from the truth considering Ada's relationship with her controlling husband.) She was required to wear an ankle monitor and report by phone to a parole officer daily.

"Ada had plenty of motive—thwarted love, revenge, money—take your pick. She had opportunity and no decent alibi. She had that prior incident reported by her late husband, not on file, but the cops remember. It does not look good," Serena said in her sweet, crisp voice. "The only thing that may save her is finding out who really murdered the two-timing bastard. We've brought in another former nun, was Sister

Brigid, now Diane Robinson, who's a private investigator specializing in women's issues."

"Turned a blind eye to abortion like you?" I asked.

"No, but Diane was a nurse, too, and something of a healer. A real sixth sense which extended itself to diagnosis. In fact, we used to call her Delphic Di. A major annoyance to physicians, as you may imagine. Nevertheless, she fell in love with an intern. Well, there are many reasons why a woman may leave the order, and they are deeply personal. I believe your daughter Becky has called upon Diane's services from time to time, to find deadbeat dads and such. Now all we need is a clairvoyant to steer us in the right direction, and you know who I mean. Diane's heard of your circle, of course. One could hardly live in Plymouth and be unaware of your exploits. You won't have to explain yourselves to Mag and Di, not that you can."

"Infamous, that's us. Let me think how best to do this, Serena. I don't usually go looking for psychic trouble. My visions often leave me enervated and even nauseous. But Ada's case is a real emergency, and besides, I got you into this. So, tell me, how's she holding up?"

"Pale and strange, but not too wan to find her own niche here. It can't have escaped your attention that the woman has style. Must have been a sizzler, so to speak, when she was younger. She's been helping the other residents to spruce up their hair and make-up, which is such a lift to the spirits, don't you think? After years spent as doormats and punching bags, many of our residents have lost their confidence in themselves as women."

"Been there, done that," I said.

"You, Cass? I can hardly imagine it."

"I was probably never as demoralized as your gals. But my real breakout was when Grandma died and left me her Plymouth cottage. Much as I mourned her loss, it meant a new life for me. Anyway, what about the arson angle?"

"The investigating officers have turned up some additional evidence linking Ada to the scene. The accelerant found at the Richter home was diesel fuel. A gallon of the stuff was found in the trunk of her car. Gloves with traces of the accelerant on them."

"My understanding of Ada's particular talent is that she wouldn't need anything as crude as diesel to get a little blaze going. Fortunately, no one's going to believe that the woman can start a fire by psychic means. I'm not sure I do. Nevertheless, someone must have planted the diesel stuff."

"It's a complicated situation," Serena said. "Perhaps we should implement a prayer ritual."

"Which reminds me," I said. "Has Patty Peacedale been around to see Ada? After all, it was she who got us into this fine mess."

"Oh, yes. Dear Patty. A scatterbrain but so well-meaning. She brought over a prayer shawl for Ada. A rather strange shade of pea green. Her first visit to St. Rita, and she was quite enthralled. I don't believe her husband, the Right Reverend Selwyn Peacedale, was quite as thrilled as Patty with the prospect of a new cause. She has not yet succeeded in getting him over here to have a look at our operation. Meanwhile, Patty has been knitting her heart out—baby comforters, sweaters for tots, and prayer shawls for the downtrodden. She has a good heart, and she believes Ada to be innocent, although she does refer from time to time to Ada's 'little problem' and she wonders how we're getting on with that. I explained we failed nuns managed to exorcise Ada's devil with a few authoritative *Begone, Thou Beelzebubs*, and Ada hasn't heated up anything more dangerous lately than a pot of her German lentil soup. So…Di is already busy poking around in Richter's affairs. How soon can you promise a psychic whammy for us?"

"Oh, *all right*," I said ungraciously. "We're going to do a banishing thing this week. I mean, our circle. I'll give it a try then when I'll have help and protection. I'll plan to stop by on Sunday morning, and we'll compare notes with whatever your people have turned up." Even as I had been protesting to Serena, an image had been flashing in my inner eye. Almost too fast to register on my brain. Something...someone ...had wanted to be rid of Richter, beside the obvious suspect, the spouse.

The banishing we held at Heather's on Saturday, a brisk October eve, proved to be liberating and energizing, as if our spirits had been dragged down by too much psychic garbage, something like a computer infested with a surfeit of spyware. I brought up Ada's situation and asked for their help in a visualization of the crime. We held hands while I stared at the fire and allowed a light trance to take over my consciousness. It was the first time I'd ever entered the realm of vision with a back-up chorus of chanting and intention. Surprising to find the pictures that appeared to me were clearer than usual and I was not as faint afterwards. I wondered why I'd never tried a circle vision before, and I knew I would try it again whenever an emergency required my powers as a seer.

"So...what did you see?" Phillipa demanded. "Who actually perpetrated the murder? I may want to let Stone in on the secret."

"Forgive me," I said. "You were all wonderful, but I want to sort out my impressions quietly for a bit. There's something much deeper here than Richter's murder, and it keeps getting mixed up with our experience in Italy. Let me just think quietly for a bit."

"Holy Hecate! What a prima donna," Heather said. But Fiona changed the subject and that's the last we spoke of it that evening.

In the cleansing ceremony that followed, we combined our sage smudging with a wild warm-up dance, then skipped down the hill to the conservatory, which was entirely lit up with Heather's quirky handmade candles.

Max Kitchener, Heather's new hired help, served wine and cheese and biscuits as soberly as if he were dishing Brussels sprouts at a royal family dinner. It was not for the perfect butler to betray surprise or dismay at anything the mistress might get up to, or her bizarre taste in companions. Elsa, his wife, popped in and out with savory hot morsels from the kitchen, seemingly able to keep the smaller canine residents, whose sleeping quarters were in the residence, out of the conservatory all the while. It appeared, on the face of it, that Heather had lucked out with her two new housekeepers at last.

"*My Man Godfrey*," Phillipa murmured, when Max had wafted out. "Or perhaps *The Redoubtable Jeeves*."

"Will we ever find out who put that explosive device in the charter plane?" I wondered aloud. The wine was, as always, excellent, and I found that I was quite thirsty after all that chanting and bouncing around on the hill.

"In one sense, we know already," Fiona replied. "In another sense, I doubt that particular crime will ever be solved. Too many people in positions of authority are in the pay of the Calabrian mafia. But if they do get a creditable lead, Guido will call me. He promised to keep in touch, dear man. Didn't he just remind you of Rosanno Brazzi?"

"Who's he," Deidre asked.

"Possibly before your time, dear," Fiona said wistfully. "And I've asked Anna Amici to see what she and her sisters can summon by way of retribution. I rather think the strega are more into payback than we are."

"Yeah, we're a little too nicey-nice, for my taste," Heather said. "I mean, what's the good of being a witch, if you're reluctant to whip up a hex."

"Nix on those black candles, my dear. Karma's a bitch," Phillipa reminded her. "Don't you think I've been tempted with that O'Reilly tribe of thieves living next door? But no. We deliberately worked a spell for *good luck* for Liam and his brood. Although I can't believe I let Fiona talk me into that one!"

"I wouldn't mind taking a psychic shot at the gangsters who kidnapped Conor," Deidre declared, sticking a sharp embroidery needle into the pillow on which she was working, *If it harm none, do as you wish.*" She looked at the words speculatively. "That was Gardener's twist on the Golden Rule. *"Harm none* is the one and only commandment of modern Wicca, thanks to the old guy. Sort of like the Hippocratic oath, *first do no harm."* Deidre paused to dimple mischievously. "But Wicca has no hierarchy, no dogma, no catechism, so I don't see why each autonomous circle can't do whatever they please. The question is, *will a hex actually work?"*

"I don't plan to find out, and I don't recommend anyone in our circle going over to the dark side." I said. I was thinking of my daughter-in-law's distress over her psychokinetic powers, which apparently had once caused an intruder with a gun to keel over in a cardiac episode. At the time, I had assured Freddie, insincerely, that she simply did not have that much power.

"Oh, thank you for your sage advice, Obi Wan Kenobi," Phillipa said.

"If it ain't broke, don't hex it," Fiona said sagely, rocking meditatively in one of Heather's white wicker rocking chairs and sipping scotch to take the chill out of her old bones. "It's like trying to blow someone up by strapping explosives to your own body. There's bound to be a negative payback."

"Don't you hate when that happens," Phillipa said.

"Yeah, well, how come the strega can do it and we can't?" Deidre whined.

"The strega were raised in a culture of vendetta. It's like taking a little sip of poison every morning in order to become immune to a large dose. I do believe that's actually possible with arsenic." Fiona said. "I think I may have a pamphlet on that in my reticule."

"Poison...explosives...mixing your metaphors but making your point, Fiona," Phillipa said.

When I related all this to Joe that night, he said, "You're going to get yourself into trouble again, aren't you? I'm not going to be pleased to accept another assignment while this murder thing is going on."

"What other assignment? You didn't tell me about that!" I should really stop putting Joe on the defensive every time he was gainfully employed on another Greenpeace expedition. After all, I had seen that impressive bank balance and was pleased with the sense of security it gave me. My own herbal business had allowed me to manage as a single woman, but it had hardly been a lavish existence. I would not, for example, ever imagined booking a week at the Danieli!

"Tuesday," Joe confessed. "The *Arctic Sunrise* is traveling along the edge of the polar ice pack in the Chukchi Sea between Alaska and Russia."

"Through ice floes and all that?" I was worried already.

"It's the Greenpeace ice breaker, so we'll be fine. There'll be an international team of scientists observing the results of climate change on walruses, polar bears, and black guillemots. Rumor has it that the walrus population is already in trouble."

"The walrus and the engineer were walking hand in hand..." I improvised.

"Three weeks. Should be a breeze."

"A chilly one. Be sure to pack all your thermal whatchamacallits." I urged the dogs out the pet door on the porch for their last run before we all turned in for the night. Wednesday the circle would be celebrating Samhain. I would do a special side-ritual for Joe's safe return.

"I'll be much more worried about you chasing down another killer" Joe said, pulling me into his arms where I always find it so difficult to argue persuasively. The very thought of soon losing my honey to good works among the walruses made me miss him already. I raised my face for a kiss that continued until we fell on the bed. Later I remembered to let the dogs in off the cold porch, and Scruffy was really pissed.

What's the good of a dog door on the porch if you leave us out there to freeze off our cojones. Madre de Dios.

"I didn't realize you knew Spanish," I said.

There was this Mexican hairless I used to hang with, Toots. Canines don't talk about their past, you know. Live in the moment, that's our creed.

"Did I say something in Spanish?" Joe wondered sleepily.

"Yes, and I want to know the name of that *senorita*," I said.

CHAPTER NINETEEN

Women are like tricks by sleight of hand,
Which, to admire, we should not understand.
William Congreve

The next day, Sunday, I visited Serena at St. Rita's and reconnected with Ada. She seemed to have blossomed out of her former wan visage and semi-comatose state to look and act more like one of those forty-something models with the marvelous cheekbones and silver-white hair cut in a smart style, women who avoid wrinkles by maintaining an emotionless mask. Still, however expressionless, Ada's awakening on any level was an improvement over looking and moving like a zombie. I didn't know whether the change could be attributed to the demise of her troublesome husband or to no longer having to fear being locked up in a mental institution.

Ada hugged me—a stiff bony hug—and we air-kissed. She seemed in good spirits for someone who was soon to be tried for murder. Ironically, the situation with Richter must have been, by comparison, an even scarier threat.

Serena poured strong black coffee from a thermal carafe into small, dainty cups and passed around a plate of chocolate biscuits. The double-caffeine had a welcome uplifting effect.

As tactfully as possible, I asked Ada about the devil Abbadon's whisper that had brought her to me in the first place. Neither of us had known at the time that I would have to dump her on Serena while I flew to Italy.

"Serena rid me of that evil influence," Ada said. "She and the others. I know I'm not supposed to call them Sisters, but... except Sister Mary Joseph. She's still a regular nun and a psychologist, too. And now we have Magdalene, the attorney, and Diane, the investigator. I feel so deeply fortunate to have such friends. Patty and Fiona and you, too, of course. I'll never forget how you and Fiona rescued me from that dreadful Tranquility place." Ada looked down at her expertly manicured nails and the wide gold band she wore on her left hand. "I'll be able to pay my way, now, at least. Jerry never got his properties back before...before...who do you think could have...? I mean, I know he wasn't well liked, especially by people he'd eviscerated in family court, but this fire...just when I was struggling with fire myself."

I thought there must be a question in there somewhere. "Who else knew about your problem with pyrokinesis?"

Ada looked puzzled but Serena, her wiry gray hair wilder than ever and her bird-bright eyes flashing, was suddenly alert. "That sleazy henchman of Richter's..."

"But what motive could Bruno have had? He had such a steady source of income with Jerry," Ada said.

"Henchman? I thought he was a PI," I said.

"Bruno Battaglia did anything that needed doing," Ada said. "Sometimes he went along with Jerry as a bodyguard if there was going to be trouble, and sometimes he dug up dirt about adversaries."

"The Good Lord knows Jerry Richter wasn't above a little blackmail" Serena said.

"I wonder about Richter and Battaglia's connections," I said. "Just something that popped into my mind." Serena glanced at me knowingly, but I ignored her, preferring not to go down that road with Ada. "Okay, here's another question. Has there been any recent divorce in which Jerry may have made a serious enemy in the Providence area?"

Ada looked blanker than usual. "He never told me anything about his cases. Even in the beginning, when he still liked to show me off and impress me with his power."

"Who would know?" I asked Serena. Even while asking the question, it occurred to me that my daughter Becky, whose practice was almost entirely family law, might be another good source of information on divorce or custody cases in which the losing party might bear a grudge against Richter. Unreasonable rage, I knew, was a fact of life in Family Law Court. Even a judge could be the target of some nutcase's lethal anger.

"Let me put Diane on it. She'll be here tomorrow with Mag for a consultation with Ada. Why don't you join us and ask your questions directly?"

Monday. Joe would be off to the Alaskan coast on Tuesday. Samhain at Heather's on Wednesday. The veil between life and death being thinnest, I wondered if Richter might appear to us, or at least to Deidre who saw that kind of thing. *Naw. Someone so soulless would hardly be spiritualized into a helpful ghost. In fact, he might be downright dangerous, and we ought not to help the genie ooze out of the bottle*

I was eager to meet both women and promised to look in at two, the time that Serena had arranged for their conference.

ᕲᕱ

There was no popping in and out of St. Rita's. The refuge was surrounded by an iron fence with wicked finials and a formidable gate where it was necessary to ring for the caretaker. I buzzed the intercom on Monday afternoon and was ushered in by Ken Wakahiro, who was not only a talented gardener but also a martial arts expert who gave St. Rita's residents pointers in self-defense to build their confidence. I wondered if he had heard rumors of Ada's unusual talents.

We exchanged greetings and reminiscences of a former resident, Rose Fiorella Abdul, whose ex-husband had attempted to abscond with their son Hari to Saudi Arabia. She was now a phlebotomist at Jordan Hospital and went by her maiden name Fiorella. Hari, who had hero-worshipped his father, was still acting out his frustration at having been forced to reside with his mother. So much grief families could cause one another in the name of love!

"I suggested a martial arts course for Hari," Ken said. "One that is deeply rooted in Buddhist principles. Perhaps it will help him learn to control his destructive inclinations. We all have to do that."

"Yes, it's the mark of maturity," I agreed.

"They're all waiting for you in St. Rita's parlor," Ken said.

I found Ada and two other women with Serena, who was serving tea and fruitcake in the Victorian parlor with its burgundy velvet drapes and heavy mahogany furniture, left over from the time when St. Rita's was a convent. The room was dominated by an ornate, gilded Bible on an oak stand and a statue of St. Rita with the thorn of martyrdom stuck in her forehead, arms outstretched in the bow window. A gold-framed painting of Jesus as the Good Shepherd hung over the marble fireplace. I had the feeling that Serena was so used to the baroque aura of the room, it would never occur to her to change it. Besides, she occasionally used that Bible for *sortes Biblicae* and was something of a good shepherdess herself.

Magdalene de Santos, Esquire, was a somewhat blousy woman in her fifties with masses of crinkly brown hair, layers of shawls and multi-colored sweaters that rivaled the Fiona look, and an overflowing briefcase that appeared totally disorganized. But when she smiled, it was as if the sun had suddenly come out on a gray day, all critiques were forgotten and forgiven. She had a soft, melodious voice with a hint of an accent. Altogether, she was as unlike Ada Richter as it was possible to be.

Diane Robinson was closer to Serena's age, early sixties, with wavy gray hair cut so short, it must have been no trouble at all to jump out of the shower and shake it into place (a convenience that I envied). Her face was round with grandmotherly pink cheeks, her eyes a compassionate brown, and her make-up barely visible. She wore tiny pearl earrings, a beige cashmere twin set, and carried a neat brown leather bag of modest proportions. I noticed at once her quality of believability, the kind of woman whose check anyone would cash and whose handbag would never be searched at a checkpoint. What an advantage for an investigator, that completely non-threatening aura!

"I can see that Ada is in good hands," I said, after introductions had been made and everyone had settled back to balance cups and plates. Ada smiled and nodded. She was wearing a soft gray sash-wrap dress that draped just below the knee. I noticed that she had a little more color than usual, and she sat with the studied grace of a princess-in-training.

"And Cass, being our clairvoyant, sees more than most," Serena said. "Which is why she's here today. If Ada is innocent, and we know she is, then someone else must be guilty, and Cass has an idea where to look, don't you, dear?" Her shrewd little eyes took us all into her confidence.

"All right. I do have the notion that Richter's killer will be found in the Providence, Rhode Island area."

"When Cass says 'have a notion,' she's referring to a clairvoyant insight, which is why I invited her to this strategy meeting," Serena said.

"Such talented women, so wonderful." the attorney said, smiling on me with great delight. When she talked, her hands were always in motion. It was difficult to picture this effusive woman in a courtroom. "Darlings, if you can help us to find a suspect who throws the shadow of reasonable doubt onto the prosecutor's case—that in itself would be a beautiful solution."

"I'll start with recent court records involving Ada's late husband," Diane said. "The obvious ones where one of the parties had good cause to feel vindictive. Perhaps I'll find a Rhode Island tie-in, although there might not be an immediately observable connection. And I'll talk to people in Richter's office, particularly his secretary Nevaeh Nichols."

Ada's expression hardened to ice. "That Nichols woman would be happy to see me hung for Jerry's death. I can't imagine that she'll be much help."

"People don't always realize that they're helping with my inquiries," Diane said with a very slight smile. "I've arranged for Ms. Nichols to receive a free massage at Armand's health club, as a promotional gift. The masseuse is a friend of mine. We worked together as nurses in the old days."

"Well, good. You might ask your friend to wring Nevaeh's neck for me while she's at it," Ada said.

Magdalene laughed gaily as if Ada were really joking.

"My dear Ada," Diane said. "You're under so much tension. Have you been suffering from headaches at all?"

Ada looked surprised. "Migraines. How did you know?"

"On the right side? Starts in the eyes?" Diane reached over and took Ada's hand. I thought maybe she was checking her pulse, but there was more to it than that. Was she reading Ada? "And perhaps an eating disorder?" Instantly, Ada pulled away.

I glanced at Diane's hands. They were as small and neat as the rest of her person, the nails cut short and buffed but not polished. I, too, could tell a great deal by touch, but more about a person's emotional state rather than her health. Diane caught my glance and smiled at me.

"Be careful," I was suddenly impelled to say. "If we are on the trail of the real killer, there could be dangers."

"Does a fruitcake have raisins?" Magdalene said, reaching for another slice. "If we can collect enough evidence on another suspect, open another avenue of investigation, I shall use all my powers of persuasion to convince the prosecutor's office to pursue it." She winked knowingly, and I was at a total loss as to what her force of persuasion might be and on whom it would be lavished. But I began to detect that she was a woman of formidable power.

As were we all.

Any other women of our ages having tea together might be comparing notes on grandchildren, shopping, and hairstylists instead of ways to hunt down a killer with our extraordinary skills, whether psychic, religious, or investigatory.

"Take heart, Ada," I said. "I think you have the real dream team here."

"Let's meet again as soon as Diane has a report for us," Serena suggested.

"I could do Thursday," I said.

"Yes, I remember that it's your high holiday on Wednesday," Serena said. "I wish you a blessed and fruitful ritual. Put in a good word for Ada to Whomever."

"That's very ecumenical of you, Serena," I said.

"Oh, I'm still a Catholic in my heart. Just a somewhat freer spirit," Serena said.

"Ah, my darlings, I drink to free females everywhere!" Magdalene toasted us with her cup as if it were a glass of wine."

Ada smiled, a rare event. "I've always wanted to cruise the Greek Islands," she said, apropos of nothing in particular. Involuntarily, my glance went to her ankle monitor. There was a great deal of work to do before Ada could realize her dream.

"Okay, Thursday it is, then," I said,

∽

Joe departed to rendezvous with the *Arctic Sunrise* on Tuesday, his bulky old canvas duffle slung over his shoulder, his Greek cap set at a jaunty angle, and a sparkle in his eye that belied his voiced reluctance to leave home. Three weeks!

"Samhain tomorrow," he said. "Say a few words of power for your staying out of mischief while I'm gone, okay?" Joe was by now well-versed in the doctrine, such as it was, and ritual of Wicca.

"I'll be saying words for your safety, honey. Stay off the ice floes and watch out for randy polar bears," I warned him.

Our lingering kiss was a warm echo of the night before, when we'd said our real good-bye in flesh and fantasy, like true lovers.

಄

Samhain, the end of summer, the third and final harvest, in the midst of the year's dark half, doorway to the new cycle of seasons. We met at Heather's to honor the Dark Mysteries and the Dark Mother in her third persona, the Crone whom we preferred to call Wise Woman. I pictured her as full-faced rather than haggard, abundantly gray-haired, crowned with a circlet of autumn leaves, sturdy and round figured, carrying a magical staff in place of a wand, and richly cloaked, surrounded by her companion animals. Well, my personal mental image of the Wise Woman might have been a tad like Fiona in full glamour— if Fiona were transformed into a divine manifestation. But I didn't think I'd tell her that rather whimsical notion.

This year, with the surrounding pine woods damp and chill, we wore our hooded cloaks in their various dark colors. Mine was green with silver clasps, one of Joe's first gifts to me. We built a sprightly fire in the center of Heather's circle of stones and lit candles in four jack-o-lanterns (carved by Deidre with her clever hands) to ward off the Wee Folk of the Forest who were out and about playing tricks, and any strangelets who were taking the opportunity to bedevil us as they had in Bermuda.

Samhain was also the night of the Wandering Dead, a time when the veil between the worlds was as thin as an autumn mist. As always, we set aside time to light a candle for each of the dear departed souls we cherished and wish them good faring in Summerland. And if any spirit desired to contact us, we were listening with quiet hearts. We kept careful watch over Deidre, however, with her newly discovered talent for seeing the dead, particularly the disgruntled dead.

As I'd predicted, though, Jerry Richter didn't show up at our Samhain fire. Deidre enjoyed a peaceful contemplation of the night, not even disturbed by her late husband Will. I felt the faint loving impress of my Grandma's spirit with the spicy fragrance of lavender that always accompanied her. Fiona waved to a shadow whom she declared to be her late husband, Rob Angus Ritchie. Heather welcomed the revenant of her Great-great grandfather, Captain Nathaniel Morgan, whose portrait hung in the mansion he'd built, probably from profits of the opium trade.

Not one to wander among the spirits, Phillipa winked at me and began a soft chant, *"All things come from the Goddess, and to her they will return..."*

As the most spiritual night of the year, it was a time for divination. Since I have what Fiona calls *an da shealladh*, the Two Sights, I am especially vulnerable to visions at Samhain, and Phillipa, too, feels her tarot readings are most inspired at that high holiday. Heather had brought her handmade divining candle, a thick purplish stub with orange streaks. Imbedded in the wax were runic symbols: the messenger *Ansuz* and the breakthrough *Dagaz*. "Mugwort and peppermint to bring out the Sybil in our souls," Heather said.

I inhaled the pungent scent of Heather's creation and deliberately gazed into the fire, something I usually avoid doing. Besides a wave of nausea, I was rewarded with the quick back view of a man in a cellar. He was wearing a hoodie, but I could tell he was about Joe's height, somewhat thicker in build. He pulled paper out of a trash container near the bulkhead, sprinkled it with a liquid, and lit it on fire. The flame raced up the cellar stairs toward the first floor. As soon as the vision disappeared, I related it to the others, or it would have dissipated from memory like a dream. A vision must be spoken or written in words at once so that no detail will be lost.

Fiona clapped her hands softly, the silver bangles on her arms chiming applause. "You see, it wasn't Ada. Some thug with a grudge, or carrying out someone else's vendetta. All we need to know now is *who.*"

"Sure," Phillipa said. "It's true that we know *what, when, where,* but how about that biggie, *why?*"

"When we know *why*, we'll know *who*," Deidre said.

"Or vice versa," Heather said.

Fiona said, "We'll just have to concentrate our psychic energy on the problem. *Believing is seeing.*" She whistled a few phrases of a melody, which as a devoted fan of old movies, I recognized as the World War II tune, *We did it before and we can do it again.*

I think we all wished we had Fiona's faith at that moment. Phillipa promised to read the tarot when we went down to the house for "cakes and ale," and we moved on to other work.

This year we took some time to conjure felicity to surround Deidre and her new lover Conor, who, like Joe, was off on another assignment, but only for a few days this time. Then we considered Ada herself. We said a spell to free her from the dangers and temptations of pyrokinesis and the suspicions that resulted in her arrest. We said words of power for the safety of Joe in the icy north and Conor in the rainforests of the Amazon *May he not be kidnapped by pigmies!* We chanted, we danced, we felt infused with cosmic energy for whatever was to come next.

Later, after we'd opened the sacred circle, we feasted on mulled wine, apple cakes, and moon-shaped shortbreads in Heather's Victorian red parlor, suavely served by Max Kitchener the perfect butler who by no glance or gesture betrayed any curiosity about our rather disheveled appearance and carelessly stashed wands. It was a good time to relate the details of my meeting with Magdalene, Diane, and Serena at St. Rita's and to get some feedback from the circle.

"Providence, indeed..." Phillipa mused. "That suggests to me that we haven't shaken off the mafia influence. Cherchez the fine Italian hand."

"Now that *is* a mixed metaphor," I said.

"What sort of a woman is this investigator Robinson?" Heather asked.

"An effectively inconspicuous, nicely-mannered lady," I said. "If she weren't an ex-nun, she'd probably fit just fine in our kind of Wiccan circle."

"We'd have been inconspicuous, too, if you hadn't made us into a crime-fighting posse," Deidre said. "No one would ever have known about *our thing* if word of your exploits hadn't been splashed all over the *Quincy Patriot Ledger*."

"You're complaining, Dee? I seem to remember that you're always the first to volunteer for a sortie," I reminded her.

Fiona picked out a tune on Heather's Steinway in the bow window, *Scots, wha hae wi' Wallace bled*...and in the Morgan kennel, converted from a former three-car garage, several of the larger canine guests began to howl, a serenade which was soon picked up by the smaller dogs in their back-of-the-kitchen quarters. We could hear Elsa Kitchener shushing them. Fiona sang on, *"Tyrants fall in every foe, Liberty is in every blow, Let us do or die."*

"Oh, sweet Isis! I suppose we're all going to be raiding some seedy vending machine social club now," Phillipa moaned.

CHAPTER TWENTY

We dance round in a ring and suppose,
While the secret sits in the middle and knows…
Robert Frost

It was Thursday, going on eleven. I was lazing in my kitchen rocking chair, having a third cup of coffee, feet up on a footstool, listening to NPR. When Joe was away, my schedule suddenly became more flexible. Loneliness has its privileges—plenty of time for meditation and mischief. Later I would wend my way over to St. Rita's to find out how Ada's team was progressing in their search for alternate suspects.

Scruffy eyed my laid-back attitude with disfavor.

Hey, Toots! We canines need regular exercise. Tones up the muscles and circulation. Gives us thick fur and bright eyes. Healthy appetites and better dispositions, I hope you've been watching The Dog Whisperer. *That tough guy says you owe it to your companions to take them for a brisk daily walk.* Nosing his leash invitingly, Scruffy pranced around the kitchen like a pup. Raffles looked at his usually dignified sire in some amazement.

Walk! Walk!

"Don't make me laugh. You guys are more like the *Before* in *Before and After obedience training*." I complained. "When's the last time you walked at heel, Scruffy?"

How do you expect me to protect you if you don't let me lead the way? I gotta be out there looking for scrappy squirrels and other dangerous critters. I'm not just a pretty pup, you know. I'm a living, breathing canine of the working class, Toots, with a mind of my own. You wanted maybe a Stepford dog?

I groaned and obligingly put on the green lumber jacket that hung near the kitchen door and donned my garden Wellingtons. Then I grabbed the two leashes and took the dogs for a long walk in Jenkins Park. In the deepest part of the woods, I let them run off leash, joyously chasing every small creature that moved. Feeling a bit hungry, I led us all the way over to Phillipa's house, which was on the other side of the Park. Puffing mightily by the time we arrived, Scruffy refrained from any more grumbles about his exercise routine. Raffles, however, was as lithe and limber as a greyhound.

Pipe down, show-off. You're giving me an earache with all that frolicking.

Frolicking! Frolicking!

I knocked at Phillipa's back door. She looked out the glass pane at the three of us standing in her "mudroom" entry and eyed the dogs with disapproval. "Come in, come in, Cass. What a nice surprise. I was just going to grill panini like the ones we had in Rome. Mozzarella, prosciutto, and roasted peppers okay for you? And I'm making a batch of those miniature cream scones that Fiona believes to be her secret recipe. I hope those mutts are not going to give poor Zelda a nervous breakdown. The last time they were here, they chased her up the china cabinet and a Meissen platter got knocked over."

That fat feline is a real klutz. Who wants to chase a hairball like that?

Hairball like that! Like that!

I was holding my lumber jacket in midair. "What happened to that clothes tree you used to have in this entry?"

"Good question. Another mysterious disappearance at the Plymouth detective's home. You'd think he'd be embarrassed. Or just plain livid, like me, at our larcenous neighbors. I wonder if the O'Reillys aren't related to those troublesome Irish Travellers."

"Be patient. Fiona says good luck will be the O'Reilly clan's undoing."

"Ha! By the time that happens, we'll be picked clean as a dog bone."

Phillipa served coffee made from freshly ground Italian roast beans, *bellissimo* panini, and glazed scones, which were *nearly* as meltingly good as Fiona's, (I wondered if Phillipa knew about that pinch of mace.) Scruffy and Raffles had homemade liver fudge. Despite her hard words about animal manners, Phillipa couldn't resist feeding treats even to four-legged friends.

She was wearing a black and white striped canvas apron over a black cashmere turtleneck sweater and black jeans with tapered legs tucked into black mid-calf boots with silver buckles. Taking off her apron after we'd cleared the lunch dishes, Phillipa offered to go with me to St. Rita's. She had not yet met Ada, although she knew her story intimately and had even been talked into consulting her detective husband, Stone, about the case.

We dropped the dogs at home, much to Scruffy's chagrin. I also took the opportunity to change out of my Greenpeace sweatshirt and grubby jeans into some decent looking tan slacks, a white cowl-neck sweater, and a camel's hair car coat. Phillipa always sets me a high standard. She was wearing a shiny black coat with a stand-up collar that framed her face. Put me in mind of Snow White's wicked stepmother.

Ken Wakahiro waved us into the St. Rita fortress, and Serena ushered us into the parlor where Diane, Magdalene, and Ada were waiting. I could see Phillipa eyeing the Catholic accouterments and the tea tray with some suspicion. More fruitcake. As it happens, I like a good rich brandied fruitcake and I've seen less and less of it in recent years. Phillipa knew Serena, of course. I introduced her to the other three, trying in a light way to explain that Phillipa was a member of *our* circle. Magdalene already knew us by reputation; Fiona and Ada had met when we'd sprung her from Tranquility Lodge.

Diane looked like a cat with a dish of cream, so I knew she'd found out something of interest. She was wearing another twin-set, baby blue, with navy slacks. "Jerry Richter was not a popular man," was her opening understatement. "If we're looking for a Rhode Island connection, I've found two possibilities. The owner of the Shady Lady nightclub was recently taken to the cleaners by his ex-wife with Richter's help. Frankie Gallo. He took the financial judgment and the loss of Frankie Jr.'s custody rather badly, I'm told. Gallo had claimed the nightclub was losing money, but with Battaglia's help, Richter exposed assets that Gallo would rather have kept hidden. Serious threats were made. When you take what belongs to a man like Gallo, you can expect payback." Diane took a small sip of tea and touched the gold cross that gleamed against her sweater like a talisman. "*But wait, there's more*, as the TV hucksters say."

"I really like this Frankie Gallo for the murder of Jerry Richter," Magdalene said, adjusting a purple fringed shawl around her plump shoulders and smiling reassuringly at Ada. A miasma of Shalimar wafted from her expressive hands. "He has the makings of a prime alternative suspect."

"What about Nevaeh?" Ada asked in her husky Garbo voice. She was wearing a designer sheath in widow's black and Ferrigamo flats with velvet bows. Classy, except for the monitor cuff around her ankle.

"Nevaeh Nichols wept throughout the free massage I arranged for her. The death of her lover..." and here Diane glanced at Ada as if gauging her hysteria level. But Ada was as cool and smooth as obsidian. "...has left her very depressed indeed. Apparently there were attractive promises, but nothing a girl could take to the bank. You know, *Why is it no one ever sent me one perfect limousine, do you suppose? Ah no, it's always just my luck to get one perfect rose?* Richter's gifts were mere trinkets, in Nevaeh's view."

Ada laughed, a deep malicious chuckle.

"Nevaeh mentioned someone else of interest to her masseuse," Diane went on. "Also with a Rhode Island connection. Not sure if it's Providence, though. The guy she used to see before she went to work for Richter. Vinnie. She wouldn't mention his last name, but she did say that he was a restaurateur. That poses rather a problem. Practically every Italian restaurant in Rhode Island is owned at least partly by someone named Vinnie."

"But the restaurant may not be Italian," Phillipa suggested. "Owned by Vinnie but some kind of upscale grill or trendy brasserie."

"I'd thought of that," Diane said. "Do you know how many restaurants there are in Rhode Island?" She unsnapped the gold clasp of her navy purse and removed a small notebook, flipping through the pages. "Over 700. Not bad for the smallest state. I expect it will take a little time to narrow down the eateries owned by someone named Vinnie, and heaven knows how many of those there are."

"This anonymous Vinnie seems less of a likely suspect than Gallo," Magdalene said. "What makes Nevaeh think he might have gone after Richter?"

"My friend the masseuse reports that, according to Ms. Nichols, arson would have been just Vinnie's style. She said he once set fire to her TransAm when she threatened to leave the state. But once Richter came into her life, with his legal expertise and the unscrupulous machinations of Bruno Battaglia, Vinnie backed off. Nevaeh said that Richter had something on Vinnie, she didn't know what."

"Honor is due, Diane," I said. "You've really given us a lot to work with."

Serena smiled. "It's that good old convent ethic: leave no scrap of dirt unturned."

Diane, Magdalene, and Serena looked at each other with sly amusement and secret knowledge that was not unlike our own circle's camaraderie. I saw that the spiritual bond between these three women was a powerful one.

Phillipa nudged me. "So glad these aren't the burning times, aren't you?" she whispered. Then she turned to Diane. "An excellent report on two live suspects. And I bet Cass can zero in on some salient details, if she's willing."

"Exactly what I'm praying for," Serena said. "After all, it's Cass who got us pursuing the Providence angle.'

"We'll all see what we can unearth," I said. "We have our ways."

"Us, too," Serena said. "Let's meet here again in—say—three days?"

As we drove home, Phillipa recited, *"When shall we three meet again? In thunder, lightning, or in rain?* For a minute there, I thought I was in the midst of a Catholic coven."

I laughed. "The word coven carries too much prejudicial baggage. A Catholic *circle* I would say."

"What about the word *witches,* then?"

"That one's unavoidable, I'm afraid. Women who work with cosmic energies to transform reality—what else could you call them?" I mused.

"Artistes du cosmos, perhaps," Phillipa mused. "Witch is considered pejorative, after all. Not among ourselves, of course."

"Wiccan is less so, but I think it's too late for us to hop back into the broom closet after all those articles about us in the *Pilgrim Times.* I remember that Tip preferred others to call him a Native American, but among his own people, he used the word Indian to refer to himself and them. Incidentally, he called us the Medicine Women. I rather liked that."

"Dear Tip. What's he up to these days?"

Tip—Thunder Pony Thomas—a young Passamaquoddy from Maine with whom I'd shared some adventures in past years, was an expert tracker and a fund of shamanistic knowledge. "Studying Native American music and archeology at the University of Maine, where he gets free tuition."

"Always on call if you need him?"

"Always my friend."

"So what are you going to do about your Providence fixation?"

"I'm not wild about inducing another vision, but with the ladies at St. Rita's depending on us, I guess I will."

"Before we meet again around the cauldron at St. Rita's?"

"That would be the deadline, yes."

We'd arrived at her house. I stopped the car, and she got out, then turned back for a moment. Her shiny black coat reflected the lowering sun. "Come over for coffee tomorrow morning, and I'll read the tarot. Maybe I can come up with something as well."

"What about the others?"

"Definitely. I'll call them tonight. Fiona can dowse the bastard. Heather can bring her divination candle. Deidre? "

"Poppets," I said. "Keep the good thought."

When she went into the house, Stone opened the door for his wife with the fond welcoming look that always greeted Phillipa. He waved to me. I drove home feeling lonesome already, but I, too, had a welcoming committee waiting for me on the living room window seat.

About time you got home, Toots. I need to pee real bad, and Junior here is driving me loco. And we're both starving. Any of that leftover beef stew?

Beef stew! Beef stew! Raffles picked up an ancient marrow bone and rejoiced in my arrival with an impromptu dance around the kitchen. I let them out the pet door on the porch. Checking the refrigerator, I took out an open bottle of red wine and the leftover casserole, beef with mushrooms *a la Grecque* enriched with Metaxa.

Greek beef stew. Before Joe came into my life, I'd given up red meat. My canine companions should feel grateful for his robust culinary influence. Heather, however, was appalled.

∽

The next morning, we got together at Phillipa's for a Wiccan coffee klatch to brew up some magic. Deidre was already there, shaking her blonde curls out of her red pixie hood as I arrived, followed by Heather with Fiona leaning heavily on her cane. Phillipa was just taking a Mexican cornbread out of the oven, a dense moist bread with the unexpected filip of chocolate morsels.

Heather set her divination candle on a pewter holder in the middle of Phillipa's long marble table and lit it while whispering a soft incantation. *Mugwort and peppermint swirling here, let the mists of mystery clear.*

After we'd all been served "coffee and...," Phillipa brought the red silk bag that kept her tarot deck safe from unwanted vibes. We were all as silent as possible, sipping and munching, while she shuffled the cards for the Celtic cross spread.

The Knight of Swords was chosen as a significator. Phillipa laid out the cards, intoning, "This covers him, this crosses him, this is beneath him..." and so forth, until the last, "this is the final outcome," which turned up a card called The Devil.

"Here's our circle, the Three of Cups," Phillipa said, pointing to the picture of maidens toasting with wine cups. "And there's danger, too, see here." One slim olive-skinned finger tapped the Five of Swords. "A cowardly attack. And here we have The Lovers. So that might indicate the elusive Vinnie, victim of unrequited passion. On the other hand, this Ten of Cups reversed does suggest a bad family situation, possibly the revengeful Gallo. And this ominous Ten of Swords, can represent death by misadventure. The Hanged Man, reversed, an arrogant ego. The Devil as the concluding card shows a theme of material gain."

"And that all means...what?" Deidre demanded.

Phillipa sighed. "It could be either one of these guys. But if I were pressed to the wall, my guess would be Gallo. The reversed Ten of Cups, the reversed Hanged Man, even The Devil."

"We mustn't expect divination to be an exact science," Fiona said. "It's an art. Like a shaman reading the meaning of dreams. Or a psychologist treating a depressed patient. We observe and interpret, that's all we can do."

Deidre said, "Sometimes we have to give signs and portents a bit of a shove." She removed two sinister-looking poppets from her workbag, which usually held some kitsch embroidery with a sweet motto. "This one will be Frankie Gallo. See how his pockets are hanging out, empty? Thanks to his ruinous divorce settlement. And this one will be Vinnie Whatshisface. He's wearing an apron and holding a menu. Also, I've given him a little red heart, like Raggedy Andy. If we come up with a sympathetic magic spell, Frankie and Vinnie will be ready."

"Holy Hecate!" Phillipa said. "Has Conor ever seen your poppets, Dee?" She busied herself setting up her elaborate coffee system to brew another round.

Deidre grinned impishly, bringing out her dimples. "My workroom is so crowded with dolls, I don't know that he'd notice that some of them are poppets. But he calls me his little Dryad, so I guess he's cool with it."

Fiona was polishing the crystal pendant she uses for dowsing. "I don't know what I'm looking for," she complained. "Cass?"

"We could start with a map of Rhode Island," I suggested.

"Oh, yes, good idea that. Got one right here." Fiona reached into her green reticule and drew out an Arrow map of Rhode Island.

"Who's surprised?" asked Phillipa. She pushed her tarot cards together to make room for the map between our plates and crumbs. Fiona's multi-ringed fingers flattened Rhode Island out on the space provided. She centered the pendant, allowing it to dangle about five inches above the table. Although Fiona's hand was now steady, the crystal began to move in lazy, aimless circles. We watched with utter fascination.

Fiona hummed to the pendant, and whispered some Gaelic words. Then she said in a louder tone we could all hear and understand, "Where will we find the man who set fire to the Richter home?"

The crystal moved more purposefully, circling Providence in smaller and smaller circles until it came to rest directly over Atwell's Avenue on Federal Hill, the historic Italian district of the city.

"Oh, goodie," Phillipa said. "Think of the cheeses, the salamis, the Venda ravioli, the pastries…!"

"Yes," Heather agreed dryly. "And let's also think of the murderer we're tracking. In fact, let's think of him first."

"Okay, but I'm bringing my shopping bags, too. Let's all remember how you gleefully canvassed the Via del Condotti in Rome when we were supposed to be concentrated on rescuing Conor."

"Let her who is without a Gucci scarf throw the first stone," Heather said.

"Oh, cut it out, you two," Deidre said. "Now Federal Hill suggests a restaurant to me, doesn't it to you?"

"Or perhaps that's where Frankie Gallo has his office," I suggested.

"Wouldn't it be more natural for him to have an office at his club?" Heather said. "We could visit the place and check it out. The Shady Lady is several blocks away from the area indicated by Fiona's dowsing. If Frankie Gallo's office is there, I don't think the pendant is pointing his way."

"*Check out the Shady Lady?* Are you out of your mind?" Deidre said.

Meanwhile Phillipa had opened her laptop on the kitchen desk and was Googling the Gallo place. "According to these reviews I'm reading, the Shady Lady is a strip club, with topless waitresses, pole dancing, lap dancing, and a nude room. One of the reviewers, a guy, complains because there is only one toilet for the women guests which the female entertainers also share. That suggests to me that women do not frequent the place. So somehow I can't see us swanning into the Shady Lady to order afternoon tea and case the joint. They have bouncers, you know."

Deidre giggled. "Holy Mother, what would Conor think if I got caught in such a place?"

Fiona tucked the crystal pendant on its chain underneath her coat sweater of many colors. She took a notebook decorated with a pentagram out of her reticule and withdrew a bic pen from her coronet of carroty-gray braids. "What's the address? I think it would be best if I went in there alone," she said. "Chances are I'll hardly be noticed."

"I guess Fiona means to take the invisibility glamour to a whole new level," I said. "But I think it's best if we all go along with her, in case. We can wait in the car. Surely there's a parking lot."

"Valet parking," Phillipa said, still reading.

"Okay, then," Deidre said. "I agree that Fiona by herself will be less obvious than if the five or us waltzed in there. But if we're nearby and Fiona gets into trouble, she can call us on her cell."

"So if we find Gallo has an office in the Shady Lady, we'll guess that he doesn't have another on the Hill," I summed up. "In which case, we'll start checking restaurants for Vinnie the Obscure."

"Sounds like a plan," Heather said. "Why don't we go now?"

"Right. And after we've zeroed in on the culprit, we could have lunch at Camille's Roman Gardens. Although I doubt if it will be anything like dining in Rome," Phillipa said.

"You realize that Cass hasn't come across with a vision yet, don't you?" Heather reminded us.

I'd been keeping a low profile. I said, "Might as well save me for the Hill, then."

Heather blew out the divination candle. We suited up and crowded into Heather's Mercedes with the dog-drool-smeared windows. Phillipa asked Fiona if she needed to borrow something black, but Fiona said she was fine just as she was in her MacDonald tartan coat, which thankfully was the muted antique hunter plaid. If push came to shove in rescuing Fiona we could always call 911 and report a robbery. Or a kidnapping.

The Mercedes made the trip to Providence in record time, just over an hour. No moss grew under Heather's wheels.

"Isn't it too early for a strip club to be open?" Deidre asked.

"Apparently not. Free admission 11:30 to 6:00 on weekdays," said Phillipa, who'd read the reviews.

"Guys must be truly desperate," Heather said as she wheeled right past the Valet Parking sign and eased into what she called "her rightful parking place, the witch's prerogative." It was right across the street from the Shady Lady's front door, facing toward Route 95, so right in line for a hasty departure. *Perfect!*

A beefy wrestler type came out the front door and tossed a small cigar into the gutter. He looked up and down the street, then went back inside.

"Yikes," Deidre said. "Would that be the bouncer?"

Before we could even assemble suitable warnings, Fiona had hopped lightly out of the car, throwing off all signs of arthritis, and was halfway across the street. Heather rolled down the window and drew in her breath sharply. "Will you look at that!"

Fiona seemed to shrink and fade as she crossed the street to the Shady Lady. I could have sworn that her coat had changed from MacDonald tartan to some nebulous gray, and there was a kind of mist around her that made me blink several times to clear my vision.

"Does she at least still have her cane?" Phillipa asked in a nervous tone.

"I can't quite tell," Heather said, "but she must have, as it's not here in the car."

The door opened and Fiona went inside. It was impossible to see who had let her in—could it have been that muscle-bound bouncer?

Every one of us had a cell phone in hand, awaiting the first panic call.

Many mortally long minutes passed.

Then Heather's phone rang!

CHAPTER TWENTY-ONE

Give me a bowl of wine.
In this I bury all unkindness.
William Shakespeare

Heather listened anxiously while we hung around her cell trying to hear. "Yes. Yes. Right. I'll have the motor running when Cass brings you out of there." She ended the call. We all looked at her with varying degrees of expectant alarm.

"She says that Cass should go in and get her now. And to call her Auntie." Heather reported.

"*Me?*" I croaked. Then a fleeting impression went across my thoughts. "Okay, I've got it. An addled Auntie. Not far from the truth."

"Cass may need help. I'll go, too," Deidre declared. She whipped off her peaked red hood, shook out her blonde curls, and quickly applied pink lipstick. "Okay, I'm all set."

Deidre and I crossed the street to the Shady Lady's front door. Not being under a charm, we had to dodge through traffic, cars honking impatiently.

The same muscle-bound, plug-ugly man we'd seen earlier opened the door just as I reached for the knocker, which appeared to be a woman's breasts. He was smoking a fresh cigar which he chewed around to the corner of his mouth to growl, "What's this? More crazy broads?" His beady eyes glared at us.

"Auntie." I said firmly. "We're here to get Auntie."

He looked at me and sucked on the smelly cigar.

"We think our dear old Auntie may have wandered in here, and we've come to bring her home," Deidre said loudly.

"That the Auntie with the cane?" he said. He rubbed the knuckles of his right hand with his left.

"Uh oh," Deidre said.

"Oh dear, I hope she hasn't been any trouble," I said. I'd become extremely conscious that I was still standing outside the club and hadn't yet heard a squeak from Fiona.

"Oh, there, you are, dearies," Fiona's voice spoke merrily behind the big bouncer's squat square frame. "I think I'm in the wrong place. I wanted to buy a nice little sewing stand. You know, with the cute drawers for notions and all? But this isn't the Good Will shop after all."

Fiona's head poked around the corner of the bouncer. She had two Shady Lady swizzle sticks in her coronet of braids and a glass of something amber in one hand. An attractive redhead pushed through beside her, elbowing the bouncer to one side. She was grasping Fiona's arm and patting her hand. Another girl, a brunette, was holding her tartan coat and cane. The girls were wearing high cut panties and ratty little fur jackets, under which it was easy to see that they were topless; their pert breasts peeking out of the jackets looked cold in the draft from the open door.

"Now you leave Auntie alone, Slugger," the redhead said to the bouncer.

"That fucking old broad smacked me with her cane," Slugger complained. "I shouldda..."

"You asked for it, Slug, trying to push her outta Frankie's office like that," the brunette said. "Anyone with half a brain could see she didn't mean any harm."

"Here you go, Auntie," the redhead said, "your two nieces are here to take you home now."

"Oh, thank you, Cherry. Thank you, Tiffany," Fiona said, pushing smartly past Slugger who was watching our tableau with an ugly scowl, his burly arms crossed. "Goddess bless you both." She drained her glass and handed it to the bouncer. "Just remember to keep your left up, Slugger."

With a nervous look at Slugger's menacing face, I grabbed Fiona's hand, put my arm around her shoulders, and hustled her across the street to the Mercedes where Heather and Phillipa were hanging out of the open windows. Deidre followed with Fiona's cane, waving it at the speeding cars to allow us safe passage.

"I must have had a few chinks in my invisibility glamour," Fiona complained as she seated herself in the front seat with Heather. Deidre, Phillipa, and I crowded into the back. Heather took off like a jet plane toward Route 95.

"Sweet Isis," Phillipa exclaimed. "Tell us everything."

"Well, dears, I can affirm that Frankie Gallo does have his office in the Shady Lady. Let me just catch my breath a little." Fiona took a tiny spray bottle out of her reticule and enveloped herself (and us) in a lavender mist.

"There! That's better," she said. "Now I know you ladies are all curious about the invisibility glamour. At first, it worked fine. I slipped in very easily, just as that Slugger fellow had turned his back to spit or something disgusting like that. *So good, so far.* I hunched over and shuffled along with my cane like a cleaning woman with a broom toward the back of the club where I thought the offices must be. And I almost made it, too, but that awful music gyrating in my head must have broken my concentration. The next thing I knew, Slugger suddenly came out of his stupor and hot-footed over to where I was starting to open the office door and threw me against the wall. Naturally, my first instinct was to defend myself. *The best offense is a good defense.* So I smashed my cane across his hand. It was simply a natural reflex action but it seemed to upset him.

Because he grabbed my throat with his other hand, and I really lost my breath there for a few moments." Fiona rubbed her throat, which was red in splotches.

"Holy Mother!" Deidre exclaimed. "We should never have let you go alone into that den of iniquity."

"Oh come now, Dee. That's a bit dramatic. That nice girl Cherry screamed at Slugger, and a man came out of the back office and shouted '*what the fuck...?*'"

"A man? Was it Gallo?" I asked.

"Slugger let me go immediately. As soon as I could speak," Fiona fished in her reticule and took out sage oil, which she dabbed on her wrists. "I explained about the Good Will store, and the man from the office laughed. Cherry had her arm around me by then, and Tiffany came over. 'Aw, Frankie, she's just a harmless old doll who got confused,' Cherry said. 'We'll help her out of here, Frankie,' Tiffany said. 'Hey, who the fuck is the bouncer around here? I'll take care of this one, Mr. Gallo,' Slugger said. So that was Frankie Gallo. Mission accomplished. *Time to get out of here*, I thought. 'Oh dearie me. Let me call my niece,' I said. So that's when I called Heather on my cell. And Cherry asked if I'd like a drop of sherry to calm my nerves, and I said, better make it a double. After that, I was all right, really. But Slugger asked how come my niece let me wander into a strip club, and I had no answer for that one, so I fainted. Always a good thing to do when you haven't an answer, don't you think?"

"I must remember that," Phillipa said.

"Cherry and Tiffany were really so sweet. They left all those men who'd been watching them dancing around the poles, which put me in mind of Maypoles. Some of the patrons were jeering and whistling and banging their fists on the bar. Slugger went over and quieted them down, though, before he went back to guarding the front entrance. Meanwhile the girls splashed my face with a few drops of club soda, got me to sit up, and helped me to the door. They really should keep some smelling salts on hand in the club, don't you think? And then Cass and Dee came to my rescue, and here we are!"

"Frankie Gallo in his office at the Shady Lady probably is not our suspect you dowsed out on Federal Hill," Heather said, "so let's have a look at the restaurant scene. I figure that Phil and I can go in the likely ones and ask for Vinnie."

"Sure, and six guys will answer every time," I laughed.

"Okay, Cass," Phillipa said. "We took off before you could do your vision thing, so now's your chance."

"Ceres save me," I said. "You want me to have a vision while Heather's driving?"

"Exactly. What do you need?" Phillipa asked.

I was sitting between her and Deidre. I leaned back and fixed my attention on the sun, which was at about two o'clock ahead of us as we drove through the arch with a giant dangling pine cone west onto Atwell's Avenue. "Just give me a minute of silence, ladies."

Fiona reached into the back seat and handed me her bottle of sage oil. I took a deep sniff and closed my eyes.

A fleeting vision of the street, and letters formed on my mind's eye. "Campobasso," I said.

"Aren't you confusing Federal Hill with the Campobasso where the Mafia kidnappers of Conor had their stronghold?" Deidre asked.

"That's all I've got. There was a bronze tablet right in the sidewalk, and above it there was a sign *Campobasso*." I said.

Phillipa said, "Have you ever been here before, Cass? Federal Hill has a number of bronze plaques commemorating street corners where immigrant grandfathers operated pushcarts many years ago."

"Campobasso, lettered in gold," I said. "Drive slowly, and let's see."

We drove past Camille's, the Civita Farnese, Joe Marzilli's, the Mediterraneo, the Blue Grotto, and Chef Ho's Chinese Restaurant. "Chef Ho? How'd he get in here?" Phillipa scoffed.

"Oh, look," Deidre cried. "The Café Campobasso. It's not some Italian nightmare after all. You guys ought to have more faith in Cass."

"I distrust all coincidences," Phillipa said. "There's always a message in a coincidence, or a warning."

Heather careened into a suddenly vacated parking place and slammed on her brakes. "Look at this! The Goddess is with us."

I was feeling disoriented and nauseous, so I said nothing.

"What a hole in the wall!" Phillipa said. "Oh well, maybe the food's good anyway. *Let's do lunch!*"

We gathered ourselves together and went into the Café Campobasso. It was a small place but bigger than it looked from the street, charming décor, with pink tablecloths, pink candles, and impressionistic paintings of the Campobasso countryside and the Old City. Delectable aromas wafted in from the kitchen. A few of the tables were occupied with late lunchers like ourselves. A slender young woman with her dark hair slicked back in a ponytail and gold hoop earrings the size of bracelets seated us at a round table near the window. She handed out menus and supplied us with a basket of fresh bread. Saucers of herbed olive oil were already on the table. She said, "Hi. My name is Angie, and I'll be your server this afternoon."

"It's nearly two-thirty, and I'm starved," Phillipa said, studying the menu as if boning up for a quiz. "Not too heavily tomato-sauced, at least."

"Do you have Prosecco?" Heather asked the waitress, who nodded *Si.* Heather immediately ordered a bottle to share, then before she could leave, questioned the girl, "Is Vinnie here today?"

"Vinnie is never here until after seven," the girl replied, the gold hoops swinging as she shook her head negatively.

"A girl we met at the health club, Nevaeh, recommended this place. She said the owner is an old friend. Ask for Vinnie, she said." Deidre looked inquiringly at the waitress.

"Oh, her," the waitress said. "Yeah, she used to hang here. She sent a message for Vinnie?"

"Ah, no," I said. "Let's everyone order, shall we?"

"She said to tell Vinnie she's in the market for a new TransAm," Phillipa said. "Ouch, Cass. That's my foot you're stomping."

"Who shall I say?" asked Angie.

"Oh, just friends," Fiona said. "Friends of Nevaeh's,"

Phillipa handed the waitress one of the promotional cards from her cookbook *Native Foods of New England*. Along with a glossy photograph of moose-and-fiddlehead shepherd's pie and a blurb about the book, it bore her name, Phillipa Gold Stern, Web site, and an email address. A restaurateur might also recognize her name as that of a frequent restaurant reviewer for New England magazines.

Angie read the card without expression, tucked it into her apron pocket, and went to fetch the sparkling wine.

"I think we should keep a low profile, dear," Fiona said to Phil.

"Oh, look who's talking. I say, we stir the cauldron and see what kind of creature jumps out," Phillipa said. "At least we've found the elusive Vinnie. What a coup!"

"What do you mean, *we*?" I said. "And we still don't know his last name."

Phillipa turned over her menu and read all the fine print, but no last name was in evidence.

The waitress returned with the Prosecco and five glasses.

"Oh, would you settle an argument for us, Angie?" Heather asked sweetly while the bottle was opened and poured. "Just exactly how do you pronounce Vinnie's last name?"

Angie looked as if Heather had taken leave of her senses. But she said, "Bennett. Vinnie Bennett."

"Oh, it's not Benedetto, then?" Heather inquired innocently. "Tall bearded guy?"

Angie looked even more suspicious. "No. Bennett with no beard."

"Oh for Goddess' sake, let's at least order some food." Phillipa said. "Angie, bring us five orders of cioppino, a large artichoke frittata to share, and the white pizza with wild mushrooms and a balsamic reduction. Is that all right with everyone?"

"And a bottle of Fiano de Avellino," Heather said. After Angie had left with our order, she continued for our edification, "An antique Roman wine from the Campania region. You'll love it. 'Wine of the bees.' Apparently bees preferred the flowers of this grape vine above all others. We can toast our recent Roman adventure."

"And our next Roman adventure," I said. "If we're not very careful here."

We were always in good hands when Phillipa and Heather ordered for us. We ate, drank, and were merry. After a few glasses of Prosecco and the lovely white wine that Heather had ordered, we nearly forgot we were sleuthing and had a jolly afternoon at Café Campobasso. Which only goes to show, once again, that clairvoyants can be as obtuse as anyone when it comes to personal danger.

CHAPTER TWENTY-TWO

As a woman, I have no country.
As a woman, my country is the whole world.
Virginia Wolfe

Two days later, as arranged, Phillipa and I met again with the Catholic circle at St. Rita's and were able to report our considerable progress. Fiona had dowsed Federal Hill, where Frankie Gallo wasn't but Vinnie was, and it was no small thing that Heather had teased out his last name, Bennett. Of course, I, too, could take modest credit for coming up with Campobasso, which had saved us from eating our way across Federal Hill to find some anonymous Vinnie's restaurant.

Serena was serving Irish Breakfast Tea and spicy, fruit-filled rock cakes made in their own kitchen. Phillipa broke off a crumb and tasted it carefully. I didn't have to be a mind reader to know she was thinking of how she could make these even tastier, but she wouldn't dream of asking for the recipe. "Mmmm," she said. "Harry Potter's favorite tea-time treat."

"Let's not tell Sully about that." Serena's bird-bright eyes twinkled. "Our cook Mrs. Sullivan's already got enough on her hands, praying for our souls to be reunited with the Church."

"Phil, Cass...you are such darlings!" Magdalene exclaimed warmly. Today she was wearing a deeply fringed white wool shawl over a cerise knit suit, and she was drenched in White Diamonds. I seriously wondered if she even owned the *de rigueur* navy "power suit" that my Becky insisted upon for court appearances. "We are now on the track of a viable alternative suspect. But we will need tangible evidence against this Vinnie before I can present a motion to dismiss the indictment against Ada."

Diane sipped her tea with a thoughtful expression. "A good starting place might be to discover what Richter had on Vinnie to blackmail him into staying away from Nevaeh. I can't very well break into Richter's office to look through his files but I will do an extensive background check on Vincent Bennett. Maybe that will turn up some possibilities."

Phillipa and I looked at one another. "I can't," she whispered. "What if Stone…"

"Heather will go along," I whispered back. "And she's got lots of experience."

Serena raised one eyebrow and looked at us questioningly. "Exactly what are you two whispering about? I hope you're not considering a foray into Richter's records yourselves."

"Whatever you do, darlings be extremely cautious," Magdalene warned. "Bruno Battaglia is still on the loose, and then there's the problem of entering a premises illegally. As an officer of the court, I am bound to report any criminal activity that I learn about *before the fact*. After the fact, of course, is an entirely different matter. If I am the attorney representing you, everything you tell me will be privileged communication."

My daughter Becky was an attorney, too, but perhaps if it were a matter of her mother being charged as a criminal… "Thank you, Mag," I said. "That's very reassuring. We'll say no more now, though. Let Diane do her thing, and Phil and I will consult—psychically."

"Oh, well," Serena said. "I may as well try a *sortes Biblicae*." She put down her tea cup and strode over to the ornate Bible on the oak stand. Phillipa pinched me gleefully, delighted to witness a new divination method. Naturally, we were respectfully silent. Magdalene and Diane bowed their heads for a moment, and then looked up expectantly.

Serena said her prayer with her hands on the Bible. She seemed to wait until moved by the spirit, then she opened the gilded book at random, and without looking, ran her finger down the page until it came to rest without effort. She read the passage to herself, and then aloud to all of us.

"Malachi, the last book of the Old Testament, Chapter 2, Verse 14," she said. "*Yet ye say, Wherefore? Because the Lord hath been witness between thee and the wife of thy youth, against whom thou hast dealt treacherously: yet is she thy companion, and the wife of thy covenant.*"

"Well, there you have it, then," Diane said. "I'll need to find out if Vinnie Bennett had a wife, and if so, what became of her. I'm assuming she's not in the picture now, if he was hooked up with Nevaeh."

Magdalene's eyes gleamed with anticipation. "Ah, darlings, what a break! Perhaps a little scandal in Vinnie's past?"

"Maybe Nevaeh broke up his marriage, as she did mine, the little bitch," Ada said in her deep Garbo voice which made even profanity sound classy.

Serena closed the Good Book and patted Ada's hand. "The *sortes* does bring us a whole new perspective on the problem, doesn't it?"

When our tea conference broke up that afternoon, each of us seemed to come away with a personal mission. Magdalene and Diane wanted to thoroughly investigate Vinnie Bennett, Phillipa was trying to persuade me not to search Richter's office, and Ada would do just about anything to trash Nevaeh.

"Ada, you wouldn't have any keys to your husband's office, would you?" I asked as Phillipa and I were heading out the parlor door. I was careful to wait until Magdalene had already preceded us into the cavernous hall where our coats were hung and Serena was taking the tea tray out to Mrs. Sullivan. Diane merely glanced at us, winked, and busied herself writing in her neat little notebook. When Diane sat quietly, one almost forgot she was there. I was reminded of Fiona's invisibility glamour.

Ada smiled with sweet malice. She really was coming to life now that she was a widow. "I made copies of the key to Jerry's office in Historic Plymouth and his office at home. He kept that locked, as well. But a man has to sleep sometimes, doesn't he? Especially after a late night with his girlfriend. You ladies just wait here for a moment."

Ada was housed in special guest quarters on the ground floor, so she was back before Serena returned from the kitchen, thrusting two keys into my hand.

"Here—I kept these under a jardinière on our patio. Ken Wakahiro retrieved them for me from the so-called *crime scene*. Such a resourceful man," Ada said. "Remarkably, the fire leaped from the cellar to the kitchen then up the back stairs to Jerry's bedroom. By then, the Fire Department had arrived and got the flames pretty much under control. The whole house is wrecked, of course, but Jerry's study is almost intact, except for the smoke and water damage. All those elegant law books... I've always thought that Jerry kept the real dirt in his safe at home. Why else keep the study door locked and not even allow the housekeeper in there? It was all very medieval. One would think he was an alchemist."

With the touch of her cool fingers, I'd felt the heat of emotions she was hiding beneath that poised persona. I put my arm around her shoulders, marveling at her fragility. "If you ever want to be rid of this pyrokinesis, Ada, you will have to let go of your anger," I warned her. "That will be the price of peace."

"I don't know if I can," she whispered hoarsely.

"Can what, dear?" Serena asked as she came back into the room.

"Anorexia," Diane said, startling me since I had almost forgotten her presence in the room. "That's the other demon that our Ada must overcome, isn't it dear?"

"I just want to be left alone." Ada crossed both arms across her breast, holding everything inside herself. "What makes you think you know so much?"

"Years and years as a nurse. Things just come to me," Diane explained.

I thought there was a little more to it than that in Diane's intuitions. *Takes one to know one.*

❧

The keys Ada had given me were burning a hole in my pocket. But before I could organize a stealthy search of Richter's files for anything he may have used to blackmail Bennett, Diane called me. The investigator had found out some dark areas in our suspect restauranteur's life with a simple Google search. I took this as a Cosmic Nudge to let my fingers do the walking more often instead of breaking into a locked premises illegally as a means of research. My daughter-in-law Freddie, an expert hacker, could be an enormous help with internet investigation.

"Perhaps we can skip Richter's law offices, after all," I said. "There's probably a night watchman, anyway."

But Heather was deeply disappointed, and even Deidre was cross that she had not been invited to go along on the raid, if we did plan one. Obviously, it would take some real action to satisfy them.

Meanwhile, we had learned from Diane that Vinnie Bennett had a questionable history, in the form of a missing spouse. (*Sortes Biblicae* had been right on!)

Ten years ago, his wife Linda, to whom he had been married for three years, had disappeared on Easter night while he was out fishing on Narragansett Bay in his 16-foot cruiser, the *Bella Barca*. Bennett told the police that they'd attended mass and had dinner with his in-laws, the Leones, then driven home to Warren about six o'clock, where Linda had stated her intention to go jogging with their greyhound Ghost while Bennett went out on his boat. Her Dooney & Bourke handbag with wallet and keys had been left in her bedroom closet. Ghost was later found running loose with a muddy leash attached to his collar.

A massive statewide search and the promise of a hefty reward had turned up no leads. Linda, alive or dead, was never found. After seven years, Linda Leone Bennett had been declared dead and her insurance policy of over a million dollars was paid to her beneficiary, Vincent Bennett, who had subsequently invested in a Warwick casino that featured video lottery terminals programmed to play blackjack, keno, slots, and three versions of poker. His new gambling partners met often at his unofficial office, the Café Campobasso, named after the Italian province from which his maternal grandparents had emigrated to the United States. Bennett prospered at his new career and bought a handsome home in Barrington on Narragansett Bay. He did not remarry but was seen with an assortment of girlfriends over the years since his wife's disappearance.

"That Diane is a whiz at research," I said. "Who needs clairvoyance when we have Delphic Di at the keyboard?" We'd gathered in my kitchen to share Diane's news and plan our next move. It was hard to even imagine Easter on such a cloudy, cheerless November afternoon. I kept the teapot full, and Phillipa passed a plate of her double-gingerbread, which had finely minced candied ginger folded into its moist molasses cake.

"Who goes fishing alone on Easter?" Deidre wanted to know, holding out her tea cup for a refill.

"What if Jerry Richter knew something about Linda's disappearance that cast the light of suspicion on Vinnie?" Heather suggested what we were all thinking. "There's no statute of limitations on murder, after all."

"That Campobasso business still bothers me," Phillipa said. "Not that I think there's an actual connection to our Italian adventure. But I distrust coincidences."

"And rightly so," Fiona decreed. "Coincidence is the Cosmos way of getting our attention. We need to step carefully here."

"Perhaps just a little look around Richter's study," Deidre said. "It isn't still a crime scene, is it?"

"Yes, and it will be until all the evidence has been gathered with which they hope to convict his widow," Phillipa said.

"Oh well, what's a crime scene anyway but a little yellow ribbon," Heather said. "I'm sure the premises are no longer actually guarded by the local police. And we do have Ada Richter's permission."

"In fact, we're probably only going in there to pick up a few items that she needs during her sojourn at St. Rita's," Deidre said. "If they weren't burned up. Extra sweaters and a warmer coat, that sort of thing. Her library books must be quite overdue. "

"I'm not listening to this," Philippa said, putting her hands over her ears.

"The place must be simply reeking of negative vibes," Fiona said. "Be sure to dust your shoes with cinnamon."

"The better to leave tracks?" Phillipa took her hands away from her ears and cast them wide in an attitude of despairing amazement.

"I'm more worried about leaving footprints in the soot or falling through burned flooring," I said.

"Let's all wear black, then," Deidre said. "So our sooty clothes won't give us away. Why don't I bring a broom to whisk away our footprints?"

Phillipa groaned. "What will Conor think when you go traipsing out in a black outfit riding on a broom?"

"Conor has his own apartment," Deidre reminded her. "We don't want to scandalize Mother Ryan, at least not yet. He spends much of his free time at my place, but always by arrangement. I just won't be available on whatever night we choose.

Heather said, "I wish we had an astrologer on board to give us a propitious date and time."

"The Twelfth of Never," Phillipa said.

"What a grand idea!" Fiona said. "We *should* have an astrologer on call for these unofficial sorties. After all, if it's good enough for a president of the United States... But for now, my dears, we'll have to make do with my own modest research." She took a dog-eared pamphlet out of her reticule, "Stealing by the Stars." Paging through to November, she said, "Right you are. The Moon will be in the Twelfth House on Thursday night, perfect for covert action. Pisces is the Twelfth House, you know. Danger of self-undoing, but good for hidden intentions."

"How very useful," Heather said. "I wish you'd been around with that book in my younger days, when I was still breaking into laboratories to rescue animals. But now I've promised Dick not to do that ever again."

"Little does he know what loopholes lurk in that promise," Phillipa said.

"Another thing, supposing Ada is right and all the incriminating stuff is locked up in his safe," I said. "How are we going to deal with that?"

"If it's a fire safe, built to protect items from fire, it will be easy, some obvious combination," Fiona said. "Too bad I'm not going with you. I do have a special facility of hearing how the lock tumbles. Not everyone can do that. Ah well." She sighed for the good old days when her skills had been useful for vigilante protest groups at Berkeley.

"Check with Ada on Richter's social security number, his birthday, his license number. Also he may have written a combination down somewhere, like under the telephone or on the underside of a desk drawer. But if it's not a fire safe, everything inside will be incinerated anyway," Heather said.

"Safecracking! Isn't that a felony?" Phillipa demanded.

"Now, now, ladies," Fiona said. "Let's all do a white light spell to protect our investigative team. Sage-smudging purification, too, I think. And a sprinkle of corn pollen, of course. Phillipa, you organize a chant, will you?"

Fiona always knew how to get us all on the same wave length. Soon we were visualizing, smudging, and chanting in purposeful unison. *She whose love is everywhere, keeps us safe within Her care.*

CHAPTER TWENTY-THREE

Be well aware, quoth then that Lady mild,
Lest sudden Mischief ye too rash provoke:
The Danger hid, the Place unknown and wild...
Edmund Spenser

Still, I did feel a flutter of fear in my third chakra as Thursday evening loomed into view. Thank the Goddess that Joe was off in the Arctic saving the polar bears and black guillemots. I felt like a black guillemot myself as I clambered into my black jeans, black hoodie, and black boots. I even tied a black wool scarf around my neck. Clipped to my belt was a black flashlight, my cell phone, and the "woman's knife" that had been a gift from Tip in a black leather sheath. In my pocket was a little notebook with all the possible number combinations that Ada thought her husband might have used to secure his safe. In my other pocket was a stethoscope that Fiona had pressed upon me in case I had to resort to listening for the lock tumbles. *Fat chance! Who did she think I was—Jimmy Valentine?*

Heather insisted on driving the Mercedes, which was probably a good choice, since it was too dirty to attract much attention. Deidre was already in the passenger seat when she picked me up, so I sat in back with a parting wave to the two disgruntled dogs watching from the living room window seat.

One look at me and Deidre began to hum *Mack the Knife.* In her size 2 black ski suit with a black head scarf tied Italian style, she should talk—she could have been a Victorian chimney sweep.

"It's only a woman's knife," I said. "Indian women used them to skin small game, clean fish, and stuff."

"And gut the odd marauding white man, I don't doubt," Heather said. "Nice get-up." She herself wore a regulation commando outfit complete with boots and beret and appeared to be someone sent down from central casting to fill out *The Dirty Dozen.* "Khaki registers as black after dark," she explained. "Parking may be a problem in that residential area, but I think we can find something inconspicuous behind the Mayflower Funeral Home. That won't be too far to walk."

"Or run," I said.

"We're supposed to be practicing the invisibility glamour that Fiona tries to teach us," Deidre reminded me. "We begin by cultivating perfect confidence that we have every right to go wherever we're going."

"You first," I said.

"And that our demeanor and actions are completely unremarkable," Deidre continued undeterred.

There were lights still on in the funeral home, but the lot was nearly empty, the only cars being in reserved parking places, possibly the embalming crew. I couldn't help but wonder who was getting the vampire treatment tonight.

Heather parked the Mercedes in the shadow of a mammoth oak, and we set out on foot to the Richter place, two blocks away. One could see that the residence had once been a handsome house of generous proportions with a columned front porch, center entrance, four tall windows across both the first and second floors, and nicely groomed rhododendrons masking the foundation. Now, of course, it was a burned-out mess, at least on one side. The yellow crime scene ribbon, however, had been removed, and a sign on the spacious front lawn bore the name of a swank local outfit, Brewster Renovations. The neighbors must have been relieved.

"The Richter heirs aren't wasting any time in getting the place fixed up," Heather whispered. "Evidently, the estate moved through probate with meteor speed."

"Let's get out of the light," Deidre said, scurrying into the shadows cast by the rhodys. Apparently her invisibility pep talk hadn't been entirely convincing. I looked up and down the street. One lone dog walker moving away from us. We followed Deidre and hunched down between the bushes.

"Connections whisked them through probate," I said. "Everything was inherited by Richter's brother and sister, except for all that real estate that was still in Ada's name." I jingled the set of keys she had given me, but softly. "One key fits every exterior lock, and the other is Richter's private study key. Ada said to try the side entrance that's relatively undamaged and to go up the front stairs to the study."

We did that, and it was easy. The side door led through some kind of family room. Everything was covered by a layer of soot, but someone had laid down heavy paper in the walkways, so we followed that to the front of the house and up the stairs. Although we had a key to Richter's study, we found that door unlocked after all. Possibly the investigating officers had left it that way.

So good, so far, as Fiona would say.

"No turning on the lamps, please. Use your flashlights, ladies," Heather decreed. We scanned the room as best we could; our lights crossing like searchbeams.

Richter's study, which had suffered less smoke and soot damage than other parts of the house, was filled with quality leather furniture, burgundy in color, well cared for but several years old. One fabric-covered chair and hassock, however, in a green and burgundy paisley print, was brand new. Probably a replacement for the easy chair that had caught fire earlier, an incident that Richter had blamed on his wife and reported to the police. The floor-to-ceiling bookcases and hefty masculine desk were mahogany, The only items on the single slab of gleaming wood were a brass letter holder and matching opener, an antique ink well and pen, a telephone, and a bronze statue, which read: "Plymouth County Attorney of the Year." An ergonomic desk chair that looked more like a throne nearly hid a mahogany cabinet in the wall behind the desk.

"Ah ha," Heather said, striding over to open the cabinet with a flourish. Predictably, inside was a gray steel safe about the size of an under-the-counter refrigerator.

"Oh, goodie," Deidre said. "Open it, grab the stuff you want, and let's get out of here."

"Not so fast, Dee," Heather said. "Remember how you begged and pleaded to be taken on this little escapade? Now there's the slight matter of figuring out the damn combination." She took some latex gloves out of her pocket and put them on, carefully, finger by finger, as if they were expensive kid leather. "Okay, shoot," she said to me

I took out my notebook and slowly read out Richter's social security number while Heather maneuvered the dial. *Nothing.*

Then we tried his birthday, his driver's license number, his license plate number, his wedding anniversary (however unlikely that he was sentimental about that one!), his parents' wedding anniversary, his telephone number at home, at the office, on his BlackBerry. Nothing again!

"I guess all that's left is to find out if he wrote down the combination somewhere," I said. "Got any more of those gloves?"

Heather handed each of us a pair and we put them on.

Half an hour later, having checked the undersides of the phone, the desk drawers, the pull-out shelves, the ergonomic chair, and everything else we could think of, we looked at each other with dismay.

"Hey, Cass," Heather said. "This would be an excellent time for a useful vision, honey."

"Oh, shit. Okay," I said.

I really loathed having to perform on cue, but there seemed no logical alternative. "Shine that flashlight over here, will you?" I pointed to the bookcase in back of me, and she obliged. I stared at but not into the high-powered beam. That particular aslant gaze often triggered a spontaneous clairvoyant episode. I tried to allow my mind go blank while I took deep cleansing breaths. The place smelled awful, I realized. Not only with smoke, but mildew was starting to form somewhere, maybe the drapes or the books. A small picture began to form in my mind's eye, my third eye. A dark green book with an engraved illustration on the cover, the way books used to be decorated a hundred years ago. "Ugh. Turn that flashlight down now," I said.

I described the book and we went looking, each of us taking a different wall of bookcases.

Deidre was the one who found it, and she gave a low whoop of joy. "Swiss Family Robinson!" she said, opening to the frontispiece, then turning to the title page, then back again to the cover. "Oh, look. There's a military number stamped inside the cover. RICHTER 6882. Someone in the service must have carried this book with him overseas. Maybe Richter's father?"

Heather was already at the safe, trying the new combination of letters and numbers. Somehow we all knew we were on the right track at last. But Heather sat back on her heels and sighed, "It's too long."

"Try just the first four letters, or even the first three," I suggested.

RICH 6882 did the trick! The gray steel door swung open. It was depressingly crammed with folders and boxes, but we'd come this far, so we sat on the burgundy sofa and matching chair (mindful that they would be easiest to wipe clean) and began to thumb through the various documents.

Time goes very slowly when you're in danger of being discovered in a burglary. But, in fact, checking my Timex, a mere twenty minutes had passed when I found the document that would have put fear of Nemesis into Bennett's heart, if he had one. "I think this is what we're looking for," I said.

"Oh what, what?" Deidre cried.

"Read it," Heather demanded.

It was a letter from Linda Leone Bennett to Jerry Richter, dated April 10, stating that she was retaining his services to obtain a divorce settlement from her husband Vincent Bennett. It advised her attorney that she would be in fear for her life once she informed her husband of her intentions. She said that he had a violent temper and had threatened her with bodily harm many times in the past. Now he expected her to finance his new casino ambitions with money she'd inherited from her grandmother, and she had refused to do so. Instead, she wanted to end their marriage, and she would ask her husband to move out sometime over the holiday weekend. She told Richter that Bennett had insisted on their both having million-dollar insurance policies naming each other as beneficiaries, but she intended to have hers secretly changed in favor of her parents. In the meantime, if anything happened to her or she mysteriously disappeared, her husband Vincent Bennett would have been responsible, even if he had an alibi, and that he had many contacts in organized crime. If harm came to Linda, she was instructing Richter, as her attorney, to bring this letter to the attention of the police.

"Well, well, well," Heather said. "If this letter had ever surfaced in the investigation, Bennett would have been charged with murder for sure. I wonder why Richter never blew the whistle on Bennett."

"Okay. Let's get out of here," Deidre said.

"Richter must have been holding this letter over Bennett's head. Probably kept it on ice until Linda's was officially declared dead, then demanded a cut of the insurance payoff," I said. "Threat of exposure kept Bennett from going after Nevaeh when she dumped him for Richter. Small wonder he was pissed."

"Let's get out of here *right now*," Deidre insisted. She began stuffing the folders and boxes back into the safe.

"Oh, good work," Heather said. She took Linda Bennett's letter, folded it back in its envelope, and tucked it into one of the many inner pockets in her commando outfit. She started handing the rest of the safe's contents to Deidre while I wiped off the leather where we'd been sitting.

"Wait! Did you hear that?" Deidre listened fearfully. Then she grabbed the rest of Richter's papers and crammed them into the safe, swinging the door shut with a sharp click.

There was a rumbling sound downstairs. We all heard it. Then the *clump, clump* of boots crossing the family room. *And coming up the stairs!*

"Holy Mother!" Deidre exclaimed. "I knew it! I knew it!"

CHAPTER TWENTY-FOUR

He who fights and runs away
May live to fight another day.
Ancient Adage

We flung ourselves back in various cowering attitudes of dismay and guilt.

"Hecate, preserve us...it's the cops," Heather whispered. "How will I ever explain this to Dick?"

"Never mind Dick," Deidre wailed softly. "How will you explain this to the police? Oh, my poor children."

"Hush! It's not the police," I said. "It's worse."

A hefty figure swathed in black, wider than he was tall, loomed in the study doorway. His head looked square, like an Aztec stone carving, with a black wool hat pulled down over his ears. A brilliant flashlight swept the room, pausing where each of our bodies was shrinking into a respective corner. *"Wha' the fuck!"*

He made a grab for the person nearest to him, who happened to be Deidre. She squealed and kicked him in the shins. The sound that came out of his mouth was more of a roar than human speech. I thought of the Cyclops dangling one of Ulysses' men in mid-air.

Grabbing for the Attorney of the Year statue to defend Deidre, I froze when I heard Heather's quiet voice behind me saying, "Put that girl down or say goodbye to your knee."

The big man dropped Deidre like a handful of hot coals. "Hey! Easy there, sister."

I whirled around, the statue still grasped in my hand. Heather was holding a handgun, rather a small one, but it certainly looked effective, and her hand wasn't wavering at all, nor her expression. The sight of Heather aiming at the guy's leg was even more shocking than the appearance of the thug in the doorway.

"Holy Mother, where did you get that thing?" Deidre was rubbing her arm where the brute had grabbed her. "Fiona?"

"Gun club," Heather said succinctly. "*Later.*"

The big man appeared to be frozen in place. "Who the fuck *are* you?" he growled.

"And who the fuck are *you?*" Heather responded in a *means-business* voice.

"Put that fucking thing down! *Who am I?* I'm the one guarding these premises from looters like you, that's who I am. Battaglia. Heard of me, have you? And just what the fuck are you bitches after?" He moved a step forward, as if testing Heather's resolve.

Not being so sure of her resolve myself, I made a fast decision. In one quick motion, I bashed Battaglia over the head with the statue in my hand. Luckily, I was almost as tall as Ugly Bruno, so Attorney of the Year hit him with a satisfying *thwack.*

To my surprise, he went down very soft and easy.

"Oh, the poor man," Deidre said. She took a throw pillow off the new chair and put it under his head. "I think he's all right. He's breathing, anyway."

"Thank the Goddess," Heather said. "I don't know if I could have gone through with shooting him. A living being, and all. Should we tie him up, do you think? Cass, your scarf?"

"No, we should get the hell out of here before he wakes up," I screamed, the kind of quiet scream you use for children misbehaving in church.

"Oh, do you think he'll call the police and give them our description?" Deidre worried.

"No, because Battaglia's not the caretaker or anything else," I said. "I think he's looking for some of Richter's blackmail material so he can go into business for himself. Now, *come on...*"

"Maybe I should report this as a robbery. Anonymously, of course." Heather reached for the cell phone attached to her broad black belt. "That way Battaglia will be found and attended to, in case of concussion, you know."

"How do you *know* the new owners haven't hired him as a guard, Cass?:" Deidre insisted, as I pulled her out the door.

"I just know *in my bones,* that's how," I thought of how often I'd heard my grandma say those very words. "If you're going to call, Heather, use the phone on the desk. I don't know for sure, but I think a cell phone call can be traced. And *hurry up!*"

Heather didn't argue, for once. She grabbed for the phone desk and dialed 911. Covering the phone, she whispered urgently. "What's the address here, anyway?"

"111 Mayflower," I whispered back.

"There's a robbery going on at 111 Mayflower," she shouted into the phone. "Better send a squad car right away."

She hung up without another word, and we fled, banging down the stairs without regard to how much noise we made, out the side door, not pausing to lock it again, and down the street toward the funeral home. In the distance, we could already hear sirens. *How would we ever get out of here without being arrested?*

But another, more immediate danger was afoot!

It appeared that Battaglia had come back from the dead and was chasing after us like a revived Egyptian mummy, cursing. I guessed I should have bashed him harder. I glanced back quickly. He was only a block away, but we could run pretty fast for our age. At least Heather and Deidre could. I came puffing after them. I definitely needed to lose a few pounds if outrunning thugs continued to be my karma.

"Holy Mother, that...guy...is...coming...to...get...us," Deidre gasped. "Hurry up, Cass!"

The sirens got closer. Two squad cars squealed to a halt in front of 111 Mayflower. Not much of a criminal nature happens in Plymouth, so you can always count on a rapid response to a distress call. *Too rapid.* As I ran I could hear the officers, opening the cruiser doors and jumping out, no doubt with guns drawn.

"Duck into the parking lot," I insisted, pushing Deidre into the shadows. Heather was already ahead of me, racing for the Mercedes.

"Hey, you there!" One of the officers yelled. "Freeze where you are!"

Great Goddess, were we caught? Since I was bringing up the rear, could I expect a warning shot over my head at any moment? As I reached the funeral home's foundation yews, I looked back fearfully. Maybe the others could escape while I took the heat.

But it was Battaglia who was caught in the cruiser's headlights.

I didn't stay to see what happened to him after that. I assumed he'd be trying to explain that he was not a fleeing thief but was chasing three women who had broken into the house.

Good luck with that one.

We jumped into the Mercedes, and amazingly, Heather found a back way out of the funeral home parking lot, sped out onto Court Street which ran parallel to Mayflower, and we were on our way out of the lovely historic district of Plymouth in a splat of gravel.

"Wow, that was, like, too close for comfort." Deidre, huddled in the front seat next to Heather, turning her complaint toward me in the back.

"There's been more than a few close calls from which we've escaped unscathed. Perhaps Lady Justice is protecting us," Heather replied for me.

"Or it's just dumb luck," I said. "You know what's worrying me? So now we have that letter from Linda Bennett, which might connect her husband to her disappearance, if we can figure out how to get that information to the police. But what is there to connect Vinnie Bennet to Jerry Richter's death? Nothing. *Nada.*"

"Well, we can't tell anyone how we got the letter, not even Magdalene. Should we ask advice from Stone? Or maybe Phil will do it for us?" Heather said.

"What we really need now is less fancy footwork and more good old-fashioned spell-work," Deidre said. "Wasn't there something in that antique Book of Shadows that we used once? "

"Fiona will know," Heather said.

"You do remember, don't you, that a spell set into motion can have unintended consequences?" I was remembering a few Cosmic surprises encountered in the past.

"It's a chance we have to take," Heather said. "We can't allow Ada to be convicted of some else's arson-murder."

"Well, at least we've established that Bennett had a motive. It seems that Richter may have forced Bennett out of Nevaeh's life by threatening to stir up new evidence in Linda's disappearance."

"If only Linda's body were found!" Deidre said.

"If only!" Heather and I agreed in unison.

∽

"Oh, sweet Isis," Phillipa exclaimed. "Do you realize what a chance you were taking, breaking *into Richter's safe?* And now you expect me to explain to Stone that you're in possession of this very damaging letter? That Richter was holding it over Bennett's head?"

"What if...?" Heather paused, as if to collect her thoughts. "What if we put it back in Richter's office, under the desk blotter or something, and Stone or someone found it there?"

"*Put it back in Richter's office!*" I exclaimed. "After we got away with it once without getting caught?" We were gathered in my kitchen for a "debriefing" the next day, and I was making a pot of Earl Grey tea. I stood holding the kettle in midair, a statue frozen in astonishment.

"Makes sense," Deidre said. Her hand hovered between the almond cookies, made by me, and the decadently fudgy brownies that Phillipa had brought. The brownies won, and no wonder. Although my almond cookies are quite nice, too, when difficult matters are to be decided, a gal does need a chocolate boost.

"Stone wasn't the investigating officer in the Richter case. Tom Moody led that team. I don't know who was involved in the Linda Bennett disappearance, it was so long ago," Phillipa said. "But I suppose Stone could tell Moody that he got an anonymous tip. They would have searched the office, of course. Do you think you might put it back in the safe? No, I guess not. If you're caught, you could be charged with a felony."

"Thanks for that good thought," I said.

"What if Ada went home to collect a few personal items, and *she* found the letter in her husband's office?" Deidre suggested.

"Ada can't leave St. Rita's while she's wearing that probationary ankle cuff," Heather said.

Fiona had been quietly sipping and munching. Now she said, "There's a simpler, but far more dangerous way to connect Vinnie Bennett with both crimes."

"Okay, lay it on us," Phillipa said.

"If we lead Bennett to believe that the letter Richter was holding over his head is now in Ada's possession, what might he do next?"

"Try to burn down St. Rita's?" Deidre suggested.

"He'd never get past Ken Wakahiro," I said. "Especially if we alert him."

"I don't like that at all," Phillipa said. "It's not a decision we should make, putting Serena and all her good works among battered women at risk. Perhaps it's time to concoct a little magic and let the Cosmos take over. There's that spell we tried on Reynard...what was it called?"

"*That the Truth May Be Revealed*," Fiona said. "Very deep stuff out of that mysterious Book of Shadows that turned up at our library sale."

"Yes, I remember. Reynard revealed himself all right, only it was in my kitchen, waving a gun and threatening me and my grandchildren," I said. "What was the Cosmos thinking of?"

"Well, we have to do *something*," Deidre said.

"I'm thinking, I'm thinking," I said, pouring more tea all around.

"Haven't you got any whiskey to kill the tannin?" Deidre asked. "Too much tea always gives me a funny tummy."

I got her the bottle of Jack Daniels that Joe keeps in the parson's cupboard. She poured a healthy swig into her cup, and Heather joined her.

"Maybe invoking Kali and using *salvia divinorum* was a bit over the top," Fiona admitted. "But there's another spell that might work. From *Hazel's Book of Household Recipes*.

Hazel's Book had a more comfortable, homey aura about it, with magical spells innocently jotted down between recipes for calf's foot jelly, eel pie, and mustard plasters. Suiting action to words, Fiona drew out of her reticule the black receipt book with purple-etched lettering, a gem discovered at some long-ago yard sale. Remarkable that it fit in Fiona's ever-present carryall. I glanced at Phillipa. She rolled her dark eyes upward. Fiona, meanwhile, was paging through, the half-tracks on her nose.

"This might work." Fiona pulled a pen out of her carroty-gray crown of braids and began to make notes on a paper napkin. *Bringing Dark Matters to Light.* Seems a fairly failsafe spell. You purify and bless a flowerpot. Hazel used a Bible quote, of course, in case anyone was reading over her shoulder. *And God saw the light, that it was good, and God divided the light from the darkness.* Genesis 1:4. You fill the flowerpot with rich dark earth and plant seeds in it. As the seeds sprout, the secret matter emerges. How magical is that!"

"What kind of seeds?" I asked.

"Poppy seeds," Fiona said. "Opium poppy."

"Same stuff we use in cooking," Phillipa said. "Stone's partner Billy Mann once flunked a urine test after consuming too many of my lemon-poppy muffins."

"Oh, poppy seeds, of course." I reached into my spice-and-herb cabinet and took out a squat little jar, unlabeled, kidney-shaped little black seeds of the opium poppy. "The problem will be getting the little buggers to geminate fast. You just press them lightly into a pot filled with good rich soil and mist them daily, but it could take as many as twenty days. Or, if we're lucky, as few as four. Meanwhile, the prosecution moves ahead inexorably to put poor Ada on trial for her husband's suspicious death. We can't afford to let the grass—or poppy seeds—grow under our feet?"

"Inconsistent metaphor," Phillipa remarked.

"That's where magic comes in, as all good gardeners know, isn't that true, Cass?" Fiona said. "We say the right words, send our heartfelt intention off into the Cosmos, and, voila! the poppies come up and the secrets are revealed!"

"Worth a try," I said. It was the work of only a few minutes to scoop some compost into a small pot. A potting table on the porch held supplies for germinating herbs and setting house plants. I set the small container on an old cracked saucer, moistened it thoroughly, and pressed some poppy seeds gently into the soil. Then I carried it into the kitchen and set it in the center of the table. We gathered around and held hands.

"*Let these poppies quickly spout, murder and the truth shall out,*" Phillipa improvised the chant, and the rest of us took it up, blowing gently on the pot as we circled the table, slowly at first, and then faster and faster.

Finally, after our merry dance around the kitchen, we slowed down and threw ourselves into the kitchen chairs, puffing. Deidre fanned herself with a copy of the *Pilgrim Times* and exclaimed, "Oh, gosh, I'm absolutely melting. Reminds me of the Sambo story, how the tigers ran and ran around the tree until they melted into pure butter to spread on pancakes."

"Transformation of danger into harmless goodness," Fiona said. "A magical story, although politically incorrect now, alas."

"Along with Huck Finn," Phillipa said. "I wonder how this danger is going to be transformed into harmless goodness, don't you?"

Fiona was still catching her breath, but she managed to say, with an air of breathless confidence, "By making this spell, we're leaving the matter of the purloined letter and Ada's rescue up to the Divine Cosmos."

"*The Purloined Letter,*" Phillipa said. "Now there's a thought. *Hide it in plain sight.*"

"What was in that brass letter holder on Richter's desk, do you remember?" Heather asked Deidre and me.

I could see something in my mind's eye; it flickered in and out. A pre-printed envelope of some kind. I couldn't be sure what.

But Deidre said, "Phone bill, stamped and ready to mail. I noticed that particularly because it reminded me I'd better pay our own phone bill as soon as I got home from breaking into Richter's. *Way* overdue."

"When the police searched Richter's office, do you suppose they bothered with a phone bill in plain sight on his desk?" Phillipa asked.

"There's a thought there, but I don't like it," I said. "Are you suggesting that we go back to Richter's and put Linda Bennett's letter in that letter holder?"

"Well...if the Cosmos doesn't come up with anything better," Phillipa said. "The Goddess helps those who help themselves."

Fiona said, "Do I remember correctly, you said the crime scene tape was gone and the sign on Richter's front lawn advertised Brewster Renovations?"

"Yes, Brewster," Heather said. "You know him?"

"I know Bernie Brewster's father, Billy," Fiona said with an enigmatic little smile. "He's retired from the business but he still keeps a presence in the office. I might perhaps talk him into giving me a tour of the premises. Billy and I went to Plymouth High together, before I went off to Berkeley. I've never had much trouble getting Billy to help when I needed him."

"I bet you didn't," Phillipa said. "So perhaps *you* could take Linda Bennett's letter on your tour of Richter's place, distract poor Billy, and 'hide' the evidence in the letter holder? Then Tom Moody would need a nudge to have another look at that desk? Stone won't like it but in the interests of justice, he will drop a hint—something he heard from an informant. His wife, but no one needs to know that."

"Bingo, baby," Fiona said, helping herself to the bottle of Jack Daniels on the table. I made a mental note to buy another before Joe returned from the Arctic and wondered if I'd become a secret drinker.

"Also, we'll want to see what comes to light when the poppies sprout," Fiona added. "That Hazel was a cunning woman—an herbal healer and spell-maker. Lucky for her she wrote her recipe book a decade after the witch trials. There's a date on the flyleaf. 1723. And a pious inscription from Proverbs 31:27. *She watches over the affairs of her household, and does not eat the bread of idleness.*

"I bet she had a big family to watch over, like me. I feel as if I know her," Deidre said.

"Reliable recipes, too," Phillipa said.

"I wonder what her last name was," I said. "And where she's buried."

"I could dowse that," Fiona offered.

"If you find her, we should plant flowering herbs on her grave," Heather said. "In spring, after this Richter business is long over and settled."

"*Her price is far above rubies*," Fiona declared.

CHAPTER TWENTY-FIVE

Oh what a tangled web we weave,
When first we practise to deceive.
Sir Walter Scott

Two days later, Fiona reported that Billy Brewster, with a little subtle prodding, had offered her a tour of the Richter place, to see how that fine old home would be restored in a manner faithful to its 19th century heritage. While they were there, poor Billy had been bothered by a pesky cinder in his eye, which had given Fiona the opportunity to tuck "the purloined letter" into an unaddressed envelope with Attorney Jerold Richter Esquire's business address printed in the upper left hand corner. She'd stood the envelope behind the phone bill.

Phillipa had a talk with Stone, who had a word with Tom Moody.

I don't know whether our chant, our dance, or constantly breathing on those seeds did the trick, but the day after Fiona's tour, the first tender green sprouts appeared in the pot on my sunny bird feeder window. I clapped my hands with triumph and immediately called everyone.

An hour after my joyous announcement, Phillipa called back. "We'll never know if there's a connection, but Stone just rang me to say that a body has washed up near the oil refinery at the North end of Narragansett Bay. Meanwhile, it appears that Tom Moody decided to take one more look through Richter's office before the renovators packed up its contents. And— surprise, surprise! there was Linda's letter right behind the unmailed phone bill So that gave Moody a reason to suspect that the body from the bay might be Linda Bennett's. After all, her husband had gone out fishing on the night of her disappearance. Moody got in touch with Travis Reeve who had been the lead detective on that decade-old case. He's retired now, so he passed on his notes to Moody who talked to the Rhode Island D.A. The case of Richter's murder has now been officially reopened in Massachusetts, with Rhode Island detectives working on the body-in-the-bay angle. The body's pretty damaged, and its hands and teeth are missing, but a DNA test will tell the tale."

"Ugh! How horrid. What a monster that Bennett must be!"

"Yeah, but we've got him now."

"Does he know it's us?"

"Good question," Phillipa said thoughtfully. "We were asking about Bennett at the Café Campobasso. Someone may have told him that. And Bruno Battaglia knows we were nosing around Richter's study. He saw our faces, too. But since he was Richter's man, I don't think he's passing on tips to Bennett."

As it soon became apparent, Battaglia had indeed taken note of Heather, and most likely, he'd identified her when a photo appeared in the *Pilgrim Times* the same week as our foray into Richter's study. *Morgan Heiress Builds New Wing on No-Kill Shelter.* And there was Heather, smiling, holding an armful of rescued kittens. Plans for the new wing included quarantine quarters for cats with feline leukemia.

Battaglia did not, however, share information about us with the cops who had questioned and released him; it might have interfered with his plausible explanation for returning to Richter's. He claimed he'd gone back into the house to recover his last invoice, still unpaid, so that he could submit it to

Richter's executors, who were also the heirs. So much we found out from Stone.

As we learned later, Battaglia had other motives he'd not shared with the cops. He wanted to get his hands on various blackmail items that he'd seen Richter stash in his safe. Working closely with Richter, he may have observed him opening his safe on many occasions and memorized the combination. But soon the restoration would begin in earnest and the contents of the study would be stashed elsewhere. Battaglia may have been furious about losing such a good source of income, but going back for another foray was too chancy.

Battaglia would have remembered one juicy prospect, however—Linda Bennett's letter. Even though Battaglia didn't have the letter in his possession, he knew the contents and could attempt to collect Bennett's regular blackmail payment, the one he had formerly paid to Richter. In case Bennett demanded to see the letter, Battaglia figured he'd pay a call on Heather, to find out if she knew its whereabouts. Possibly he watched the Morgan place, because he chose Wednesday to confront Heather.

Wednesday being the morning that Maxwell and Elsa did the shopping, and with Dick busy at the Wee Angels Hospital, the coast was clear for magic. Heather liked to spend that time in the little tower room in the mansion's widow walk, where she meditated on any crusades that were afoot, burned the appropriate candles, and chanted to the Cosmos. During those personal hours, her canine companions were shunted outdoors, weather permitting. It was, however, a dreary, wet, wild November morning when Battaglia came to call, so the dogs were all keeping safe and warm in the conservatory.

He broke the glass panel in the kitchen door, using a towel to muffle the sound. Heather's canine crew, being in the conservatory at the other end of the first floor, shuffled about nervously, but they did not bark. Drawn upstairs by Heather's assertive chanting, Battaglia finally zeroing in on the widow's walk tower, which could be entered only through a trap door and pull-down ladder. The next thing Heather knew, his ugly square head loomed in the door of her sanctum, and he appeared to be waving a club in one hand, something like a sawed-off baseball bat.

Heather shrieked and, with great presence of mind, threw some melted wax from one of the larger lit candles at the intruder. He bellowed with pain, clutching his face. Immediately, he caught hold of her foot, pulling her unceremoniously down the ladder with him. Then he belted her in the jaw with his massive fist, and she went down for the count.

Battaglia dragged her by that long bronze braid she wore to the nearest bathroom and poured a glass of water over her head. "When I came to, there was this thug's ugly face leering at me, demanding to know if I had Linda Bennett's letter and were we working for Ada. He called Ada *that skinny slut*. If I could get him the letter, he wouldn't tell Bennett that we had set him up with Ada's help. I could hardly think, but when he slapped me across the face, one side and then the other, I not only saw stars, I saw a glimmer of an idea. So I told him, *yes*, we had taken the letter, and it was hidden in the conservatory."

"And the whole pack of dogs was in there!" Deidre exclaimed. She adjusted the ice pack on Heather's ankle. "Didn't Battaglia hear them?"

"You never know with dogs, what they understand without words. They must have heard some scuffling but they were as quiet as a nest of little mice until that bastard opened the door." Heather groaned and rubbed her scalp. "Maybe I should have my hair cut. This braid is just too easy to grab."

"Sophia's Serene Salon. You'd look smashing in a chin-length bob," Phillipa said. "But never mind that now...what happened next?"

Confronted by a dangerous stranger dragging their beloved person, who was obviously battered and in pain, they did what dogs do. Dempsey sprang for his throat, Honeycomb and Vader, a black lab, battered him in the belly, and two miniature poodles, Abbott and Costello, sank their teeth into his ankles. Right behind the advance team, Holmes and Flashdance, a couple of rescued greyhounds, Trilby, the ancient bloodhound, and a Yorkie named Marilyn set up a howl for help.

"If I hadn't intervened, I think they would have killed him. After I got him away from the pack, he went for me again, but I ran like Hades for my study and retrieved my Lady Smith from the lock box—you remember I mentioned that I'd joined a gun club? I find that I really enjoy target practice, and I'm rather a good shot, as it turns out. So anyway, once Battaglia saw that I was armed, he backed away down the hall into the kitchen. I told him, in my best magical voice, that if I ever saw him on my property again, *he would die.*

"My magical voice isn't as good as Phil's but must have been good enough, because I could see a flash of fear in his eyes, and he fled out the back way. I think he was muttering 'damned witches', but it might have been 'bitches'. The dogs had made quite a mess of him, anyway. The arm of his shirt was torn, and his trousers were in tatters."

"Did he say anything else?" I asked.

"Something about letting the cats out of the bag. I didn't quite get it."

Fiona sprinkled a fine dust of corn pollen over Heather and the chaise lounge on which she was reclining. Her Wedgewood green bedroom with exquisite creamy plaster moldings of nymphs and whatnot was nearly as large as my entire first floor. Heather was wrapped in a russet velvet robe. Her face looked bruised, and she was wearing enormous Jackie Kennedy dark glasses.

"It's really just as well that he got away, don't you think, dear? You didn't call 911?" Fiona asked.

"*No way*. I didn't fancy explaining to the Plymouth Police that Battaglia was after something he thought we'd stolen from Richter's when we broke in there on the same night they'd picked him up on Mayflower Street. My head hurt, and I wasn't sure that I could think fast enough to answer questions."

"With appropriate lies, you mean," Phillipa said. "Well done! I'm really relieved that I don't have to explain our current misadventures to Stone."

"When the Kitcheners got home, I told them that I'd fallen on the back step and broken the glass door panel by accident. Maxwell replaced it almost at once. The man is a miracle worker, *My Man Godfrey*. I don't think he believed me, though. I specifically told him not to alarm Dick, who's trying to cope at the hospital with only a veterinary nurse to help him, but I didn't mentioned you gals. So he took it upon himself to call Cass while Elsa was helping me wash my various cuts and bruises—and here you all are! I don't think the ankle is sprained, anyway. Just sore where it twisted under me."

"What do you suppose Battaglia will do next?" I said.

Fiona said, "Obviously, he wants to continue Richter's blackmail of Bennett. But as soon as this new investigation breaks in the news and Linda's body is identified, he'll know that the letter must be in the hands of the investigating detectives."

"He'll be pissed at us, but what can he do?" Deidre said.

"He can tell Bennett that we're the ones who blew the whistle," Phillipa said.

"He probably doesn't know that the rest of you are involved," Heather said. "I don't even know how he recognized me."

Phillipa reminded Heather of the article and photograph that had appeared in the *Pilgrim Times* the same week we broke into Richter's—all about Heather and the new wing at Animal Lovers. "If you read all the way to the last paragraph, there's a mention of Heather's involvement with a local circle of amateur crime-solvers who are reported to be Wiccans."

"Uh oh," Deidre said.

Maxwell, the perfect butler, appeared at the bedroom door toting an enormous tray laden with tea, sherry, cakes, and little sandwiches, which he set on a folding base he carried over his arm. "I thought you might enjoy a little light refreshment, M'am," he said. "Shall I pour the Amontillado?"

"Oh, for goodness sake, Max, call me Heather," she said. "Yes, we could all do with a little stiffener. How are the dogs?"

"Yes, M'am," Maxwell said. "The dogs seem to be in fine fettle after their skirmish with the intruder. They ran outside, marked all the bushes, and came straight back inside. It's still raw and rainy. Elsa has passed out congratulatory biscuits all round."

"Fine. Good. But not too many treats. All those extra calories." Heather sank back and closed her eyes. The tide of adrenaline had ebbed, leaving her weak and depleted. Fiona held her hand and patted it from time to time with a soft tinkle of silver bangles. Deidre laid a cool cloth over Heather's brow.

"Do you think it would be all right," Heather said in a weak voice, "if I burned just one little black candle to hex Battaglia?"

" No!" "No!" "*No!*" Deidre, Phillipa, and I chorused.

"Heather is naturally a little upset right now. Let's all hum for healing," Fiona said.

And we did.

❦

It took almost two weeks to identify the DNA of the body in the bay. Meanwhile, Tom Moody dropped into the Café Campobasso to speak with the owner. Bennett was disagreeably surprised that old suspicions had resurfaced, thanks to Linda's letter to Richter. He'd certainly read about the body that washed up from the bay and probably hoped against hope that it wasn't Linda, or if it was his wife, that the measures he'd taken to remove her identity would be sufficient.

Just about then he must have received a call from Battaglia who was furious and would have taken pleasure in telling Bennett that a gaggle of Plymouth amateurs (us!) had stirred up his present troubles, aided and abetted by Ada.

Meanwhile, unaware that we had become targets of Bennett's ill will, I was satisfied that things were moving in the right direction and decided it was high time to update Ada, Serena, and her team on all that had occurred.

Because Deidre was a widowed young mother, and we tried to protect her from harmful situations, she sometimes felt left out of what she called "the witchy fun," So I'd suggested that she go with me to St. Rita's, and Fiona, too. Deidre was delighted and gave us both a lift in her aurora blue Mazda 3. Serena had arranged a morning coffee klatch, and at Ada's suggestion, had also invited Patty Peacedale.

Deidre had brought Ada a protective amulet in the form of an amber bracelet. "Amber is formed from organic resin," Deidre explained, "the substance that trees use to heal and protect themselves, and possibly the earliest known jewelry. It will protect you as well," Deidre explained.

Ada touched the stones thoughtfully. "I've always loved amber," she said in her dramatic Garbo voice. Wearing slim black pants and a gray silk blouse, she was looking nearly healthy, if still thin as a green bean.

One of Serena's resident protégés served us coffee and rugelach. The rugelach were still warm. Apricot and raspberry. *Yum.*

Taking one look at the resident's battered face, Deidre dug into her workbag and came up with an amber pendant, closing it into the woman's hand. "Keep this with you," she whispered.

"I have a lovely Celtic cross that these ladies gave me," Patty patted her beige blouse beneath which the cross was well hidden. "Very reliable blessing it has proved to be, too." Pausing only for occasional sips of coffee, she was busily knitting a deep purplish brown prayer shawl for Ada.

"A color we don't see very often. Puce," Fiona said, admiring the shawl. "Color of a flea's belly."

Diane Robinson grinned. I didn't think puce was a color she'd ever wear. Today's cashmere twin set was pale lilac. "I happened to see some of the police reports about the body surfacing in Narraganett Bay," she said. (I wondered how she'd managed *that*.) "The suspicion is that the body belongs to Linda Bennett, Vinnie Bennett's long-lost wife."

"But now, darlings, we need to connect the murderous Bennett to the arson that killed Jerry Richter." Magdalene flipped her deep crimson scarf over one shoulder and a mist of Joy perfume wafted through the room. *The woman must own a scent shop.*

"A miracle, then." Serena touched her blouse at the neckline where, I assumed, a discreet cross was in hiding. She may have been drummed out of the Church, but she was still deeply religious.

"Oh, we mustn't wish for a miracle, dear," Patty said, her eyes on her work as she knitted placidly on, whispering the occasional prayer. "That's like asking God to do all the work. No, I think we can safely leave this problem in the hands of our local circle of Wiccans." I wished I had Patty's confidence.

"And Diane, too, of course. A private eye did you say you were, Di?" Patty continued, turning the shawl for another row. Deidre watched her closely. No doubt imagining some knitted spell-craft of her own devising.

"I prefer the term *investigator*," Diane said."

"I'm a finder myself, dear," Fiona said. "Have you ever tried dowsing with a crystal pendant?"

Diane smiled. "No, I'm afraid my methods are much more mundane. Contacts, surveillance, research."

"There's no magic like Google," Fiona said.

Before we left, I told them about the break-in at Heather's, and about Battaglia's threat to tell Bennett we were all involved in retrieving Linda's letter.

❧

That night I was surprised by a panic call from Serena. As soon as my cell woke me up with its tinny little tune, I looked at the clock. *Past midnight.* This had to be serious business.

"Someone got into our grounds tonight," Serena whispered urgently. "It could have been any one of the crazy husbands we deal with, but I'm betting on Bennett. We must get our fence alarmed as soon as possible. It's not fair to expect Ken always to be on the alert."

"What did the intruder do? What happened?" All vestiges of sleep fled; I was wide awake now.

"Ken got up, probably because his Akita started pacing. Saw someone moving around the house so he flipped on the floodlights. Whoever it was dropped the can he was carrying and ran like hell. Later, Ken found the main lock broken and the gate ajar. And Tadashi, his dog, smelled the diesel fuel, of course. A gallon container lying on its side right by the kitchen door. I think we had a close call there."

"He must have been after Ada. Did you tell Ada that it was an arson attempt?"

"Ada was awake and looking out her window. She says she saw someone slinking around the corner of the house before the floodlights came on. Told me she had bad thoughts about him, by which I think she means she may have given him a hotfoot."

"How appropriate. What did Ken think?"

"Ken said the intruder was limping when he crossed the driveway and made it out of the gate."

"Best to notify the police, right?" I said. "Deisel was the accelerant used in the arson that killed Jerry Richter."

"I already did, reluctantly. I always fear that the identity of the women sheltering here may be carelessly revealed. A number of officers are swarming around here right now. Maybe Bennett left prints on the can?"

"That would be great, but I doubt he did," I said..

"You'd better watch out at your place, too," Serena said. "I'll say prayers for all of us."

"*Pray to God and hammer away*, as the Spanish say. Get that alarm installed."

CHAPTER TWENTY-SIX

Bring all the wanderers home to the nest,
Let me sit down with the ones I love best.
Edgar Guest

Joe came home from the Arctic the week after the break-in at St. Rita's, and life warmed up. After many days apart, kissing him hello—his generous mouth and teasing beard—was always like the first time.

Hey, Toots, why is it we have to sleep in the kitchen when the furry-faced guy is here? Is that fair? Who's going to protect you from squirrels and mice?

Squirrels and mice! Squirrels and mice!

Put a sock in it, kid! I'm trying to make a point here. Scruffy didn't understand why the house rules were changed when Joe was home. Sometimes, if we were noisy in the bedroom, Scruffy leaned against the closed door and barked, often at the worst possible moment.

Feminist though I may be, I felt infinitely safer in the arms of my brawny sensible husband, sure that he would watch out for our well-being. I relaxed (as much as a gal can relax when being stalked by a vendetta-crazed Italian arsonist) and began to enjoy planning for Thanksgiving.

Adam, Freddie, and the twins would be joining us, also Becky and *whomever*, and Fiona with her grandniece Laura Belle, who noticed everything but spoke rarely. I hoped the children wouldn't be too fussy about having a later dinner. As usual Joe and I had been conned by Patty Peacedale into serving at the Gethsemane Thanksgiving for the Lonely and Elderly at the Presbyterian church-around-the-corner. Meanwhile, the turkey would have to baste itself, which is perfectly possible if you skewer a slab of chicken fat on top of the breast and lay a sheet of foil loosely over the bird.

∾

After Linda's body was identified and suspicion once more fell on her husband, her outraged family, the Leones, demanded justice. But Rhode Island detectives had to move carefully in collecting ten-year-old evidence from witnesses who had no wish to be involved. Finally, the former manager of the Wickford Marina, now retired, admitted to having seen Bennett carrying a bundle the size of a large duffle bag over his shoulder when he got on board his boat to go fishing that long-ago Easter night.

An old girlfriend of Bennett's, assured that she would not be charged with complicity, was more cooperative now that the romance was long over. Vinnie had bragged to her, she said, about being a millionaire once his wife was dead. He'd talked about his dream to invest in a casino. But when Bennett's wife mysteriously disappeared, the girlfriend had become uneasy, and the romance had cooled. At the time, she'd been questioned by detectives, of course, but had decided not to repeat Bennett's idle talk. Married guys always made exaggerated remarks about their wives, and in her experience, were not to be believed.

Evidence against Vinnie Bennett was circumstantial at best, and the Rhode Island district attorney Rocco Conti still didn't connect him with any death other than Linda Bennett's.

Ironically, we had Bruno Battaglia to thank for Ada's finally being cleared of the Massachusetts murder charge that had been hanging over her head for months. Battaglia got himself into a brawl at the Shady Lady in Providence and broke a bottle over his unarmed opponent's head. The victim was in the hospital in a coma. Charged with assault in the second degree, a possible five-year sentence. Battaglia bargained his way out by offering Conti additional information about Vinnie Bennett. He told Conti that Richter had stolen Bennett's girlfriend, Nevaeh Nichols, and had been blackmailing him with Linda's accusatory letter. Bennett often settled scores with a can of diesel, Battaglia said. Conti passed along the tip to the Plymouth County prosecutor, Stan Steemer.

On further questioning, Nevaeh Nichols told Tom Moody about the incident in which Bennett had set fire to her TransAm. As additional evidence against Bennett came to light, the charge against Ada began to look more and more insubstantial.

None of us had ever seen the femme fatale who'd caused so much ill feeling between Richter and Bennett. But Phillipa happened to be at the station in Middleboro to pick up her husband when Nivaeh was brought in by Tom Moody for questioning. She described Nevaeh as a striking young woman with straight blonde hair that brushed her shoulders, turquoise blue eyes, and white peach skin. She was wearing some kind of metallic dress that clung dramatically to her slim but curvy figure.

"*La Belle Dame Sans Merci.* She'd be right at home on any red carpet, but there didn't happen to be one at Plymouth County Detective Unit," Phillipa said.

Once they went looking for it, Tom Moody found further evidence to connect Bennett to Richter's death. Apparently a man out walking his dog on the night of the fire, had told canvassing officers about a man lurking around the Richter house, but detectives concentrating on Ada had ignored that report. A dishwasher at the Café Campobasso had noticed Bennett putting a gas can into his Chevy van. Another neighbor on Mayflower Street, had observed a black Chevy van parked near the Richter's place on the night of the fire. She remembered the license plate especially because it began with her own initials, CMP. She didn't remember the rest, but the license plate on Bennett's van was CMP-784 and it was black. Ada was released and Bennett was charged with both killings. Battaglia would testify to the blackmail motive.

All of us, including Serena's crew, would breathe sighs of gratitude and relief when Vinnie Bennett was in custody at either the Plymouth or Cranston, Rhode Island, correctional facility.

When the Providence police went to arrest Bennett for his wife's murder, however, he'd already fled. The slender, dark-haired waitress Angie told the officers that Bennett had driven a rented gray Dodge Caravan into the Café Campobasso parking lot that morning. His hair looked different—bleached or something—and he'd been seen to load a backpack into the car's trunk. Then he'd taken all the cash in the safe, she didn't know how much but he'd filled a zippered travel bag before he sped off. Detectives working on the case speculated that Bennett was going to make a run for it to Mexico. The rental car had come from Enterprise Rent-a-Car in Providence; the make, model, and license number were immediately broadcast in an APB.

The Dodge Caravan was found abandoned at the Warwick Mall, leaving no further trace of the fugitive. Tom Moody in Plymouth County agreed with the Mexico theory and thought Bennett had either stolen a different car or continued his journey by hitching rides. Providence detectives began a check on cars stolen that day in the mall area; stolen cars can be traced. But Bennett had been smarter than that. As soon as Linda's body had surfaced in Narragansett Bay, he'd stashed a privately purchased getaway car at the Warwick Mall, an old and undistinguished Toyota Corolla. All he had to do was to switch cars.

Perhaps he did intend to head toward Mexico. Before he escaped to another country, however, he dropped in on his former girlfriend, Nevaeh Nichols. Maybe he hoped to persuade her to flee with him, but (as we learned later) she put him off with kisses and excuses, promising to follow him as soon as she could sell her condo. They would need all the money they could gather for a fresh start. At any rate, before they parted, Neveah told Bennett how the infamous letter had mysteriously disappeared and then reappeared in Richter's office. Bennett said he already knew about the circle of busybodies responsible.

That would be us.

Bennett should have given up the notion of payback and really fled the country, either to Mexico or Canada. He'd have needed a new identity, but someone who was connected in Providence would naturally know where to obtain new papers.

Go figure! After Neveah's helpful tip, somehow Bennett had fixed on me as the ring-leader of the "busybody" circle.

෴

It was now the Friday before Thanksgiving. Joe had taken the dogs with him to Home Warehouse to pick up lumber for his latest do-it-yourself project, a genuine woodshed near the porch door, and I was already cooking dishes that could be frozen in advance. I'd made Cranberry-Blueberry-Ginger Sauce, a butternut casserole, and Grandma's nine-herb stuffing for the turkey. My oldest child Becky called to say she had hooked up with Johnny Marino again and would it be okay to bring him to our family Thanksgiving. Of all Becky's revolving boyfriends, I'd always liked Johnny best (he reminded me of Joe, only darker in some way) and I was delighted. Also, he'd be bringing that lovely cannellini and mushroom soup, redolent with onion, garlic, fresh sage, and rosemary, sparing me from having to devise a first course.

While I was still packing up stuffing for the freezer, Phillipa called me, gloriously excited. "I'm thankful," she caroled. "Blessed Brigit! I'm so fucking thankful!"

At first, I thought she was having some kind of Thanksgiving epiphany. But, as it turned out, it was a wish come true...finally.

"I'm happy for you, Phil. Did something special happen?"

"The O'Reillys won the lottery! Hooray, hooray! Not the megamillions, but something in the hundreds of thousands. They've put their house on the market, and they've bought a place in Chatham! And Chatham doesn't even know who's moving into their exclusive community—ha ha!"

"Phil, you're sounding a little hysterical. Are you okay?"

"Barely. I will never, never doubt Fiona again... *'wish 'em good luck,'* she said, when all I *longed* to do was to hex them into oblivion. Oh, that odious loud-mouth daughter and her thieving brothers...ha ha ha ha!"

She *was* hysterical. "Listen, Phil, is Stone at home?"

"He's in the shower. He brought the good news home, and I jumped on his bones, I was so thrilled. Oh, and now I can return the bodacious Boadicea to Heather."

"You mean she finally managed to foist that cantankerous boxer off onto you."

"Oh, you know Heather. She insisted the old girl would keep the neighborhood petty thieves away and 'round out' our domestic bliss. How can anyone resist an enthusiastic Libran in search of balance and joy for all? I think she expects me to adopt the mutt."

"Will you?"

"I'll think about it when we get home from Vermont. We're spending Thanksgiving with Stone's Mom who never cooks and won't allow anyone else to mess up her kitchen. So

I've made reservations for the three of us at a well-reviewed little inn in Maine that offers a special Thanksgiving weekend deal. The Bone Rock Inn."

Should I tell Phillipa that I knew the Bone Rock Inn? That when Joe and I had stayed there, Cecile and Nigel Usher, the innkeepers, had been rather proud to be haunted by the ghost of Grace Meade, a murderous herbalist? *Perhaps not.*

"Sounds like a lovely plan, dear. You'll enjoy that scenic ride along the coast."

I went back to my cooking chores with a pleased smile. Another problem solved! Flipping on the light, I headed down to my cellar workroom with my freezer packages. The freezer was located in the former cold room where my grandmother had once stored a winter's supply of root vegetables.

Coming upstairs, I was humming *We gather together...* without a hint of foreboding, which just goes to show the irony of being a clairvoyant. *Clueless* when it comes to danger to oneself.

Quite suddenly, my ordinary five senses kicked in. An ominous dark figure was looming in the doorway to the kitchen. I almost lost my footing on the stairs. When his head turned, light fell on his face. An excruciating thrill of fear snaked down from my neck to my first chakra. I recognized him from the recent newspaper articles. The hair was lighter but the intruder definitely was Vinnie Bennett—and here I was trapped in the cellar!

Well, almost trapped. There was an old door from the cold room to the back yard. I hadn't opened it for months, but... I backed up cautiously.

"*What do you want? Get out of here!*" I demanded. "I'll call my husband! *Joe, Joe...*"

"Shut up, you interfering bitch. There's no one here but you. I watched them leave—waiting for this..." Bennett took something out of the pocket in his jacket. It was a switchblade. He flipped the knife open.

I moved farther back toward the cold room, holding my two little fingers in front of me, the power of magic against bare steel.

Who am I kidding? I'd gladly trade all my magic for Grandma's rifle hanging over the fireplace.

"I'm going to slit your lying throat." He spat his words at me and eased down the top step.

Joe. Scruffy. Raffles. Where are you when I need you? my mind screamed.

I just have to have faith in the power of my craft. And a freaking big cloud of protective white light!

Bennett came down another step. He was smiling, sort of. "I know about you," he snarled. "I know you're the one who gave that miserable slut Linda's letter to the cops."

"No, no. I really didn't do that. The letter was found in Richter's study." I remembered a news story I'd read about a quick-thinking woman talking a killer into giving himself up. They'd ended up reading the Bible and praying together.

Oh, yeah.

"Richter kept that fucking letter in his safe." Bennett's tone ranged from accusatory to deranged as he kept advancing. "Battaglia told me it was *you* and the other witches who burgled the safe and left the letter where it was sure to be found. And Nevaeh knew where you live. Nevaeh loves me and she's going to join me as soon as everything falls into place."

"Don't you realize that Nevaeh's afraid of you and she'll say anything to get you out of her life" I said. "She's already told Tom Moody that you set fire to her TransAm."

Bennett snarled and leaped toward me. One look at his face turning apoplectic suggested that revealing Nevaeh's duplicity was not the best strategy.

Making a sudden jump into the cold room, I tried to slam the door shut. It was an old door that hadn't been used since the days before supermarkets, and it no longer fit the frame. But it did close. I pulled over a heavy little bureau to hold it shut.

That will last about one minute!

With my one-minute reprieve, I raced to the other door, the one that led to the backyard, and gave it a mighty shove. But it wouldn't budge. *What in Hades?*

And then I remembered. We'd moved aside wood stacked outdoors for the fireplace so that Joe could construct the woodshed. We'd piled it against the house, and the cold room door! *How dumb was that!*

Bennett was already pushing aside the bureau-braced door. I picked up a jar of olives and held it at the ready. With the other hand, I grabbed a bottle of extra-virgin olive oil.

The door opened, and an evilly grinning Bennett came in, holding the narrow stiletto blade that caught light from the workroom. But the cold room was dark, and I could see him better than he could see me. I hurled the olives, followed by the oil. *Ambidextrous, not bad.* The olives missed and broke on the stone floor with a strong smell of brine, but I got a direct hit with the oil. *Good. I've clipped his head*, I thought. *Why doesn't he fall down?*

The bottle broke open and spilled down his shirt. Bennett yelped, "*You bitch!*"

I picked up two cans of tomatoes. I've always thought you can't have too many cans of tomatoes on hand, and I was right.

Bennett moved another step closer.

I screamed and hurled the tomatoes at him, one after the other. He ducked and laughed, the kind of laugh you never want to hear when you're trapped in the cellar.

Then we both heard another noise—the sound of two dogs barking! Joe was home! I launched another couple of cans and yelled "Help! Help!"

The crash of wood being heaved aside—the backdoor to the cold room opened with a flash of sunlight. Joe's strong hands grabbed hold of me and pulled me out without ceremony, almost throwing me into the backyard. I fell on my knees, breathless with terror and relief. Scruffy and Raffles rushed into the cellar right after Joe.

As Heather had discovered, it's always surprising what dogs know. My dogs knew that this man was an attacker, and they didn't hesitate to jump him. Raffles grabbed his leg, Scruffy bit into the arm that held the knife.

Cursing, Bennett shook them off and stabbed at Raffles with his knife.

I screamed, *"Oh, Joe, watch out for the dogs! There's broken glass in there!"* Afterwards I realized that protecting the dogs was the least of our problems at the moment.

Bennett rushed back up the stairs to the kitchen and out the way he'd come in, the door to the porch, rarely if ever locked.

But Joe was already racing around the house to grab Bennett, Scruffy and Raffles right on his heels. Joe was brandishing a stick of firewood. Bennett ran faster, but Joe did whack him a good one once before the younger man sprinted out of our driveway onto the main road, jumped into his old Toyota, and floored it.

"Z27-486," Joe said, taking out his cell phone to call 911.

I was examining the dogs' paws. Luckily, no shards of glass, but Raffles had a knife slice on his shoulder. He didn't seem to know it, but Scruffy did.

Hey, Toots. We got a wounded warrior here.

"Don't worry. I've got some good herbal stuff to put on that cut. What a monster that Bennett is!" My voice got a bit muffled as I buried my face in Joe's shoulder and his comforting arms held me close. "How did you know I was in trouble?"

"That old car up on the main road. Something about it didn't look kosher. And I could hear you yelling."

"Right through the cellar door?"

"Maybe I have some extra-sensory skills, too."

Later, we got to tell the whole grim story to Plymouth officers, Ken and Barbie (who didn't like to be called that). They remembered previous brawls with murderers at our house, notably the one in which Joe got brained with a cast iron frying pan.

Phillipa and Stone were packing his silver-gray Audi for their Thanksgiving trek to Vermont and Maine when he heard a report on his radio about the fracas with Bennett. Phillipa insisted that Stone and she race over to hear the news first-hand and to see if we needed help—or food.

Stone and Joe stood out in the front yard talking with *Kenneth and Barbara* (as they preferred) while Phillipa took over in my kitchen and made pots of coffee and tea.

"Why did the murderous thug come after you?" she demanded, unpacking smoked salmon sandwiches, brie en croute, and a double-gingerbread from the picnic basket she'd stored in the Audi for their trip.

"I don't know for sure. At first he blamed Ada and tried to burn down St. Rita's with her in it. But apparently Nevaeh told him about the business with Linda's letter, that it only came to light because of us."

"Sweet Isis! I don't know what I'd do if someone with a stiletto backed me into a cellar wall. How in the world did you defend yourself?"

"I threw stuff at him. A jar of olives, a bottle of extra-virgin, a few cans of tomatoes, and some other stuff. Artichokes and cannellini, I think."

"Hmmm. Sounds like the start of a tasty pasta sauce."

"A good cook never runs out of options," I said. "And weapons. Say, Phil, are we going to eat all that stuff you're setting out there?"

"I called the others while Stone was driving me over here. Heather's bringing some restorative beverages."

"Of course."

Soon I was relating my narrow escape to Heather, Fiona, and Deidre amid cries and murmurs of commiseration. Heather poured some excellent brandy into my pressed glass tumblers, and after a time we became quite merry over my canned goods defense.

Joe got a mug of coffee, laced it with brandy, and went back to stacking the wood he had hastily tossed out of the way earlier. Scruffy and Raffles dogged his footsteps eagerly. *Let's get out of here, kid. More screeching than a flock of blue jays.*

Blue jays! Blue jays!

Then Stone came in and helped himself to a sandwich and a cup of Earl Grey. Bennett didn't get far, he told us. With his car's make and license number now known, Rhode Island patrol cars forced him to a halt on Route 95 South. He was still drenched with extra-virgin olive oil.

∾

After Thanksgiving dinner, while Becky and Freddie were wrapping up leftovers, the children and dogs curled up in our bedroom watching a video, and Adam, Joe, and Johnny Marino loafed in the living room catching football scores, Fiona got me aside in my office, the old borning room.

"I happened to come across a little background on the Kitcheners," Fiona confided. "It may be that the reason Max and Elsa act the part of the quintessential butler and cook is because they are actually actors. Apparently they were touring with a repertoire company in South Carolina when there was some kind of unfortunate run-in with the local constabulary, and they were forced to split. It wasn't a theft or anything like that. Something to do with beating up an officer of the law who was beating up a suspect, a young black fellow who worked backstage at the theater. There may even still be a warrant out for the Kitcheners' arrest."

"And no one ever caught up with them before they went to work for Reynard? What about references?"

"Well, dear, they've changed their names and I don't doubt forged their references. In other words, I believe they're *lying low*, as the expression goes."

"Well, how on earth did you discover all this, Fiona?" Knowing Fiona, I shouldn't even have asked.

"I was just Googling around when Omar pounced on the keyboard. The little darling was trying to whack a moth that was attracted to the monitor. We had those two unseasonably warm nights, you know, and white moths appeared out of nowhere. If you had an outside light on, they simply swarmed into the house. Anyway, have I ever mentioned to you that I believe Omar is a true sensitive? A dear familiar, in the old religious sense of the word."

"Yes, you have mentioned that Fiona, once or twice. But let's get back to the Kitcheners. How did you—and Omar— catch on to their act?

"With one swipe, my clever kitty had linked me with *The Union Daily Times,* a South Carolina newspaper. Knowing Omar's prescience, I was curious and began trolling through the archives. And there it was, the whole assault business. The officer asserted that the boy was resisting arrest. The Kitcheners said he was lying on the ground, nearly unconscious, and the officer was stomping him. The story was illustrated with the officer's official photo in uniform and another of the Kitcheners being arrested. I recognized them at once, although the names were different. Lawrence Leroi and Julie Jones. Stage names, sounds like. Who knows what their real given names may be?"

"Oh, Good Goddess, do you think we should tell Heather?"

"I've pondered that, and on balance, I would say no. That poor girl has had enough trouble with housekeepers. Let her enjoy the perfect couple while she can, I say."

"At least, Julie...or Elsa...is a pretty fair cook. And a good hand with canines," I said.

"Oh, the doggies love her," Fiona said. "That's enough of a reference for me."

CHAPTER TWENTY-SEVEN

Unable are the Loved to die
For Love is Immortality.
Emily Dickinson

After the warm gathering of Thanksgiving and the merriment of Yule, the rest of the winter became a bleak test of endurance that buried us in storm after storm, turning the trees into white marble statues of themselves. Usually Plymouth and the rest of the South Shore are only lightly touched by blizzards when the rest of Massachusetts is up to their windowsills in drifts, but on years when a pattern of Cape storms develops and takes hold, the situation is reversed. Such was the case in the months after the Bennett affair. Fortunately, Joe had bought himself a vehicle—at last cutting his dependence on rentals. The red Toyota Tacoma, although small for a pickup, was a sturdy truck onto which he could attach a plow when needed, and it was needed plenty that winter. He kept our place, Phillipa's, Fiona's, and Deidre's in passable shape. Heather had her own landscape crew to manage her estate.

Although warned sternly by Heather never to allow this, Scruffy and Raffles adored riding in the back of the Tacoma, and Joe took them on short runs from time to time to collect more supplies from Home Warehouse, including plenty of ice melt. Our canine companions complained mightily, however, about the freezing outdoor accommodations in which they were expected to relieve themselves.

The neat little woodshed was finished, holding our supply of logs dry and handy for the cozy blazes that kept our kitchen and living room cheery through the long dark winter months.

In March the temperature finally warmed to the forties and rain washed away the last of the endless snow. The Spring Equinox, the circle decided, would be the perfect time to search out Hazel's grave. We wanted very much to visit her final resting place and express our gratitude for her recipe book that had so enriched our natural magic.

But there were a few small problems; we needed to find out who Hazel was, where she lived, and when.

Finding, however, is Fiona's special talent. With her crystal Fiona dowsed all the local maps until she found Hazel's plot. The pendant indicated it was somewhere in Burial Hill, a historic Plymouth cemetery, but the map wasn't detailed enough to pinpoint which part. And we still had to discover Hazel's surname. We wanted to pay homage to her for the carefully worded spells that had seen us through many an investigation, even though, in truth, we knew that only the shell of the person remained in her grave, the spirit had flown to Summerland.

It was the twentieth of March, and a light rain was falling aslant in the cemetery. After we'd wandered around Burial Hill trying to read weathered and mossy gravestones for a half hour or so, Fiona took a forked willow dowsing stick out of her reticule, closed her eyes, and followed its invisible prompting. Invisible to us, that is. Fiona said she felt the wood tremble in her hands and tell her which way to proceed, something like the childhood game when our friends would shout out "warmer" or "colder." We trudged behind, following her hooded tartan coat zigzagging through the markers, gradually leading us to the north end of the burial ground. Only Deidre ran ahead, her peaked red pixie hat bobbing between rows. She had a closer relationship to the world of spirit than the rest of us, coming late to an ability to see ghosts, which she claimed she in no way enjoyed. Today, however, she used this spiritual empathy to put her hand right on the stone we were seeking. It was a thin, leaning slab of granite, its engraving barely readable: *Hazel Morse Eastey, 1695-1752. Wife of Phineas Eastey, mother to Thomas, Benjamin, and Sarah. Good heart, good deeds, a friend to all in need.* She was buried beside Phineas, who had died seven years earlier.

With a sage oil-scented besom, we brushed away weeds and debris around Hazel's plot and planted fragrant rosemary, thyme, and lavender. Phillipa composed a thank-you chant *Dear sister Hazel, so wise in quiet ways, we thank you for your gifts with heartfelt praise.* Fiona kept time on her Navaho drum as we chanted and danced to raise a cone of energy, sent into the Cosmos to bless Hazel's spirit wherever it might be.

"Eastey and Morse," Fiona said thoughtfully while we were driving home in Phillipa's BMW, "Those are both names associated with the witch trials in Salem. Of course, Hazel was born later."

"I don't believe in coincidences," Phillipa said. "She was our timeless friend, quiet and clever. Without raising any suspicion, she worked her magic and left us her spell book as a legacy. She may even have foreseen our circle."

"Speaking of coincidences we distrust, how about this," Heather said. "Have you been reading the news of Bennett's trial in the Patriot Ledger?"

We all had, but not as avidly as Heather. She'd followed up on a mention of his family with internet research. Bennett was the grandson of Vincenzo Benedetto of Campobasso, Italy.

"What comes around, goes around," Fiona said.

"No connection, of course, but it *is* eerie," Deidre said, shuddering at the memory of Conor's close call and our Italian adventure.

"The Cosmos works in wondrous ways, its mysteries to perform," Fiona added sagely.

Phillipa shook her head as if to clear the cobwebs. "The long arm of an Italian malediction," she intoned soberly, winking at me.

But I was lost in my own chain of curious implication. "You know, that thing about Hazel Morse Eastey...we ought to dig up something more about that."

At once, I fell into a light trance like Alice down the rabbit hole. As I tumbled into darkness, I felt the graininess of dirt all around me. And I was digging, digging, digging.

Then, just as suddenly, the light returned, and mighty welcome it was, too. "Here, dear, take a whiff of this," Fiona was saying, holding those acrid smelling salts under my nose.

"Taking a little trip, were we?" Phillipa inquired as she turned into Heather's circular driveway.

"Yes," I said faintly. "And I wonder what all that was about. Better stop the car for a minute. I'm feeling rather nauseous."

"What you need is a good strong cup of tea," Heather said. "Why don't you all come in for a while and give Cass a chance to recover."

As soon as we were settled in the conservatory, Maxwell wafted in with a tray of tea and scones. "I thought you'd be wanting some refreshment, M'am," he said, smoothly. He set out a bottle of sherry and some lovely crystal glasses, then glided back to the kitchen.

"Oh, shades of *Gosford Park*," Phillipa said. "Is that clotted cream?"

I glanced at Fiona. The shake of her head was barely visible.

"Yes, I think I have really lucked out at last," Heather said.

"Luck is moot, dear. It all depends on which plane of existence you're living in at the moment," Fiona said.

"Planes of existence?" Heather paused in the act of pouring sherry into those elegant glasses.

"Five, and you can choose among them."

"Is this, like, the new physics or something?" Deidre looked skeptical.

"No, dear, it's the old metaphysics," Fiona said. "At the base, there's a shadow plane where imps of fear, anger, willful passion and so forth are granted power. We've all been there. Above that is the plane of earthly pleasures. And very nice it is, too. Third, there's the plane of connection with others, empathy, and our work in the world. That's where our circle finds its power. Fourth, the plane of inspiration and creation, the sense of a guided life. That one is always personal and unique. And the highest plane, pure existence in divine consciousness. Maybe we have a glimpse of that on our best days. Mostly we coast between planes like driftwood with the ebb and flow of the tide, but when we become conscious beings, we can learn to flow from plane to plane deliberately."

"Suppose I ask you how to do that—is there an answer?" I wanted to know.

"Focus on a smaller or greater outlook," Fiona said. "And zoom away!"

"Metaphysics, microphysics, macrophysics. I knew it would be another obscure notion," Phillipa said. "It's like the glamour. Easier said than done."

"Speaking of glamour," I said, "Serena tells me, now that Ada has been exonerated of any complicity in her husband's death, she's off to New York to resume her modeling career."

"At her age?" Deidre asked in an amused tone.

" Yes, there's life after menopause after all, Dee. It seems that Ada's former agent called with an offer to represent her. Mature models are suddenly in demand, and Ada has the gorgeous cheekbones and silvery hair, along with the anorexic figure, that are marketable with our aging Baby Boomer. Ada Feuer. She's resumed her maiden name."

"Fire," Fiona said. "Feuer is fire in German."

"Figures," Phillipa said. "One way or another, Ada could be hot stuff in New York."

"Should we do a spell or something?" Heather wondered. "Cool waters sort of thing."

"In every crusade, there's a time to let go," Fiona decreed. "I certainly wouldn't want to quench a woman's hidden fire. You never know when she may need to give someone a hotfoot."

"Yeah," Phillipa agreed. "Any pushy art director better watch his step."

༄

A few days later, when the sun had a chance to warm the woods and dry up some of the mud, Joe and I and the dogs went for a walk to that secret place in Jenkins Park where a stand of pink lady slippers came up every spring. Joe and I sat on a fallen log and contemplated the emergence of the delicate plants from a bed of rotted leaves, while Scruffy and Raffles rushed around in the woods fluttering the birds and scattering the squirrels and rabbits.

At that moment, our trip last fall to Italy seemed as unbelievable as some fantastic dream. "Did all of us really dine on the Danieli rooftop overlooking the Grand Canal by moonlight?" I asked.

"Yes, and the memory is ours forever," Joe said. "Along with a number of amusing photographs. Do you remember that Fiona…"

He didn't have to finish the sentence. We were already laughing. The dogs came back to see if we were all right and leaned against our legs. A fit of merriment in their human companions is cause for serious worry among canines.

Hey, Toots! You sure sound funny, barking like that. Are you okay? Maybe it would be a good idea for us to take you home now. Isn't it almost time for dinner?"

Dinner! Dinner!

I thought about the contents of my refrigerator, how Joe would transform that humble ground beef into *Keftedes,* Greek meatballs with mint and oregano. And I would make a salad with feta cheese and garbanzo beans. Scruffy and Raffles would get a meatball cut up into their dinners. We would open a bottle of undistinguished red wine and drink it from our pressed glass tumblers. There would be many toasts, much laughter, and a cozy fire in the kitchen fireplace against the lingering chill of a New England spring evening.

Maybe, it wasn't going to be the Danieli rooftop restaurant by moonlight, but things don't have to be perfect to be perfect.

The Circle

Cassandra Shipton , an herbalist and reluctant clairvoyant. The bane of evil-doers who cross her path.

Phillipa Stern (nee Gold), a cookbook author and poet. Reads the tarot with unnerving accuracy.

Heather Devlin (nee Morgan), an heiress and animal rescuer. Creates magical candles with occasionally weird results. Benefactor of Animal Lovers Pet Sanctuary in Plymouth.

Deidre Ryan, recent widow, prolific doll and amulet maker, energetic young mother of four.

Fiona MacDonald Ritchie, a librarian and wise woman who can find almost anything by dowsing with her crystal pendulum. Envied mistress of The Glamour.

The Circle's Family, Extended Family, and Pets

Cass's husband **Joe Ulysses**, a Greenpeace engineer and Greek hunk.

Phillipa's husband **Stone Stern**, Plymouth County detective, handy to have in the family.

Heather's husband **Dick Devlin**, a holistic veterinarian and a real teddy bear.

Deidre's new love, **Conor O'Donnell**, a world-class photographer and Irish charmer.

Cass's grown children
Rebecca "Becky" Lowell, the sensible older child, a family lawyer, divorced.

Adam Hauser, a computer genius, vice president at Iconomics, Inc., married to

Winifred "Freddie" McGarrity an irrepressible gal with light-fingered psychokinetic abilities and they are the new parents of twins, **Jack and Joan Hauser**.

Cathy Hauser, who lives with her partner **Irene Adler,** both actresses, mostly unemployed.

Thunder Pony "Tip" Thomas, Cass's Native American teenage friend, almost family, whose tracking skills are often in demand.

Fiona is sometimes the guardian of her grandniece **Laura Belle MacDonald,** a.k.a. **Tinker-Belle.**

Deidre's family
Jenny, Willy Jr., Bobby, and Baby Anne
Mary Margaret Ryan, a.k.a. **M & Ms,** mother-in-law and devoted gamer.
Betty Kinsey, a diminutive au pair, a.k.a **Bettikins.**

The Circle's Animal Companions
Cass's family includes two irrepressible canines who often make their opinions known, **Scruffy,** part French Briard and part mutt, and **Raffles,** his offspring from an unsanctioned union .
Fiona's supercilious cat is **Omar Khayyám,** a Persian aristocrat.
Phillipa's **Zelda,** a plump black cat, was once a waif rescued from a dumpster by Fiona.
Heather's family of rescued canines is constantly changing, and far too numerous to mention, except for **Honeycomb,** a golden retriever and so-called Therapy Dog who is Raffles' mother.

Ada Richter's German Lentil Soup

2 tablespoons vegetable oil
2 yellow onions, chopped
4 stalks celery, sliced
3 carrots, sliced
1 large clove of garlic, minced
1 package (1 pound) dried lentils, rinsed
8 cups water (or more if needed)
2 tablespoons granular chicken bouillon (or salt to taste, probably 2 teaspoons)
¼ cup minced fresh flat leaf parsley
1 bay leaf
Ground pepper to taste
1 pound frankfurters, lightly grilled and thinly sliced
2 tablespoons cider vinegar

Heat the oil in a large heavy pot, and sauté the onions, celery, and carrots until they are fragrant. Add the garlic and sauté for 1 more minute. Add the lentils, water, bouillon, parsley, bay leaf, and pepper.

Bring the soup to a simmer and cook, stirring often, until the lentils and carrots are tender, about 45 minutes to 1 hour. If the soup thickens too fast and is in danger of sticking, add another cup of water, or as much is as needed.

Remove the bay leaf.

When the lentils are tender, add the sliced frankfurters and vinegar. Simmer 5 minutes longer to develop flavor. Taste to correct seasoning, adding more salt, pepper, or vinegar to your taste.

Makes a gallon or more. Leftover soup can be frozen and is mighty nice to have on hand.

Philipa's Mexican Cornbread

It's important to use yogurt so that the batter will be thick enough to support the chocolate.

1/3 cup butter
1 ¼ cups all-purpose flour
1 cup stone ground cornmeal
½ cup sugar
2 teaspoons baking powder
½ teaspoon *each* baking soda and salt
½ cup plain non-fat yogurt
¾ cup milk
1 egg
¼ cup chocolate chips
Cinnamon Sugar

Heat oven to 400 degrees F. Melt butter in 9 x 9-inch pan and remove promptly.
Sift together flour, cornmeal, sugar, baking powder, soda, and salt. If you use regular cornmeal, stir it in after sifting.
Whisk together yogurt, milk, and egg. Whisk in melted butter. Fold in chocolate chips.
Combine liquid ingredient with dry. Spoon into pan and smooth top. Sprinkle with cinnamon sugar.
Bake in the top shelf of the oven for 20 to 25 minutes, until risen, lightly browned, and dry inside when tested with a cake tester.
Makes 8 or more servings

Joe's Greek Meatballs

2 scallions or 1 shallot, chopped
4 to 5 sprigs fresh flat-leaf parsley, stems removed
2 sprigs fresh mint, stems removed
1 teaspoon dried oregano
2 tablespoons grated Parmesan cheese
1 teaspoon salt
½ teaspoon black pepper
1 cup fresh bread crumbs
1 pound ground beef or lamb (ground turkey can also be used)
1 egg
1 tablespoon lemon juice
½ cup roasted red pepper, chopped small (from a jar, Pastene is a good brand)
olive oil to cover the bottom of skillet
3 peeled cloves garlic

By hand: In a bowl, mix together the scallion or shallot, parsley, mint, oregano, Parmesan, salt, pepper, and bread crumbs. Blend with the ground meat, egg, and lemon juice. Fold in the roasted red pepper.

With a food processor: Chop the scallion or shallot, parsley, and mint with on/off turns of the motor. Blend with bread crumbs, oregano, Parmesan, salt, and pepper. Add the meat, egg, and lemon juice, and mix with on/off turns of the motor until just blended. Add the roasted red pepper and pulse once or twice.

Remove the mixture from the bowl and form into twelve patties. This can all be accomplished in advance. Refrigerate until ready to cook.

Heat the oil and garlic slowly. When hot, add the meat patties and fry on medium-high heat until browned on both sides, 4 to 5 minutes a side. Check the inside of one of the patties to make

sure it's just cooked through. Overcooking makes the patties tough.
Makes 12

Fresh bread crumbs: Best made in a food processor. Tear off hunks of slightly hard Italian or French bread. With the motor running, toss the hunks down the feed tube one at a time until all are reduced to crumbs. Store in freezer until needed. Very useful for making meatballs, meatloaf, or topping baked fish.